'The Glory Hole. It's a... ....g.... p.... ... ...-man's land –
the trenches were so close here they could bomb each other all
the time without artificial aids. But don't ask me why it's been
left, I don't know why.'

Nikki craned her neck at the Glory Hole. 'There's a sign
saying "For Sale" on it.'

'Is there?' He drove on slowly. 'Well, I don't think I'll put in
a bid. With all the unexploded shells and grenades still in the
ground there it doesn't strike me as a desirable property.'

'Unexploded?' She twisted in her seat to look back. 'Do you
mean they could still go off?'

'I do indeed! And if we go walking across any ploughed fields
or through any woods I wouldn't go kicking any clods of earth
or odd-looking piles of leaves, either. They've been known to
go off bang.'

Anthony Price was born in Hertfordshire in 1928, was educated at King's School, Canterbury, and studied history at Merton College, Oxford. Apart from some peace-time soldiering he has been a journalist all his life, beginning as a reviewer of historical books, going on to become crime reviewer on the Oxford Mail, then Deputy Editor and finally Editor of the Oxford Times, from which position he retired during the summer of 1988. He won the Crime Writers' Association Silver Dagger for his first novel *The Labyrinth Makers*, and the Gold Dagger for *Other Paths to Glory*, which has been shortlisted for the Dagger of Daggers Award for the best crime novel of the last 50 years. All his novels reflect his intense interest in history and archaeology, particularly military history.

Other Paths to Glory

Anthony Price

PHOENIX

A PHOENIX PAPERBACK

First published in Great Britain in 1974
by Victor Gollancz
This paperback edition published in 2010
by Phoenix,
an imprint of Orion Books Ltd,
Orion House, 5 Upper St Martin's Lane,
London WC2H 9EA

An Hachette UK company

1 3 5 7 9 10 8 6 4 2

Reissued 2010

A CIP catalogue record for this book
is available from the British Library.

ISBN 978-0-7538-2828-1

Printed and bound in Great Britain by
Clays Ltd, St Ives, plc

The Orion Publishing Group's policy is to use papers
that are natural, renewable and recyclable products and
made from wood grown in sustainable forests. The logging
and manufacturing processes are expected to conform to
the environmental regulations of the country of origin.

www.orionbooks.co.uk

For Brian Farrelly

In a few years' time, when this war is a romance in memory, the soldier looking for his battlefield will find his marks gone. Centre Way, Peel Trench, Munster Alley, and these other paths to glory will be deep under the corn, and gleaners will sing at Dead Mule Corner.

– John Masefield, 'The Old Front Line'
(First published 1917)

Part one
Your Country Needs You

The Angel of Death, looking to call his roll in Picardy on the morning of September 27th, 1918, would have been hard-pressed to find the village of Fontaine-du-Bois.

It had never been very big, just a little church and a few houses set in a pattern of fields on a gentle slope. But then one day, as the rumble of gunfire to the south grew louder, a German staff officer noted its convenient contour lines and marked out his trenches across it and all around it. And now, viewed from the heights of Heaven, it was as though it had never been: the church and the houses were a formless scar in a moonscape of craters and even the line of its one road was broken and indistinct. Between them the British and the Germans had reduced it to a map reference.

Yet if Fontaine-du-Bois was no longer visible from above, the same was not true of the leading company of the West Hampshires who were attacking it. Advancing in the open with the rising sun behind them they showed up all too clearly as pale blobs with long tails of shadow pointing towards their objective.

Less obvious, but still clear enough, were the three small groups of blobs – blobs with no shadowy tails – which were waiting patiently for them, snugged down in shell-holes just behind the empty front line: the Hampshiremen had only a few more steps in the mud and a few more breaths of life before they ran into the hidden machine-guns of the German rearguard. In half an hour all this vital outwork of the Hindenburg Line would be in British hands, but thirty minutes would be a thousand years too late for the assault company.

Mitchell laid aside his magnifying glass sadly, listening in the silence to the sound of the machine-guns in his imagination.

This was one of the bad moments when the absolute peace of the Great War Documents Room of the British Commonwealth Institute for Military Studies turned sour on him. When he had first established himself in the furthest corner of the room, concealed behind the very material through which he was bur-rowing, it had seemed the ideal hole for him. Not even the loudest London noise could penetrate such defences, losing its way hopelessly among the bookshelves of the Douglas Haig Library next door, which barred its way.

Yet it was here that he had discovered the difference between silence and tranquillity. He had been prepared for the dull days, when never a thought came to him unstamped by its passage through some other brain, and by now he was far too old a hand at the game to hope for anything spectacular. What he had not expected and what still ambushed him were the moments like this, when the weight of death and pain in the piles of dusty papers and long-forgotten diaries suddenly closed in crushingly on him, destroying his critical ability and breaking down his discipline and training.

This ought not to have been such a moment. Outside, the autumn sun had returned after a week of rain, slanting down through the high window to cheer him up. He had known from the start that the letters of General Sir Henry Chesney contained nothing of interest beyond the much-quoted passage about the Fontaine-du-Bois success, when the West Hampshires and the 401st United States Infantry had in the end performed together

4

so creditably; to read the General's own meticulous copperplate was more an act of piety than an essential piece of research.

And then, at the very bottom of the box, he had come upon this faded air photograph.

There was really nothing very special about it; the inscribed date and the map reference pinned it down exactly to an event about which everything was already known. He had seen others like it before. Yet for some unfathomable reason it had altogether destroyed his peace of mind.

There was no doubt in his mind that this was where the machine-gunners had cut down the attackers, right in front of the village. A few seconds after this photograph had been taken they had opened fire, only to be outflanked and killed in their turn by the second wave a few minutes afterwards. For all the little blobs on the photograph, British and German, this was the last hour of the last day of their war, and this their corner of the foreign field. And it was pointless to mourn men whose fatherless children were now grandfathers.

He pushed the photograph to one side and drew towards him the Fontaine-du-Bois map, with its tracery of trench lines in red and blue. With maps like this he was safe; it had been just such a map, illuminated by a single flash of pure intuition, which had launched him on this project and had won him one of the Institute's coveted grants. He had been congratulating himself on his ability to distinguish at a glance a British trench system from a German, despising the haphazardness of the former and admiring the interlocking logic of the latter. And then, out of nowhere, it had dawned on him that he'd got it all back-to-front –

'Mr Paul Mitchell?'

Mitchell looked up in surprise at the two strangers who had appeared without a sound in the gap between the filing cabinets. Yet it wasn't so much the stealth of their approach which astonished him as their ability to reach him unaccompanied by a messenger. Ever since the outbreak of arson at the Imperial War Museum the Institute had locked its doors and screened its visitors with care, and neither gold nor threats overawed the ex-Guards sergeant-major who patrolled the entrance hall.

'Mr Paul Mitchell?'

Number Two spoke this time. And whereas Number One was a huge, rumpled soft-spoken Oxbridge type, Number Two had 'soldier' written all over him, from his carefully cropped red hair and the mirror-shine of his shoes to the bark of his voice.

'I'm Mitchell, yes.' Mitchell stood up slowly. It was odd that no messenger accompanied them and even more odd that the sergeant-major should have allowed anyone to disturb him against his express instructions. In fact the more he thought about it, the odder it became. 'What do you want?'

'If you could spare us a few moments, Mr Mitchell, I'd be grateful,' said Number One.

That shift into the first person singular marked Number One as the senior partner. But then he would have guessed that anyway, and it had nothing to do with either the man's words or his size. If Number Two radiated the confidence of his profession, schooled both to command and obedience, Number One's confidence existed on a higher plane, subordinate only to his own will.

A soldier and a professor, maybe. But though neither was out of place in the Institute together they made an incongruous pair, and also a curiously disquieting one. Momentarily Mitchell found himself looking down at the photograph; it was almost as though the last quarter of an hour had been a premonition of their arrival, the barometer falling before the storm's appearance.

'My name is Audley, Mr Mitchell, and this is Colonel Butler,' the large man took possession of the silence before Mitchell had decided how to react. 'The Imperial War Museum people have directed us to you. We think you may be able to help us with a small problem we have.'

'The Museum?' Mitchell frowned, irritated with himself for having missed the point where he could object.

'That's right. A Mr Crombie there told us where to find you.'

Curiouser and curiouser. Alex Crombie knew where he was to be found, sure enough. But Alex was as scrupulous as the sergeant-major about the 'Do not disturb' rule, and only the direst emergency would cause him to bend it.

He eyed Audley cautiously. That 'small problem' hardly sounded like a dire emergency, but then neither of these two had the look of men who concerned themselves with small problems anyway.

'He said you were an expert on the First World War, Mr Mitchell – the 1914–18 War,' continued Audley smoothly.

'Hardly an expert.'

'But you are writing a book on it.' Audley's eyes took in the littered table.

'On one piece of it – I'm gathering material for a book, that is,' Mitchell nodded. It was flattering to be classed as an expert, even by a Second World War man like Alex, but he was still far from reassured about the circumstances of the recommendation.

'Just so . . . Well, you see our little problem relates to your war, Mr Mitchell.' As he spoke Audley unzipped a dark blue plastic case. 'We rather hoped you might be able to tell us something about this – ' He offered Mitchell a single sheet of paper.

An ancient childish memory stirred in Mitchell as he reached forward with instinctive curiosity – *Never take anything from a stranger, Paulie. You never know what he'll want in exchange* – but it was too weak to stop his fingers closing on the paper. Whatever Mother thought, Paulie was a big boy now.

No paper though, but a photocopy of a charred rectangle of map. Or, more precisely, a photocopy of a photocopy, with the gradations of each copying as telltale as the irregular burnt edges of the original.

And no very big problem either, but just a little one, like the man said.

'If you can't identify it, then perhaps you know who could, anyway,' murmured Audley.

'Oh, I can identify it easily enough.' Mitchell dropped the fragment carelessly on the table. 'But what exactly is the little problem?'

Audley regarded him silently for a moment, with a cool, appraising look which made it abundantly clear that he knew he was being needled. 'You know what it is then?'

Mitchell smiled. 'It's a piece of German trench map.'

Again the big man paused before speaking. 'Yes ... well, we did get that far – since the only words on it are in German that was within our powers of deduction.'

Mitchell made an elaborate pretence of examining the fragment again. 'Quite so ... *Schmutziger Graben* – "Dirty Trench" – almost certainly a masterly understatement.'

'And the words in the corner?' Audley's patience was remarkable.

'*In die vorderen?* That's just part of a standard exhortation on this type of map – *Diese Karte darf in die vorderen Stellurlgen nicht mitgenommen werden* – "This map must not be taken into the front lines".'

'That's it. But in this instance someone was careless.'

'This map was captured, you mean?'

In face of such patience Mitchell's resolve to be as bloody-minded as possible evaporated. Besides, there was something just a little daunting in such restraint in the big man when he could sense a rise in the blood pressure of the red-haired colonel.

'It was, yes. Central Somme, October 1916. The railway track is the Albert-Bapaume line and the stream beside it is the Ancre – those trenches at the top lead to Thiepval, if I remember correctly.'

Audley relaxed. 'You know the actual map?'

'I've seen it, certainly,' Mitchell shrugged. 'The Somme isn't my special field, but I've done some work there in the past.'

'While you were Professor Emerson's researcher?'

Mitchell stared at him in surprise. 'That's right. How did you know?'

'They told us at the War Museum,' said Audley casually. 'And as a matter of fact I rather think I know your old tutor at Cambridge – Archie Forbes.'

'Yes, he was – my tutor.' Mitchell's caution reasserted itself. There definitely was something not quite right, or at least not quite academic, about Audley which cast doubt on his first impression without completely contradicting it. But he couldn't put his finger on it. 'You're at Cambridge, are you?'

'No. Now about this map – ' Audley brushed the question aside ' – have you a copy of it here?'

'There may be one somewhere, but I've not seen it. Your best bet would be the Museum.'

'I see. But what could you tell us about it in the meantime?'

'It all depends what you want to know. We lost one hell of a lot of men trying to take this bit of ground – this is just about where the Ulstermen attacked on July 1st, or maybe they were a little to the north.' Mitchell glanced down at the fragment again, struck as he had been so often in the past with the impossibility of computing how much any one piece of that muddy chalkland in Picardy represented in British and German blood and treasure. More than the choicest sites in Piccadilly and the Unter den Linden, certainly.

'Is this anywhere near Beaumont Hamel?' asked Colonel Butler suddenly.

'Not very far. But then nowhere's very far from anywhere on the Somme. It's a very small battlefield, you can walk from one end to the other in a day quite easily – ' Mitchell stopped as he marked the shadow on the red-haired soldier's face. 'Why, do you know Beaumont Hamel?'

Butler shook his head slowly, still staring fixedly at the map. 'My father was there on July 1st. He was with the Royal North-East Lancashires.'

'The Royal Lancs?' Mitchell paused as the textbook facts assembled themselves in his memory. Beaumont Hamel had been another pure nightmare, with the Hawthorn Ridge mine exploded too early and the open slope swept by machine-gun fire from end to end. He couldn't place Butler's father's regiment in that holocaust, but the very fact that Butler was here established his father as one of the lucky ones.

'They never got past the wire,' said Butler.

Mitchell knew exactly what he meant, and what he had left unsaid. Like so many other units that terrible morning, the East Lancashiremen had left their dead hanging on the unbroken barbed wire among the dud shells and unexploded Stokes mortar bombs to mark the high tide mark of their hopeless attack: the memory, passed from father to son, was written on Butler's face.

Audley cleared his throat. 'So there's nothing very special about the map, it's not a rarity?'

'Not a rarity, no. More a curiosity . . . But I'm not an expert on the Somme – you'd do better to read Farrar-Hockley's book, or the Official History if you've the time.' Mitchell paused. 'Or if you really want to know every last detail you should talk to Professor Emerson. He knows that ground backwards.'

Audley grinned at him suddenly in a lopsided, surprisingly boyish way. 'Well, if you're not an expert then he really must know every inch of it.' He reached down for the map and slipped it back into his case. 'I'm most grateful to you and I'll try not to bother you again like this.'

That was a curious way of putting it, thought Mitchell quickly: it was almost as though Audley was deliberately leaving the door ajar for a further visit – again like this. And what was plain was that the man had taken quite a deal of trouble to find out more about him than was strictly necessary for the solution of his little problem.

'I doubt if I could help you much more anyway,' he replied guardedly. 'I only know that map because I've seen Professor Emerson use it – he's your man for the Somme. He's only just come back from there as a matter of fact – '

'From the Somme?' Audley's movement towards the corner of the shelves slowed and then stopped. 'He's been over there?'

Mitchell began to feel slightly guilty about throwing Emerson's name back into the conversation, thereby exposing him also to such equivocal characters.

'Professor Emerson has just returned from France, you mean?' Audley rephrased the question casually.

The guilt increased. He knew nothing about them because he hadn't really tried to find out, but had let himself be over-awed all too easily.

'This is the best time of year to see the ground, after the autumn ploughing,' he began, groping for a way of bringing Audley back within range of the unasked questions again. 'But exactly what is it that interests you about the Somme, Mr Audley?'

The disarming grin was switched back on. 'I'm not writing a book about it, don't worry.'

'I'm not worrying. But I'd still like to know what you are doing – and who you are, come to that.'

Audley considered him equably. 'Let's say I'm just someone with a piece of German trench map, that's all.'

He nodded and turned away, leaving Mitchell no alternative but to ask the same question of the red-haired colonel, who as yet showed no sign of following him.

Yet before he could re-formulate the question Butler himself spoke, gesturing to the maps and papers on the table. 'What makes anyone want to write about – all this – nowadays?'

'Anyone?'

'You then.'

Coming from Butler it seemed a strange question, and he hardly knew how to handle it.

'Curiosity, maybe.'

'Curiosity? You mean morbid curiosity?'

'No, I wouldn't say that.'

Butler frowned at him. 'We lost sixty thousand men on the first day of the Somme . . . But of course – you're not interested in the Somme, I remember. So what are you interested in?'

'The Hindenburg Line.'

'Why that?'

'My grandfather was killed breaking through it, near Bellenglise on the St Quentin Canal. He commanded the 1st/6th West Mercians.'

Butler looked at him for a moment. 'This professor of yours, Emerson – where would he be at the moment?'

The abrupt change in questioning wrong-footed Mitchell. 'Why do you want to know?'

'You say he's the expert on the Somme. And you say you aren't.' Butler's voice was expressionless. 'Is he at home?'

The man was as bad as Audley. 'You tell me why it's so all-fired important and I'll tell you where he is, Colonel.'

Butler shook his head. 'We can find out easily enough, you'll simply be saving us time, that's all.'

'You sound like a policeman, Colonel.'

Butler's lip curled. 'Then perhaps I am one, Mr Mitchell.'

'But you don't intend to tell me?'

'Our business is official, not personal – will that do?'

Emerson would curse him, thought Mitchell impotently, but there was no point in refusing. Anyone who could penetrate the Institute would make short work of tracing someone.

'His telephone number is Farley Green 21242.'

'You mean he's at his home?' The colonel's eyes were as devoid of expression as his voice. 'You're sure?'

'There's a call-box in the entrance hall . . .' The hell with it, though; he was tired of being interrogated. 'He was at home this morning. He said he was going to work there all day.'

'Thank you, Mr Mitchell.' Butler half-turned, and then stopped just as Audley had done. 'Your grandfather commanded the West Mercians in 1918 . . . What did your father do in the last war?'

Again an abrupt change in the direction of the question. Only this time Mitchell had the feeling it wasn't accidental; indeed, that none of the questions had been unplanned, but that the whole script had been planned with some obscure objective of their own in mind. And how many of the answers had they known in advance?

'He worked on a farm in Wiltshire,' he replied evenly, trying to match Butler's tone. 'He was a conscientious objector – a pacifist.'

He stood for a time, staring at nothing. Then he picked up the phone on the windowsill.

'Can you get me Farley Green 21242, please?'

There had been a question on Butler's face at the end, but he hadn't turned it into words, so there was no telling whether it was the right one. But then when he thought about his grandfather, a colonel at twenty-six and a dead hero at twenty-seven, and his father, who'd reached the rank of under-cowman at the same age, he wasn't sure what the right question was. Or that the answer would be in any book, even the one he was writing.

The phone rang.

'Your call, Mr Mitchell – there's no answer. It sounds as though the phone's out of order. The line's dead as a doornail, sir.'

2

As he invariably did when he came home by train, Mitchell finished the last lap of his journey by the short-cut along the towpath.

Actually it was no longer a short-cut, because he had outgrown his schoolboy habit of cutting through the goods yard, squeezing between the last line of hoarding and the beginning of the iron railings, and sliding down directly on to the path by way of the river bridge embankment. But it was still the coolest and most pleasant route in summer and the quietest and most relaxing one in winter, giving him an undisturbed quarter of an hour in which to consider the day's events and the evening's possibilities.

This evening was ideal for short-cutting: dark, but not too dark, with the towpath lamps catching the mist as it rose from the dark river like steam and picking out the puddles ahead; in fact just light enough to walk and think without fear of stepping off into the water, just dark enough to discourage casual walkers, and just chilly enough to drive courting couples under cover.

Only for once he regretted the reflexes which had automatically taken him along it, rather than among the bright lights and distractions of the town, because the day's events had been disturbing and the evening, like all evenings since his arrangement with Valerie had broken up, was very likely to be a drag.

And the bloody inescapable thing about this was that the drag was neither his nor Valerie's, but entirely in Mother's mind, probably because her married life had been such a succession of contrived tragedies that she was no longer able to identify a happy ending when she met one. For Mother, boy meets girl had to be one extreme or the other – happy ever after or paradise lost. She just couldn't accept that rather than get married, girl wanted to become a publishing tycoon and boy wanted to write a book on the Hindenburg Line.

But that was not what was worrying him now – in fact it was not even important, only irritating. What was important was his failure so far to raise Professor Emerson at Farley Green in order to warn him about the afternoon's mystery men, and to apologise in advance for his big mouth. It might not matter at all, because Emerson wasn't the sort of man to take offence so easily, but that only made him feel more guilty. So if the phone was still dead he'd just have to get the car out and drive over there himself after supper, no matter how much it offended Mother.

As it undoubtedly would offend her. And as he'd now reached the first of the weir bridges he had only another five minutes in which to frame an explanation . . .

He moved to one side to allow a wide berth to two men he could see approaching from the other side of the bridge, the first he had seen since he had come down to the riverside. The water, he noticed, was not quite as high as might have been expected after the previous day's rain, with no more than half the curved weir gates raised. But then it had been a dryish autumn so far.

He needed an explanation for Mother – it would be no good telling her about the enigmatic Dr Audley and his uninformative colleague, because she'd only make a great dramatic production of it straightaway. But a mention of the professor would be like a red rag to her; she was quite irrationally jealous of the poor man.

'Mr Mitchell?'

One of the two men checked his stride as they came alongside him.

'Eh?' Mitchell looked at him in surprise, fearful for an instant that he was about to be asked for the price of a cup of tea. But the educated voice and respectable overcoat reassured him. This was evidently a day for strangers.

'It is Mr Mitchell, isn't it?'

'Yes. But I don't believe – *oooof.*'

Two hands grasped him from behind simultaneously, the first gripping his arm at the elbow and pulling him towards the railings while the other, in the small of his back, turned him sideways, face to the river. Their combined force slammed him into railings brutally. His briefcase was wrenched from his fingers.

Oh, God! he thought despairingly, terrified not for the £20 in his breast-pocket, but for the three months' work in the briefcase, *muggers – mindless thugs who would as soon empty its contents into the river as give it back to him once they had found it all to be valueless –*

'Please don't – ' he gasped. But the words were cut off as the man who had spoken to him grabbed his free arm, bending him double over the top rail so that his feet almost left the ground.

The hold on each of his arms tightened, but the pressure on his back slackened as the hands there shifted down his body to the inside of his thighs. He found himself staring down uncomprehendingly at the olive-green water six feet below him, where it first rippled against the closed weir gate on his left and then slid in a smooth cataract into the open one directly beneath. The roar of the weir was deafening.

Even before the hands on his thighs betrayed his assailants' intention the sight and sound of the water had sounded an alarm signal in his brain, tensing his body into rigidity.

Not his briefcase – oh, Christ! Not his briefcase and not muggers –

Then he was flying up and over, arms and legs released, flailing and kicking wildly against nothing, darkness and light whirling and the water and noise coming up to meet him –

exploding in his face – dragging him downwards. His knees struck the concrete lip of the weir spillway and he was instantly swept over it, his shoulder striking the first leg of the bridge with a bone-cracking shock. He felt himself tumbling and rolling helplessly, and then something slammed into the pit of his stomach – one moment he had been part of the torrent, and the next it was bursting over him, battering him and filling his eyes and nose and mouth. He fought the unbearable pressure on his lungs until his chest seemed full of fire and consciousness was only pain.

Then, unbelievably, he could breathe and breathe and breathe, each breath a wonderful burning agony. He was still somehow suspended in noise and darkness and water, but in an incomprehenisible bubble of air.

Where am I?

There was a slimy hardness under his cheek and under his fingers. He groped slowly over the slime until he felt a solid object – a stanchion of some sort? A pillar?

God! He was still under the bridge – under the bridge and wedged in the angle of a supporting pillar and an iron cross-girder, wedged like a piece of river flotsam. The lower half of his body was held against the upright by the solid cataract of water racing through the open gate, a stream now buffeting him and cascading over him in a great arch of spray. But the upper half was lying in the protection of the closed gate, in the mere trickle coming from underneath it; it had been that diverted spray caused by his own body which had been drowning him as he struggled instinctively to raise his head above it, and only in beginning to lose consciousness had his mouth and nostrils dropped into safety below it.

Slowly he tested the pieces of his body. Each piece moved, although he was now aware that the freezing force with which he had been rammed against the pillar had been tremendous. In fact, he could feel nothing except a roaring, numbing cold spreading through him, beyond pain and fear. He had to get out of it, away from it, or it would kill him just as surely as the river itself had tried to do.

But it hadn't been the river ... a vague memory of events which had occurred seconds before he had been swept under the bridge asserted itself. Someone had deliberately thrown him into the weir, deliberately and unbelievably ... casually.

No, not casually –

'*It is Mr Mitchell, isn't it?*'

The noise all around him was so scarefying that he couldn't hold his thoughts together.

'*It is Mr Mitchell, isn't it?*'

It was Mr Mitchell, and no one else but Mr Mitchell, who was meant to be drowning now, drifting at the bottom of the Conservancy basin below the weir – or tumbling round and round in the undertow in that crashing water a few feet away.

The thought of it was blurred and confused for a moment, and shot with panic as he realised that they must be standing directly above him, scanning the basin in the bright light of the lamps on the bridge. And then the panic turned to anger which was like a small fierce fire inside him, a point of spontaneous combustion in the heart of a block of ice.

He twisted his position, shrugging off a new jet of water and holding his breath as he searched for something solid to hold. He wasn't going to drown for them, and he wasn't going to surrender to the cold for them, and above all he wasn't going to die for any murdering bastards, not if it was the last thing left in the world to do.

One way or another, he just wasn't going to give them that satisfaction.

3

It wasn't until he reached over for the bolt on the inside of the back-garden door that Mitchell understood how frozen he was.

He could feel the outline of the metal, but his fingers wouldn't grasp it: it was like trying to pick up a needle while wearing a thick woollen glove. In the end he abandoned the attempt and clambered over the door instead, no longer worried about his ruined suit and remembering too late as he dropped down on to the concrete path on the other side that he had only one shoe on.

As he limped towards the kitchen door he realised that there was no chance of unlocking it and getting upstairs without alerting his mother. If he couldn't operate the bolt he certainly couldn't turn that awkward little key, even supposing he could establish in the darkness where it was on his key-ring – supposing too that his keys were still in his pocket.

Which meant she would see him in all his glory – poor drowned Phlebas the Phoenician, a fortnight dead – upon which sight she would probably either fall into hysterics or drop instantly in a dead faint, preferably the latter. But in any case, the light was on behind the kitchen curtains, so there was positively no help for it. It was Mother or pneumonia.

He thumped with his numbed hand on the door and stood back a pace, praying for the gift of tongues. There would be a time and a place and a person for the truth, but here and now and Mother fulfilled none of the necessary conditions: now was the time for straight, quick and unashamed lying.

The door shivered and swung open, the brightness of the interior making him blink.

'Now, Mother – '

'Paul, oh Paul – thank God!' Her voice cracked with emotion. 'Thank God!'

'Now, Mother – I'm quite all right – I simply f-fell into the river – ' His excuse lost impetus as he registered something very wrong with her reaction. She shouldn't be thanking God . . . she should be going white with horror and surprise.

'Oh, my darling, thank God!' She wound her arms round his neck before he could stop her, ignoring his saturated clothes. It was as though she hadn't heard a word he'd said.

'M-mother – ' he gritted his teeth ' – I fell in the river, that's all.'

It shouldn't have sounded so completely unconvincing – it was the goddamn truth that was outlandish – but somehow his words carried no more conviction than if he'd tried to pass off his appearance as the result of his usual evening swim.

She half disengaged from the embrace suddenly, though without letting go of him, as if she still needed physical contact to reassure her that he was flesh and blood.

'Of course you did, darling. You just fell in.'

He stared at her in absolute bewilderment, but she avoided his eyes. There was a damp patch now in the front of her dress.

'You fell in the river, sir?'

Mitchell swivelled his head to his right, towards the door into the hallway.

A policeman.

'You're Mr Mitchell, sir? Mr Paul Mitchell?'

'It is Mr Mitchell, isn't it?'

A policeman? A policeman with the same question as the thug on the bridge?

Before he could think about answering, his mother broke the moment of silence.

'That's right, Constable. My son fell in the river.'

Just as the policeman's voice had been disbelievingly neutral, so his mother's tone was too emphatic to be convincing. Which could only mean that he was going crazy, that he had hit his head and was in delayed shock – or that everyone else was crazy. It had to be one or the other.

'What's going on? What – ' Mitchell winced as his mother tightened her grip on his arm. That was one bit of him that had taken a knock on the bridge, and not the only bit either. His shoulder was a raw, throbbing ache. 'Mother, what's happened?'

The grip didn't slacken, but her eyes were blank. 'Now, darling, you're soaking wet and you'll catch your death of cold if you don't get these wet things off. So you just run upstairs and get into a hot bath at once.'

He stared into the obstinately expressionless face for one second to confirm the suspicion within him. She was now behaving so wildly out of character, with her emotions so completely battened down, that it was obvious she was trying to protect him from something. And being Mother, she was thereby making it a cast-iron, copper-bottomed certainty that whatever it was, it would get him for sure.

He looked at the policeman: youngish, fresh-faced, but sharp-looking . . . for all his apparent neutrality, with a predatory glint in his eye, as though he'd maybe got his teeth into something worth chewing.

'Constable, can you kindly tell me what's happened?'

'I was hoping you'd tell me that, sir, actually.'

'Paul, darling – '

'Shut up, Mother.' Without looking back at her he loosened her fingers from his arm. 'What do you mean – I'd tell you? Tell you what?'

'Paul – '

'Tell you what?'

The young policeman considered him thoughtfully. 'You said you'd fallen in the river, sir. You mean you fell into it by accident, I presume?'

Someone must have seen something – seen it, and maybe phoned the police. But then that was maybe twenty minutes or more since, and they'd have surely gone straight to the weir first, and when he'd finally climbed back on to the bridge there hadn't been a soul in sight. He'd made sure of that.

It didn't make sense, it made nonsense. But the time for lying was over – Mother would just have to take the truth on the chin. Or at least as much of the insane truth as there was.

'What would you say, Constable, if I told you that two men tried to kill me this evening? That they grabbed me on the bridge over Godsey Weir and threw me in?'

He heard his mother's sharp intake of breath beside him.

'Is that what you're saying, sir?'

'Would you believe me?' He was a little surprised at the young man's reaction. From polite disbelief he should have graduated to irritation on being handed such a cock-and-bull story, but instead he now seemed remarkably understanding, almost sympathetic.

'You were attacked on the towpath, sir? By two men?'

'On the weir bridge.'

'On the weir bridge – just so. They pushed you in.'

Mitchell nodded uneasily. He had expected to be disbelieved when he first told the story, not to be believed.

'Then you're very lucky not to have been drowned, sir. That weir's a very dangerous place. You must be a very strong swimmer indeed.'

'No, I – I'm not much of a swimmer at all. B-but I was lucky, you see.'

'Lucky?'

'I g-got caught under the bridge, on one of the pillars. They threw me in next to one of the gates that was lowered – closed – and the current pushed me to one side, where there was hardly any water coming through. It's quite easy to climb back on to the bridge from underneath.'

He looked at the policeman pleadingly. 'Do you know the weir?'

'Yes, sir. I know it well. And you simply climbed back on to the bridge from underneath?'

'Yes – '

'And these two men – the two men who attacked you – where were they?'

'Where – ?' The question caught him unprepared. 'Ah – well, you see – I waited underneath – I waited until I thought they'd be sure I'd drowned. I m-must have waited ten minutes or quarter of an hour. I m-made sure they weren't there before I came out.'

The policeman nodded. 'You showed great presence of mind.'

'Paul – you mustn't – '

'Please, Mother! '

'I think you'd best leave this to me, Mrs Mitchell,' the policeman said quickly – and much more sharply. 'Now, Mr Mitchell –' his voice decelerated again ' – these men, can you describe them?'

'Describe them?'

'Did you see them?'

'I only really saw one, and I didn't see him properly. But I'm sure I don't know him because he didn't know me.'

'How do you know that, sir?'

'Because he asked me if my name was Mitchell. He asked me twice, in fact. They wanted to make sure it was me, that's why. And when they were sure – '

They stared at each other, the same question in each look, Mitchell knew instinctively.

'Do you know why anyone – that is, why two complete

strangers, would want to throw you into the weir, sir?' The policeman paused. 'Because this is a very serious allegation you are making, you know. If we – ah – apprehend anyone for doing such a thing, then the charge could very well be attempted murder. Can you think of any reason why anybody would want to do such a thing?'

That was the incomprehensible beginning and end of it, which had started turning over and over inside his brain even while he'd crouched shivering in the darkness under the footbridge.

'*It is Mr Mitchell, isn't it?*'

Why?

'No. I can't.'

'Neither can I, Mr Mitchell. And that's why we must talk man-to-man now – if you would leave us for a moment, Mrs Mitchell.'

'Man to – ?' Mitchell frowned, looking from the policeman to his mother. 'What the devil do you mean, man-to-man?'

'Oh, Paul, my poor darling – he means that we know.'

'Know what, for God's sake?'

As he watched her he saw her face break up, her eyes brimming with tears. It was at last the face he knew, lined ready for tragedy and sorrow.

'You must tell the truth, darling.'

'But that's what I've been doing.'

She shook her head. 'No, Paul. You see – '

'All right, Mrs Mitchell,' the policeman cut in. 'Your mother's right, sir. If you tell the truth everything will be quite all right, and there won't be any trouble. It isn't like it used to be at all – that's why I haven't even taken my notebook out of my pocket.' He patted his top pocket to match the words. 'Not one thing goes down until you want it to, and then we're only here to help you. Because that's what you need, sir – help.'

'You're darned right I need help,' Mitchell felt his anger re-awakening as he spoke. 'Somebody bloody well tried to murder me, I'm telling you – to murder me. You can put that in your book for a start.'

A muscle tightened on the young policeman's cheek as though he was beginning to find it difficult to control his own impatience. 'Is there any way you can substantiate that statement, sir?'

Mitchell gaped at him. 'Any way? Good God – just look at me! Do I look as though I've been out for a stroll?'

The policeman shook his head slowly. 'No, sir, you have obviously . . . been in the water.'

'Well, that's marvellous. And if I didn't fall in – and I certainly didn't jump in – can you suggest any other way of g-getting in the river?'

'But if I remember correctly, you did say you fell in, when you first came into the house.'

'That was just for my mother's sake. I didn't want to frighten her.'

'I see. And you didn't jump in?'

'Why the blazes should I jump in?'

'I wasn't asking you why, sir.'

'But you're implying I did.'

'Not at all, sir. I'm simply asking you – did you jump in the river?' The patience was perceptibly draining out of the young policeman's voice, to be replaced by a formality which made him at once much younger and much more hostile.

'And I'm simply telling you I was thrown in – thrown in by – '

'Yes, sir.' The policeman deftly lifted a notebook out of his breast-pocket, extracting a folded sheet of writing paper from it. Methodically he unfolded the sheet and offered it to Mitchell. 'And in that case, perhaps you'd care to explain this, sir?'

Mitchell took the paper mechanically, recognising its feel as he did so: it was exactly like his own best-quality calligraphic paper.

The signature jumped out of the page at him before he could take in the few typed lines above it.

It was his own.

Dearest Mother,

Professor Emerson has told me today that it is no good my continuing with my work. There are others whose research is further advanced and very much better than mine. I think I have known this for some time, but I managed to shut my mind to it. Now it's no good pretending any more, and without Valerie there's nothing left worth living for, nothing.

Forgive me.

Paul

For half a minute he stared at the paper – his own paper. And his own typewriter, or one exactly similar. And even his own thick black ink for the signature.

His own signature.

'B-but – ' Momentarily his thoughts overran his tongue, coming out incoherently as he met the policeman's steady gaze. 'But – I didn't write this.'

'You didn't write it, sir.'

It was the tone again, rather than the words, which pointed to the man's meaning. He wasn't asking a question; he wasn't even echoing a statement. He was making an unthreatening sound to give Mitchell a last chance to admit something perfectly plain, something that had been plain from the very beginning.

'But it is your signature, isn't it, sir?'

Another gentle question, almost apologetic. Only now Mitchell understood what had been happening to him and around him, and was desperately aware of the nature of that knowledge: so far from setting him free it merely showed him the bars of the trap into which he'd tumbled. There'd not only been something wrong with his mother's reactions from the start, there'd also been a fumbling and unnatural sequence to the young policeman's questions. A strange caution which he had mistaken for kindliness.

But the poor devil had come to check up on a likely suicide, only to be faced by the suicide himself – Phlebas the Phoenician indeed! – who'd surfaced again en route from the river bed to the psychiatric bed at the General.

'My signature?' Must answer. 'Yes – I mean *no*, damn it!' Steady now. 'I mean, Constable, it looks like my signature, but it isn't. Because I didn't write it.'

Now, for the very first time, the young policeman did look rather disconcerted – and so did Mother, Mitchell saw with a quick side-glance. Disconcerted and even in some crazy way disappointed, Mother was, because her tragi-happy ending was going wrong. And as for the poor copper, he had an awkward loony on his hands now who refused to accept defeat, and come quietly.

Only the loony didn't feel like playing games.

'I c-can't prove I didn't jump in the river, unless someone saw what happened, which isn't likely,' he said carefully. 'But I can damn well prove this – *this* is a pack of lies.'

The policeman seemed half-hypnotised by the paper fluttering under his nose.

'Could I have that note back, sir, please?'

'By all means. You'll need it for the name – Professor Emerson, who allegedly thinks my work's no good. All you have to do is phone him up – 326–21242 – and he'll tell you. Only he won't tell you that.'

In any other circumstances that would have been game and set, if not quite match. Except in his dilapidated state Mitchell didn't feel ready to celebrate any victory, but was only relieved that he was about to be taken seriously at last.

And then the awkwardness of the lengthening silence in the kitchen began to disturb him, draining his confidence. Inside his damp clothes he was chilled, yet he could feel the warmth of the boiler on his face. The overall effect was of an unwholesome clamminess – Phlebas being warmed up.

More silence.

'What's the matter?'

His mother spoke, unwillingly. 'It was in the paper this evening, Paul – in the *Evening Mail*.'

'What was?'

'The fire. Then you haven't seen it?'

'Seen it? Seen *what*, Mother?'

'Professor Emerson's house was burnt down today – it was on the local news on the radio too. He – '

'Mrs Mitchell – !'

This time she beat the policeman down.

'He died in the fire, Paul.'

4

To his shame, Mitchell experienced a shock-wave of selfish dismay before he registered sorrow.

Then cold commonsense came to his rescue, rationalising the selfishness. It wasn't just that the living always jostled the dead out of the way, but that Charles Emerson's death was a thing too stunning, too unacceptable, to take in.

What was real was the awkward present, in which there was no Professor Emerson now to bear witness to a truth that would have nailed that lying piece of paper for the clumsy forgery it was. One word from him would have done that – but now all he had was Mother, who had opposed the Hindenburg Line project from the start, and who saw his parting from Valerie as a direct and tragic consequence of it.

In fact, it was no longer clumsy: he saw, as he stared into her distraught eyes, that the clumsiness had been transformed by this hideous accident and her own imaginings into a diabolical cleverness which was about to enmesh him if he didn't think quickly.

They were both staring at him, waiting for him to react. And the more they stared, the less he knew what to say or do, so that silence built up in the stuffy kitchen like leaking gas searching for a spark.

It was the policeman who fumbled finally for the safety valve. 'What would Professor Emerson have told me, then, sir?'

The gentle voice was back – the loony was being humoured again. So the loony had better be damn careful.

'He would have told you that my research is going fine,' he said deliberately. 'He is – he was very pleased with the way it was shaping.'

'Indeed, sir?'

Indeed ... but that was too vague to carry conviction. Policemen needed facts.

'Have you ever heard of the Hindenburg Line, Constable?'

God! Don't let him ask if it has anything to with railways!

'I can't say that I have, no.'

Mitchell breathed a small sigh of relief. 'It was a system of German defences in the 1914–18 War – defences in depth, miles of barbed wire and pillboxes and strong points, almost impregnable.'

The policeman nodded. 'Like the Siegfried Line – in the Second World War.'

'Ah – yes ... that's right.'

What am I doing, trying to explain the Hindenburg Line to a policeman? Only a loony would do that!

'Yes, sir?'

Mitchell decided to cut his losses. 'Well, that's what I'm going to write a book about.'

Silence again.

'That's very interesting, it sounds.' The policeman nodded encouragingly. 'And you were talking about er – the Hindenburger Line to Professor Emerson this morning.'

'That's right. We discussed some of my ideas, and he said they seemed to make sense – ' That didn't sound right ' – that I was on the right line – ' That sounded even worse: the right line on the Hindenburg Line, change here for the Siegfried Line, the Maginot Line and all stations to Waterloo and Trafalgar Square, and don't forget to jump in the river on your way home.

'What time would that have been, sir?'

Mitchell frowned. 'Time?'

'How long were you with the professor?'

'How long?' Mitchell realised he was repeating the words stupidly. 'I suppose about an hour. I caught the early morning bus to Farley Green, so I got there about 9.10 – just over an hour that would leave.'

'Before what?'

'Before I caught the London train. For God's sake, what's all this got to do with – ' Mitchell stopped abruptly as he saw, appalled, exactly what it had to do with: the loony had visited the professor, and now the professor was dead in the ashes of his house.

'*Constable!*' Mother's voice bit into the latest in the sequence of disastrous silences like a sharp sword drawn quickly in his defence. 'My son has been standing here in his wet clothes answering questions for far too long. And there's no need for you to waste any more of your valuable time anyway, because it's all been a false alarm – and now I can see that it's all been my fault, too, because I didn't understand his note and – '

'Mother – ' Mitchell saw too late that she had made the same terrifying deduction and was reacting with her usual disregard for the real world around her. The young constable was no longer her ally, but an enemy to be dismissed or, failing that, ignored. Her suicidal son had returned, and if he'd burnt a few houses and outwitted a few would-be murderers or gone for a swim in the black river en route, that was nobody's business except his and hers.

The effect was totally disastrous, but before anyone could react to it the front door knocker hammered out.

'Now, who could that be? Paul, dear – ' She looked at him for a moment, balancing the need to separate him from the Law against his bedraggled appearance. 'No, I'd better go. But don't you say one word until I get back, dear.'

The policeman watched her out of the room impassively before flipping open his notebook.

'Well now, Mr Mitchell ... there's just one more point. I believe you are acquainted with a Miss Valerie Newton, is that correct?'

Mitchell nodded. There was at least some hope that Valerie would ridicule the contents of the note; under ordinary circumstances he would have depended on it, but he no longer had any confidence in anything going right. It could just as easily be, on this losing streak of his, that her career had gone sour and that absence had made her heart grow fonder again.

'You do?'

A murmur of voices in the hall drew his attention away from the question, his mother's voice and a male one he couldn't place.

'You were engaged to her – is that right?'

He pulled himself back to the question. 'No, it isn't right. We were – ' he mustn't say *good friends*: that was always taken as a euphemism for extreme intimacy – 'we were very friendly. But the idea of an engagement was my mother's, not ours. We were just friendly, that's all.'

He frowned. Put like that there was a basic untruth in it, because they had been more than friends. It was just that modern language hadn't caught up with modern relationships. But at least the policeman belonged to his own generation, and this might be his only chance to undo some of the damage Mother had certainly done.

'There simply wasn't – ' He broke off guiltily as he saw his mother appear in the doorway. Naughty Paul caught in the act of speaking to the policeman.

'Dear, there's a gentleman who insists on seeing you,' she said quickly, with an emphasis which suggested that this was one time when any intrusion ought to be welcomed. 'He's a Doctor er – '

' – Audley,' supplied a voice from the passage behind her.

There was nothing much left now, thought Mitchell, which really could be said to be surprising except maybe that Audley himself seemed remarkably unmoved by what he saw as he came into the kitchen: the presence of the policeman and his own appearance together apparently rated no more than one slightly raised eyebrow.

'Mr Mitchell,' Audley's head bobbed. 'You must forgive me again for intruding. I'm afraid I must break my promise.'

Mitchell stared at him. He couldn't recall any promise.

'What do you want?'

'To talk to you again.' Audley's eyes shifted momentarily to the policeman. 'Has there been some kind of – accident?'

'No accident.' Mitchell was suddenly very tired of questions. 'No accident.'

The policeman stirred. 'You're a doctor, sir?'

'Not of medicine.' Audley didn't look at the policeman as he spoke. 'No accident?'

'Two men tried to kill me, that's all.'

'Paul – '

'I was about to take a statement from Mr Mitchell,' said the policeman heavily. 'If you're not his doctor then I'm afraid your business will have to wait until I've finished, sir.'

'And I'm afraid it won't wait,' replied Audley equably, reaching inside his coat with his left hand. He drew out a small black folder and handed it to the policeman, his eyes never leaving Mitchell's. 'Tell me what happened, Mr Mitchell.'

Mitchell swallowed nervously. Whatever it was, the black folder had stopped the policeman dead in his tracks – he was staring at it with a look of frozen concentration.

'I m-met two men on the weir footbridge. They – one of them knew my name. Then they threw me into the weir, or they tried to.'

'Tried to?'

'Well, they did. But I got stuck under the bridge, where they couldn't see me.'

'And they thought you'd drowned?'

The man was quick. And what was more, there wasn't a shadow of disbelief in his voice.

He nodded. 'I waited until they'd gone.'

The policeman cleared his throat, 'May I speak to you privately, Dr Audley?' he said.

'I think you'd better, Constable – ?'

'Bell, sir.'

'Constable Bell. Perhaps we could use another room, Mrs Mitchell? And your son could get out of his clothes into something dry while I'm talking to the constable.'

Mother took a step forward, facing up to Audley resolutely. 'Will you kindly tell me who you are, Doctor – Audley? And what you're doing?'

'Ministry of Defence, Madam,' Audley accepted the black folder from the constable, but tucked it back into his pocket without showing it to her. It seemed that he considered the one answer covered both questions, and that the policeman's deference was confirmation enough of its truth.

'And what has that to do with my son?'

Audley looked down at her for a moment, as though undecided about his reply. 'Madam,' he said finally, with a gravity which only just fell short of pomposity, 'it seems that someone wants your son dead. Consequently he needs defending. Constable Bell and I will discuss how best that may be achieved. Have I your permission to use your telephone?'

'But – ' She compressed her lips suddenly as though she had decided to put her mouth under restraint. Mitchell knew the expression of old, just as he recognised her dilemma: she had realised at last that what had happened could neither be shrugged off nor ignored, but that meant she must either accept or deny his story in the certain knowledge that she was opening the door to nightmare whatever she did. She simply didn't know what to do.

'The phone's in the sitting room, Dr Audley,' he said, resolving her dilemma for her. 'Down the hallway on the left. I'll show you.'

'It's not necessary, sir,' said Constable Bell. 'We'll find the way. If you'd follow me, Dr Audley.'

'Very good, Constable. Say about a quarter of an hour, Mr Mitchell?'

Mitchell and his mother looked at each other.

'Paul, what's happening?'

'What's happening now, I haven't the least idea. What happened on the way here was exactly as I told it, Mother. Did you really think I jumped in the river?'

'I didn't know what to think – there was that note – '

The note. That at least was something real which told him he hadn't simply fallen in and hit his head and dreamed the whole horror all by himself.

'How did you get it?'

'It was lying there on the mat. It must have come through the letter-box – it wasn't there when I went to switch on the news. When I came out to start your supper I saw it there.'

'And so you phoned the police?'

She looked at him so brokenly that he instantly regretted the harshness of his words. And, damn it, what else could he expect? His paper, his typewriter, his ink and his signature, all fitting in with her own prejudices.

'Did you go out today, Mother?'

'Go out, dear? You know I always have lunch with Betty Tyler today.'

Lunch with Mrs Tyler, then an afternoon's shopping.

'So the house was empty most of the day?'

'Only in the afternoon, dear. Mrs Johnson's here until one o'clock.'

Still plenty of time for anyone to search the place for what they needed after the cleaning woman had gone. But why?

Why did it have to be suicide? And why did it have to be Paul Mitchell, out of millions?

'Darling, I – ' her voice quavered ' – I didn't mean to – I didn't know what to do.'

Suddenly he wanted to hug her. Everyone always took it for granted that Mother had a way of turning accidents into disasters, but – Christ! – this wasn't an accident, but pure murderous malevolence, cold and calculated. It was no wonder she'd proved no match for it.

'Poor old Mum!' he draped a damp arm round her shoulders. 'You aren't the only one who doesn't know what to do – and who doesn't know what's happening.'

She looked at him doubtfully, dropping her gaze to his suit when she found no consolation in his face. 'But you must get out of these things – I don't know whether they'll ever be good enough to wear again – ' She tugged vaguely at the crumpled lapels. Then the moment of merciful practicality passed, presumably as she remembered how the clothes had become unwearable. 'But Paul, what are we going to do?'

He gently disengaged her hands. 'We're going to see what our friend Dr Audley has to say first, Mother. That's what we're going to.'

'Then you really do know him?'

'Did I look as if I didn't?' The suspicion on her face reminded him that there were times when she could see clear through a brick wall with disconcerting accuracy. 'As a matter of fact I met him for the first time just this afternoon.'

'At the museum?'

'At the institute. But don't ask me what he wanted, Mother dear.'

'Why not?'

'Because you wouldn't believe me if I told you. And even if

you did, you wouldn't be able to make head nor tail of it. Just you make us all a lot of hot, strong coffee while I get myself respectable. I think we're going to need it.'

Introducing Constable Bell to the Hindenburg Line was enough for one night, without trying to take Mother back even further, to the forgotten battle lines of the Somme.

By avoiding the second and fifth treads on the staircase and timing the click of the door to coincide with the chimes of the hallway clock, Mitchell reached the sitting room without alerting his mother in the kitchen. With any luck, he reckoned he had maybe five clear minutes before her patience gave way to suspicion.

Their business, whatever it had been, was completed. Audley sat relaxed in the big armchair beside the fire, the Terraine biography of Douglas Haig open on his knee. Constable Bell hovered within reach of the telephone, as though expecting a call on a line which might have become hot.

The big man shut the book decisively and stood up. '"The educated soldier"?' He held the book up, weighing it speculatively. 'Was he educated before the war or by it?'

Mitchell recalled the afternoon's dialogue; Audley wasn't always interested in getting answers to his questions – he used them also like covering fire to keep his adversary's head down while he developed his line of attack. And the only answer to that was to fire back, ignoring them.

'Why does someone want me dead?'

Audley smiled slowly. 'You can't think of any reason?'

'No.'

'Then neither can I – yet.'

Maybe that was something less than the truth – in fact the man's presence contradicted it – but the 'yet' promised a pin-point of light at the end of a long dark tunnel.

'But you do believe me?'

'Why shouldn't I?'

Mitchell looked at Constable Bell quickly, then back at Audley. 'Have you seen my suicide note?'

'I have, yes.'

'Then you obviously don't believe it – why don't you believe it?'

'You're right, Mr Mitchell . . .' Audley paused, then shook his head. 'I don't believe it.'

'Why not?'

'Shall we say – your old tutor has confidence in your scholarship, and I have confidence in your tutor's judgement? And in my judgement you exhibited no suicidal tendencies this afternoon. You seemed to be working quite happily.' Audley paused again, his head on one side. 'And I have even more confidence in my own judgement – does that satisfy you?'

It was pure flummery: not so much a smokescreen as a little probing attack to test how easily he could be turned inside out, with no awkward questions asked. But it wasn't going to be like that at all; because the cold between his shoulders wasn't only fear, it was a reminder of the bitter chill of the river, which he had towelled hurriedly but hadn't subdued. The river had been real, and death had very nearly been real, just as this man Audley was real now. And all three realities were somehow linked together.

Only there was a difference now. Three times he'd been taken by surprise, and quizzed and half-drowned and taken for a lunatic, or maybe something worse. This time he wasn't going to be so easily dealt with.

'No, it doesn't satisfy me one little bit. I want to know what's going on.'

Audley shrugged. 'And supposing I couldn't tell you?'

'Couldn't – or wouldn't?'

'Whichever you like. What would you do then?'

Mitchell turned to Constable Bell. 'What do you plan to do now?'

Bell frowned. 'Me, sir?'

'That's right. What are you going to do about an attempted murder? Aren't you going to report it?'

Bell looked at Audley uncertainly.

'Well?'

'We aren't sure there's been one yet,' murmured Audley. 'We haven't got any proof.'

'All right. Then an attempted suicide – does that count as worthy of mention?'

'Constable Bell might remember the first thing you said when you came in, Mitchell,' said Audley coolly. 'You had a little accident in the dark.'

The rules of the game had reversed themselves very curiously, thought Mitchell. Or it might be that the new player simply didn't bother with such things as rules.

But two could play that sort of game.

'Then maybe he'll also remember accusing me of arson.'

'I didn't allege any such thing,' protested Bell.

'You didn't quite get round to it, but you meant to. So why not ask me some more questions now?'

'The questions I ask are up to me, sir – with respect.'

'Then I'll find someone who will ask them. And perhaps I'll find a journalist who'll take more interest in attempted murder than you do.'

Audley gave a derisive grunt. 'After one look at your suicide note, Mitchell, there's not a journalist on God's earth who'd touch your story with a barge-pole, believe me.'

'Then I'll try Constable Bell's superiors.'

Audley looked at his watch. 'I'll tell you something. At this moment I'd guess my boss is getting on to Constable Bell's Chief Constable. The truth is that your options are somewhat limited.'

Mitchell realised suddenly that he'd let his own problems and fears blind him to a question he would otherwise have asked much earlier. Something had happened to bring Audley back to him so quickly, and it was inconceivable that it had anything to do with ancient military history.

But it must be urgent, whatever it was, because Audley was now offering him a straight trade – credibility in exchange for co-operation – and was making damn sure he couldn't reject it.

'Just what is it you want to know?'

Audley stared at him for a second, then his face relaxed into the same boyish grin he'd produced to soften the afternoon's interrogation. Only this time it seemed more genuine, as though he was grateful to Mitchell for drawing the right conclusion at last without any more arm-twisting being required.

'I thought you'd never ask.'

Mitchell didn't feel like returning the grin. 'I'm sorry to seem so slow, Dr Audley. Perhaps it's the effect of being half-drowned. I'm just not used to it.'

'I can believe that. I never found compulsory cold baths at school invigorating, myself, to be honest.' The grin broadened, and was then slowly withdrawn. 'You got out of the river without anyone seeing you. Are you sure of that?'

'I made sure the two bastards who threw me in weren't there, if that's what you mean.'

'But did anyone else see you? When you came home here, I mean.'

Mitchell shook his head. 'I came in the back way, across the allotments. I didn't see a soul – it's pretty dark there, too.'

'Good. Now, this is – ' Audley was cut off by the fierce double ring of the telephone.

They all turned towards it instantly, but before Mitchell could move Constable Bell had staked his claim.

'44988 – Mrs Mitchell's residence – ' he began eagerly. Then his face fell. 'Who is that speaking, please?'

'Who is it?' said Audley sharply.

'One moment please, Madam.' Bell lowered the receiver to his chest, his other hand blanking the mouthpiece. 'It's a Mrs Tyler and she wants to speak to Mrs Mitchell.' He stared at Mitchell. 'She wants to know if there's any news of you.'

'Christ! She's a friend of Mother's – and she's got a tongue like a cow-bell,' groaned Mitchell. 'It'll be all over town now that I've committed suicide.'

'It will?' Audley took three quick steps across the room and snatched the phone from Bell's hand. 'Mrs Tyler? Good evening, Madam. You wish to speak to Mrs Mitchell? . . . She did?'

Mitchell heard the door open behind him.

'This is Inspector – ah – Haig,' continued Audley, his eyes directed past Mitchell. 'I think it best for you not to speak to Mrs Mitchell at this moment . . . That's right, Madam.'

Mother's face was a picture of incredulity, tinged with incipient outrage.

'No, Madam, I'm afraid there's nothing I can tell you under the circumstances. We are doing all we can . . . Yes, I will most certainly give her your message . . . Thank you, Mrs Tyler . . . Yes, I will – good night, Madam.'

The click of the receiver released Mother's tongue. 'Dr Audley, could you kindly tell me what you're doing – and why you're saying – ' she looked around for support ' – what you're saying?'

Audley was not at all abashed by her anger. 'I'm doing exactly what I said I'd do, Mrs Mitchell,' he replied mildly. 'I'm protecting your son.'

'By telling lies?'

'Not only telling them, spreading them too, I hope. Mrs Tyler is a friend of yours, I take it?'

'Yes, but – '

'And you told her your son was missing?'

'I asked her for advice. She knows Paul – ' she broke off, uneasily aware of Mitchell's eyes on her. It had always been his impression that Mrs Tyler had never quite forgiven him for not growing his hair down to his waist and relishing pot, like her own half-baked offspring. She would undoubtedly have made a meal of any sign of his mental instability.

'So she advised you to telephone the police?'

'I would have phoned them anyway.'

'Of course! So she'll be reassured to know they're on top of the job. Did she undertake any other help?'

'Why, no ... except she offered to ring round one or two places where Paul might have gone, to do it tactfully – I was so nervous myself.'

Audley beamed at Mitchell. 'Better and better! Don't look so sad, Mitchell. Mrs Tyler's doing our work for us, and far more convincingly than we could hope to manage.'

What he was driving at was inescapable. 'You mean I'm – dead?' However inescapable, it was still hard to grasp all the same.

'Not dead, no,' said Audley happily. 'To be dead requires a body. Stay rather "missing" – "missing, presumed killed in action", as you might record yourself. Rivers have a way of holding on to bodies for days on end when they've a mind to. And of course you didn't actually say you had that in mind.'

'I didn't actually say anything.'

'No, but your would-be murderers didn't indicate your preference either, so they can't expect the police to know where to look. As long as they think they know where you are they're not going to worry – providing we can get you out of here as efficiently as you got in.'

'You want my son to go into *hiding*?' Mother had got there remarkably quickly, but she evidently couldn't believe it was a real destination either.

'That's exactly it, Mrs Mitchell. He's going to hide, we're going to help him, I'm depending on you to help us.'

'But – the police – ?' She looked at Constable Bell.

'They will help too, naturally. A lie like this requires all the help it can get.'

Bell shifted from one leg to the other, as though his boots pinched him. 'I told you I can't undertake that without consulting my superiors, sir, I gave no undertaking.'

'But they will, Constable. They will. If your chief constable wants his OBE in the birthday honours and an invitation to the next Royal Garden Party, and a pat on the back from the Home Secretary for being a good fellow – I'll bet you a pound to a penny he's on to your superintendent at this very moment.' He smiled from Bell to Mitchell. 'The office of chief constable is one of the great bulwarks of our democracy, because he isn't subject to politics. In fact it really isn't subject to anything, democracy included, and that does make it marvellously vulnerable to the old boys' network – a word and a nod from the right quarter, you understand. Believe me, I've seen it work.'

Flummery again: he was talking to them, but at her, using safe words of authority to reassure her – *OBE, chief constable, Royal Garden Party and Home Secretary.*

Only with Mother even that wasn't quite good enough.

'But Dr Audley – I mean, can't they protect him?'

'From whom, Mrs Mitchell? We don't know. And from what? We don't know that either.' The flippancy had gone from Audley's voice, to be replaced by a sudden seriousness which was all the more chilling by contrast. 'We don't even know why.'

They were back to the same blank wall behind which Audley had hidden earlier, and this time Mitchell himself almost accepted its solidity. But then the cracks in it gaped at him: twice in one day this man had come looking for him, and certainly not because he had developed a sudden interest in the battle of the Somme. And (what was nearer the bone) he had accepted the truth of the towpath story without question, almost as though he had been expecting it.

'I can't believe this is really happening to us – it's like a nightmare.' Mother shook her head despairingly. 'I don't know what to think.'

'Think how your son came home to you, Mrs Mitchell,' said Audley brutally. 'And think how next time he may not come home at all.'

She stared at him as though she only half understood what he had said. 'But there must be some mistake – '

'There was a mistake right enough. The men who tried to kill him made it when they botched the job this time. Next time he won't be so lucky, you can depend on that – next time there'll be no mistake.'

She was getting the shock treatment now – Audley had cast her as a distraught mother and he was making sure she understood her part properly –

This time?

The double meaning hit Mitchell like a blow in the stomach.

This time, next time – *last time*!

He hadn't been the first victim, but the second – that was why Audley hadn't been surprised, by God!

Charles Emerson had come before him.

5

Mitchell lay on his back, watching the pale grey light of dawn advance and recede as an intermittent breath of wind stirred the bedroom curtains.

He had long passed the waking moment of confusion, when for a few seconds he had not known where he was, but only that he lay in a strange soft bed in a strange quiet room. The moment had been instantly followed by a feeling that he must still be asleep, lapped in a vivid and intricate dream, and that by shutting his eyes again he could drift away on the dark tide again until his mind was ready to open itself to reality.

But the warmth and snugness of the bed was too real and the lavendery smell of the strange room was too strong – no dream had ever smelt of lavender before, no dream had smelt of anything at all. And the fragrance of it, the genteel odour of middle-class England, was still all around him.

He had the distinct impression that he had been intellectually seduced – primed with words and liquor and soft lights, and taken for all he was worth . . . and before that he had been physically battered too –

'Tell me about the Somme, Paul – may I call you Paul?'

Physically battered. He reached gingerly inside his pyjama jacket again to examine the strapping on his left shoulder. The ache had gone, but there was still a mildly painful stiffness to remind him of noise and rushing water and numbing coldness.

He didn't want to think of that . . .

'Tell me about the Somme, Paul – '

They had driven out of the town on the western road, and then turned a little to the south, after which he had seen no familiar landmarks in the darkness through the rain-blurred windows. He had still had most of his wits about him then, but he'd been concentrating on matters other than geography.

'First you tell me about Professor Emerson, Dr Audley.'

'You think there's something to tell?' Audley leant forward to concentrate on the road ahead. 'There's a turning just here I don't want to miss – ah, there's the sign.'

'Isn't there?' Mitchell paused to let him complete the manoeuvre. 'You didn't come back tonight just to ask me about the Somme. You came back because something happened after you left me.'

'Y-ess,' Audley nodded at the windscreen. 'You're quite right, of course. Something happened. I rather fancy you've already guessed what it was – your old tutor warned me you never needed two and two to make four.'

'He didn't die in the fire, did he, Dr Audley?'

'It'll be easier if you call me David . . . No, he didn't.'

Mitchell stared at the outline of the hedgerow picked out in the headlights. He didn't know whether it made Emerson's death more or less bearable that it should have been murder, not accident. What had changed was the focus of his own anger.

'So the fire was just to cover up?'

'Not just to cover up, to destroy also. He was struck from behind, and then arranged at the bottom of the stairs. But the fire was started in his study, among his papers.'

Mitchell drew a sharp breath. Somehow that made it worse, far worse: to destroy not only a man, but also his work. The maps and the files and the carefully documented papers he knew so well . . . and above all the manuscript, the great work of love and scholarship. That was the ultimate, unforgiveable vandalism, like the destruction of something on the point of life.

'They'd thought it out quite neatly,' continued Audley, 'the scenario . . . Emerson upstairs, smelling the fire maybe, then losing his footing and knocking himself out. It just might have worked.'

'But it didn't.'

'No,' Audley grunted. 'And when you're trying to cover up a murder a miss is as good as a mile.'

'Why didn't it work?'

'Ah – well, basically for two reasons, one of which you will certainly understand.' Audley took his eyes off the road for an instant to nod conspiratorially at Mitchell. 'It isn't difficult to kill people if you've a mind to, as the Irish are so fond of proving to us. And with Professor Emerson and yourself notched up in one day, these people have certainly demonstrated their enthusiasm for it.'

'You're pretty sure it was the same pair?'

'Not necessarily the same pair, I don't know about that yet. But the same guiding intelligence, I'm sure of that. Because whoever composed your little suicide note must have already known your professor wasn't going to contradict it.' Audley paused. 'But that isn't a reason why their plan didn't work out, of course . . . No, the general reason is that while it's easy to murder it's bloody difficult to *fake* a murder – there are too many things to go wrong once you complicate a basically simple act.'

'You mean luck?'

Audley shook his head. 'I prefer not to think of luck coming into it. It's just that you limit your control of the sequence of action . . . Take your own case, for example – '

Your own case. The sound of the dry, academic voice faded for a moment as Mitchell felt his chest tighten. He still couldn't hold reality steady for more than a few minutes at a time, and every time he succeeded he liked it less.

' – could have cracked you on the head first. And you know why they didn't?'

It was Paul Mitchell they were discussing, the Paul Mitchell he knew and loved so well, who lived in a very ordinary, rather boring world and worried about girls and money and making a modest name for himself.

'Because you were going to be a suicide, so you had to drown,' continued Audley conversationally. 'They were probably afraid to mark you, because marks make policemen suspicious. Or maybe they were afraid of hitting you too hard, because every schoolboy knows that dead men won't drown. So they left it to the weir, and the weir didn't do its job properly. It was out of their control, quite simply.

'Now, Professor Emerson's case illustrates the same thing, but in a different way. They killed him with a blow on the neck – which the fall downstairs was supposed to account for. But the fire was also intended to obliterate everything, and the fire let them down just like the weir.'

'You mean, it didn't burn? The papers weren't destroyed?'

Audley sighed. 'No, I'm afraid they did manage that. By the time the fire brigade got there the study was like a furnace.'

'Then how did the fire let them down?'

'Ah, well that's the other reason why faked murders don't work: people do tend to underestimate the efficiency and the intelligence of the experts they hire to look after them. Like the firemen, for a start – just because they wear uniforms and ring bells it doesn't mean they're idiots.'

'I don't follow you.'

'You will, believe me . . . You see, someone spotted the blaze – someone on the top deck of a double-decker bus that was passing. And so the fire didn't have time to reach the body. Then as soon as the police and the firemen put their heads together they didn't like the look of things. The firemen reckoned the fire in the study had started in more than one place, and the police couldn't understand how Emerson had given himself a karate chop on the banisters. That's simplifying what they told me, but it all added up to the same thing: the fire let the murderers down – it wasn't as efficient as the fire brigade.'

Mitchell digested the information in silence. It was evident that Audley had barged straight in, waving his little black book with the same magic effect as it had had on poor Constable Bell, who must be even now lying unhappily like a trooper to his sergeant. Whatever agency the big man served, it opened and closed official doors with disturbing ease – and either accidentally or by design he had just warned Mitchell not to underestimate 'the experts', of whom he was obviously one. And a rather senior one at that.

Yet there was something distinctly odd about the time sequence of it all ... They had come to him and he had sent them to Emerson, an action which he had regretted at the time, but which had turned out to be a fortunate one for him. Yet Emerson had already been dead by then and his own death had been decided on ...

'You said you got my name from the War Museum?'

Coincidence, that was what was odd. He had felt somehow that Audley was sparking events, but that couldn't be the way of it any more. They'd been converging on him independently from both sides. Audley and – the unknown ones.

'I did.' Again that sidelong glance. 'If I read you right I rather think it's time to admit that we weren't quite – ah – straightforward with you this afternoon, Colonel Butler and I.'

'I never doubted it,' Mitchell tried to sound more knowing than he felt. 'But I found your obsession with the Somme – well, confusing, to say the least.'

It seemed to be Audley's turn for silence now; he drove slowly, though not very expertly, for about a mile before speaking again, as though the effort of becoming more straightforward was a considerable one.

'Y-ess . . . well, you see, Paul – it wasn't your name we started off with. It was Emerson's.'

'Emerson's?' Mitchell was suddenly at a loss for words.

'That's right,' Audley said gently, as though he was aware that he might be injuring his listener's self-esteem. 'And the War Museum gave us his telephone number, but we couldn't get through to him – his phone was dead.'

The phone had been in the study, Mitchell remembered.

'So we called the Museum back, and they told us about you. They said you'd be in the Institute, and if anyone knew where Emerson was to be found, you would . . . They also said you were the best young researcher in the business, if that's any consolation.'

It wasn't really so ego-bruising. He had been a little surprised as well as flattered by their arrival at the Institute, but to be overshadowed by Charles Emerson was no disgrace.

'Why didn't you ask me straight out where he'd most likely be?'

Audley gave a small shrug. 'We prefer not to advertise our intentions unless we have to. I suppose you could say we make a habit of using the indirect approach.'

Again Mitchell subsided to digest his latest shreds of information. The fragment of Somme map was the only tangible clue he'd seen, and he knew now at least that Audley's interest in the battle was no smokescreen, but the starting point of whatever he was doing. He knew also that Audley and the killers had been concerned with Emerson, not with him. He was reduced to a bit player, almost an innocent bystander.

But a victim nevertheless.

'Why the hell do they want to kill me?' he exploded angrily, outrage supplanting fear as he stared down again into the river.

There came a dry grunt, almost a chuckle, from beside him. 'For the oldest and best reason in the world, my lad – you know too much!'

'But, Christ – '

'And you know the wrong man, too. At the wrong time, as well – because you were there this morning, weren't you?'

This morning. God! It was unbelievable that it had only been this morning.

'Talking to him in that conservatory of his next to the study for all to see – for them to see,' went on Audley. 'Looking over papers, poring over maps – did you do that?'

'Yes, but – '

'You were setting yourself up, Paul. That is, if you weren't already set up.'

'But *why*?'

'Well, let's look at it from their viewpoint. Emerson knows something they don't want anyone to know. So he must die. But then there's his former research assistant, Master Paul Mitchell, who did half his leg-work in France last year and still comes to see him twice a week. It's a damn good bet that what Emerson knows, Paul Mitchell knows. So Paul Mitchell must die too – simple.'

All the outrage was gone as Mitchell felt himself cringing inwardly with panic. 'I don't know anything worth being killed for.'

'Huh! That's what you think, not what you know. You told us you weren't an expert on the Somme, but from where I sit you look uncommonly like one.'

'Well, that's not worth being killed for either. It can't be.' Mitchell heard the disbelief in his own voice, and knew he must take hold of it. Reason went out of the window as disbelief came in. However strange, the common denominator between Charles Emerson and himself was their knowledge of the 1914–18 War. And there was only one thing that eliminated three and a half of those four bloody years, zeroing attention on the Somme. 'Where did you get that piece of map?'

'From a Frenchman by the name of Edouard Antoine Barthélemi Ollivier, a very good friend of mine. We were at Cambridge together after the war as a matter of fact – that's where I first met him. We were both reading history, like you.'

Mitchell hadn't been expecting such a direct answer. 'He's a historian?'

'No. He's a sort of liaison officer between their Prime Minister's office and the Police Nationale. I've worked with him two or three times in the past ten years.'

'So you *are* a policeman.'

'Good gracious, no! Neither is Ted Ollivier.'

'But you said he works with the police.'

'The Police Nationale – and that's an organisation with as many mansions as heaven itself. Ted Ollivier's been a good many things in his time – he was in the French Resistance when he was fifteen and worked for us. He was the only survivor of his group, too – the Gestapo killed all the others – but he's never been a proper policeman . . . No, officially he's a civil servant, a glorified PRO-cum-errand boy.'

'And unofficially?'

'He's a senior operative in the Service de Documentation Présidentielle.'

'Never heard of it.'

Audley gave a grunt. 'I'm not surprised. It's the ultra-secret security agency in the French set-up, responsible only to the President himself. The great General set it up after the Martel scandal back in '62 when he found out the Russians had penetrated everything else in sight. It's run by a man named Gensoul now.'

'It doesn't sound ultra-secret.'

'Because I know about it? Ah, but you see it's my business to know about it, just as it's yours to know about the Hindenburg Line – and it's Ted Ollivier's to know about me . . . which is why it's very interesting that he should have sent me that bit of map and the name Charles Emerson.'

'What did he want you to do with them?'

'Find out if the map belonged to Emerson, and if so what he'd done with it – whether he'd lost it or given it away, or what.'

'Well, I can't tell you that. He certainly had a copy of that map, but then he had a hell of a lot of maps.' The past tense was the operative one now, thought Mitchell sadly. Past for the maps and past for poor Emerson. It didn't really bear thinking about.

'What exactly was Emerson doing in France this time?' asked Audley.

'Doing? I think he was looking over the ground along the Ancre Heights, by Grandcourt and Miraumont. Where the winter fighting took place. When I saw him after he came back he was – ' Mitchell stopped suddenly as the memory of Emerson's excitement came back vividly to him.

'He was – what?' Audley picked up the hesitation quickly. 'Let's have some of that phenomenal memory of yours.'

'Who told you it was phenomenal?'

'Everybody. Your tutor, Forbes, for one . . . Your friend Crombie for another.'

'You've done a lot of checking on me, it seems.'

'Naturally. It's routine, you know.'

'And was it routine to tell me about Edouard Antoine Barthélemi Ollivier?'

The silence which followed the question confirmed the suspicion in Mitchell's mind which Audley's frankness had aroused. At the Institute, and again at home, he had stonewalled every inquiry; but now he was answering questions which hadn't even been asked, supplying information which he ought to have withheld.

Which made no sense unless –

'What is it that you want me to do?' asked Mitchell.

Audley laughed. 'Let's say I may have work for an expert on the battle of the Somme – how's that?'

'There are others who know far more than I do, I've told you that already.'

'Then let's say I also need an expert on Professor Charles Emerson, and there aren't a lot of those around.' Audley paused, then continued in a much harder tone. 'In fact there's only one.'

Mitchell frowned at the dark road ahead. He seemed to be travelling on a pre-determined journey in more senses than one.

'You said "work" – you don't mean just information.'

'I said "work", yes.'

'What sort of work?'

'Nothing too difficult, you're well qualified for it by temperament I should say.'

'But – supposing I refuse to do it?'

'Don't you want to see Emerson's murderers dealt with – and the gentlemen who sent you for a late swim?'

'Of course I do.'

'Of course you do. I never doubted it.' Audley paused. 'And I think you're being very sensible, because if I don't look after you, no one else will . . . and that would be – sad.'

Mitchell looked at him unbelievingly in the darkness.

'Whereas along with me – ' Audley paused again.

It was true: he was being given the choice of hunting with the hunters or being thrown to the wolves.

'The fact is, Paul, Your Country Needs You – and the safest place for you happens to be the front line.'

The door of the bedroom opened wide. A large cardboard box – several large cardboard boxes – appeared in the opening, canted dangerously as the door was kicked shut, and were lowered to reveal Audley's beaming face.

'Your uniform, Captain Lefevre,' he said.

God! He hadn't dreamed it all.

6

Mitchell looked at his new watch again.

'It's almost 11.15,' he said.

Audley nodded. 'Don't worry, he'll be here on time. Jack's nothing if not punctual, and in fact he's a great deal more than that. You mustn't be deceived by appearances with Jack – people tend to be, and then he has them on the hip. I rather think he trades on it, not being at all what he looks like. He's a very shrewd fellow, our Jack.'

It was a very expensive watch, the sort they advertised as not missing a second whether at the bottom of the sea or whirling about in space, he had recognised that at once when it had tumbled out of the manila envelope with the other things, the wallet and the identification card and banker's card and the half-used cheque-book . . . and the letters from people he didn't know, who probably didn't even exist. There had even been a letter from a girl.

He had remarked on it –

'This is a very fine watch, David.'

'I'm glad you like it. A small token of our esteem.'

'My own works perfectly well.'

'But this is your own. The new you mustn't have anything belonging to the old – it's a standard precaution.'

That was more like it: a precaution rather than a token of esteem. And also a reminder.

Involuntarily he felt his upper lip, gingerly at first, and then with more confidence. It felt firm and it looked real – and now he was brushing the thing just as he had seen others do. He had always taken the action as a piece of affectation designed to call attention to what was there, but now he wondered if they weren't simply reassuring themselves about its existence, as he was doing.

'But he really is a soldier?'

'Jack Butler?' Audley looked up from his paperback. 'Oh yes, and a good one too – we're not all frauds. He won a very good Military Cross in Korea, and I believe he was a first-rate regimental officer. It says a lot for the army that they let us have him.'

He sounded more like a collector of rare objets d'art than a – but then Mitchell still wasn't too sure who 'us' were. Apart from that comparison with the Service de Documentation Présidentielle, which obviously wasn't what it sounded like anyway, he had disappeared in a cloud of vague generalities every time they had approached the subject.

'And here he is – on time to the minute,' observed Audley triumphantly. 'We'll leave my car here and let him do the drive, come on.'

As they crunched across the granite chippings which covered the surface of the lay-by towards the dark grey Rover Mitchell reflected that any event which delivered him from Audley's driving couldn't be all bad. It wasn't so much that the big man drove dangerously – and at least he drove slowly – as that he gave the impression of someone who was determined to give only a quarter of his mind to a job which required at least half of it. Colonel Butler might not be brainier, whatever Audley claimed for him, but he was bound to be more competent in this.

For a moment he thought Butler must feel the same way and was simply waiting for them to join him, but as they approached the car the driver's door clicked open.

He could see at once and exactly what Audley had meant by appearances. In the Institute the day before the colonel had worn a countryman's city suit and a look of even-tempered neutrality; now, in tweeds and deerstalker and with an expression of apoplectic anger on his face he resembled the very pattern of the Angry British Officer disguised thinly as a civilian.

'Audrey, what the hell are you up to?' he exploded.

'Good morning, Jack,' said Audley brightly. 'Have you got the reports and the maps?'

'Maps be damned!' Butler stabbed a blunt finger towards Mitchell. 'What the hell are you doing?'

Audley grinned. 'This is Captain Paul Lefevre of the 15th Royal Tank Regiment, Jack.'

'Lefever – ?' Butler gagged on the next word.

'Spelt "Lefevre" but pronounced "Lefever",' added Audley helpfully. 'A good French Huguenot name anglicised by three hundred years of English speaking – since the Revocation of the Edict of Nantes, to be precise. In the year 1685 – '

'Damn the year!' Butler spluttered. 'You're up to your old tricks – you can't do it. Not again.'

'I can and I will – and I have,' said Audley. 'And I don't think you're in any position to quibble, Jack. Not with your record.'

Butler's eyes flashed. 'That was – '

'Different?' Audley pounced on the momentary hesitation. 'Necessary, I would have said. And it's necessary now – necessity has once more been the mother of invention. I have invented Captain Lefevre.'

There was something like pain as well as anger in Butler's eyes now, as though he could see a defeat ahead which was being inflicted on him by a dirty trick.

'Why?'

'Why?' Audley stared at Mitchell for an instant, then turned back to Butler. 'Where's the village of Mametz, Captain Lefevre?'

'East of Albert, and just east of Fricourt.'

'Who took it on July 1st, 1916?'

'The 1st South Staffords and the 21st Manchesters.'

'What division were they?'

'The 7th.'

'What corps?'

'XV – Fifth Army.'

Audley paused. 'Who took Vaux-le-Petit on July 14th?'

'The West Mercians.'

'All right!' Butler barked. 'You've got yourself a Somme expert. But there are books on the Somme.'

'I haven't finished. Who owns Vaux-le-Petit Wood?'

'Monsieur Pierre Ducrot.'

'And Sabot Wood?'

'Madam Grenier, who lives in Bapaume. Number 14, Rue Palikao.'

'There are directories too,' Butler snapped.

'But not walking ones.'

'Tchah!' Butler turned to Mitchell. 'Man – do you know what you're letting yourself in for? Apart from wearing the Queen's uniform, which you've no right to?'

'I still haven't finished,' said Audley, his voice suddenly taking on authority. 'Why do you think I arranged to meet you here – because I like the open air?'

Butler glowered briefly at Mitchell, then switched his attention back to Audley. 'I assumed you'd tell me in your own good time.'

'And so I will. Or perhaps I'd better let Captain Lefevre tell you. Go on, Paul.'

Mitchell cleared his throat nervously. Yesterday, at their first meeting, he liked Butler better than Audley. His feelings about the big civilian were still equivocal, but he felt too far committed to the action plan to withdraw now. In any case, Audley was obviously the top man, and by the contents of this morning's fancy dress boxes, a man who could get things done quickly.

He pointed down the hill. 'That's Elthingham, Colonel.'

Butler's gaze followed the finger towards the huddle of houses in the valley, set in its chequer-board of fields and woodland. In the clear stillness of the morning the smoke from a dozen chimneys rose peacefully above the roofs: Elthingham was like a picture postcard of an English village.

'Yes?' Butler growled.

Mitchell forced himself to look directly into the hostile face. It wasn't his health and well-being that Butler was worried about, he sensed, but his ability to look after himself. He was being tested.

'I saw Charles Emerson twice last week, once on Tuesday, the day after he came back from France, and then yesterday. On Wednesday he went to see someone in Elthingham.'

'Who?'

'I don't know, Colonel. And I don't know why, either. But what I do remember is that he was excited about it.'

'How – excited?' Butler sounded as though he somewhat disapproved of excitement in a sober scholar whose enthusiasm ought to be tempered by gravity.

'I don't mean he was dancing up and down. But he said it was a pity he'd had to come back from France on Monday – he had a lecture to give at the Staff College on Tuesday evening – because he'd stumbled on a very interesting thing which he was following up.'

'Something in France?'

'Yes. But he said it did at least give him a chance to check it up at this end before he went back.'

'He planned to go back to France again?'

Mitchell nodded.

'Because of what he'd just learnt?'

'Yes, I gathered that was why.'

'But you didn't ask him?' Butler made this lack of curiosity sound a mortal sin.

'Well – the whole thing only came up incidentally to what we were talking about – '

'Which was the Hindenburg Line, I take it,' said Butler drily, 'and not the Somme. Go on, Mitchell.'

Mitchell swallowed. Butler had put it bluntly but accurately. And yet somehow unfairly all the same. 'Professor Emerson was advising me . . . he was getting me some American maps – their 27th and 30th Divisions were attached to our Fourth Army in 1918 – and we were going to study them together on Wednesday. That's what we'd arranged to do, anyway. But he asked me if we could put that off because he wanted to go and see a man in Elthingham in connection with this thing he'd found out – '

'The very interesting thing?'

'Yes.' It dawned belatedly on Mitchell that he was being interrogated rather than allowed to tell his own story. Where Audley's tactics over the same ground the night before had been to let him run on, encouraging him to speak his thoughts aloud, Butler evidently favoured continuous harassment. 'I didn't ask him about it because I was more concerned with my own work – and because if he'd been ready to tell me he would have done so without my asking. We agreed to meet yesterday morning instead.'

Butler pounced. 'And he evidently wasn't ready to tell you about it then either. So maybe it wasn't very interesting any more?'

'You can make that assumption if you like, Colonel,' said Mitchell tartly. 'I think it would be the wrong one, but you're welcome to make it.'

'What would the right one be, then?'

'Charles Emerson never went off at half-cock. If he said something was interesting – or very interesting – then that's what it was.'

'And therefore still is,' interposed Audley mildly. 'Well, Jack – are you satisfied?'

Butler gave Mitchell a final lingering look, his lips slightly parted now where they had been pressed together before. 'Does he know the score?' he snapped.

'He knows Emerson was killed.'

'Does he understand what that means?'

'If you mean do I know someone wants to kill me too, Colonel Butler,' cut in Mitchell, 'I've already been given a demonstration, you know.'

'And that didn't frighten you?'

'It scared the hell out of me, frankly.'

The lips parted another quarter of an inch. 'Well that's something, I suppose. And you think a khaki uniform will put them off next time?'

'Oh, come on, Jack,' said Audley. 'They think he's dead, or they will when the newspaper announces he's missing. You knew he was alive – but did you recognise him straight off? Did you?'

Audley was trading on that half minute they had walked across the lay-by, before the Rover's door had burst open.

'You think a uniform and a hair-cut and a blond rinse and a bloody stupid little moustache will do the trick?'

'Why? Christ, Jack – I think he looks perfect! '

Butler took a step back, scanning Mitchell up and down appraisingly. 'Hmm . . . If I didn't know *you* so well, Audley, I might have taken longer spotting him, it's true. I must admit the moustache looks lifelike . . .'

'And you're trained to look carefully. As far as we know they've only seen him close up once, and that was in artificial light at night – even then they had to make sure by asking him who he was.'

'You brought in Perman to handle his appearance?'

'Naturally. He said the haircut and the fair hair would alter the shape of his head – take your beret off, Paul – see, Jack? And the moustache broadens his face. Add the uniform and you've got a different person altogether – a soldier.'

Butler scowled. 'That's the trouble: a soldier is what you haven't got. That's what gave him away just now – he doesn't march, he doesn't walk – he slouches like a pregnant washerwoman on a wet Monday. My God, man – you may not be an infantryman, but you're meant to be an officer in the Royal Tank Regiment, and that means you can't drag yourself around on all fours. Stick your chest out. Get your shoulders back and pull in your stomach. A uniform doesn't make a soldier: it's the man inside the uniform who is the soldier. At the moment you're just so much *stuffing*.'

Mitchell drew a deep breath, his cheeks burning.

'That's better. Now salute me – go on, salute me. I'm a colonel and you can't wave at me as though I'm your girlfriend – *salute me!*'

It had been the first thing Mitchell had done in the privacy of his room at the hotel when Audley had left him alone: he had stood in front of the full length mirror and had saluted himself. Longest way up, shortest way down – he remembered the formula. It had looked gratifyingly military at the time. And it hadn't looked like anyone he'd ever met.

'Good God!' exclaimed Butler. 'Where did you learn to salute?'

'I used to play soldiers in the Cambridge University OTC, Colonel Butler,' he answered with insulting politeness. 'I've also played Raleigh in the college production of *Journey's End* and Carrington in the Godsey Players' version of *Carrington VC.* I'm a real veteran.'

Butler gave him a hard look. 'For your sake I hope you're half as good as you think you are.'

'I hope so too.'

'*Sir.* As of this moment you call me "sir" in public when you're in uniform. And when you're in mufti you call me "Jack" – I take it your Christian name is still the same?'

'I've been left that, yes.'

'*Sir.*'

'Sir.'

'And whose bright idea was "Lefevre"?'

'Mine,' said Audley. 'It's his second name and his mother's maiden name, so he's not likely to ignore it . . . But if you've finished the drill lesson I suggest we get down to business. I want to hear those reports.'

'And then?'

'We have an appointment down there with a Mr Hutchinson.' Butler looked at Mitchell. 'The man Emerson visited?'

Mitchell discovered that it was impossible to shrug while holding his shoulders back, the reflex instinct to do so producing only an awkward twitch. 'He may be, but I'd guess he's more likely to be the wrong generation.'

'Sir.'

Damn it! 'Sir.'

Audley shook his head with a sign of irritation. 'Come on then. We haven't got all day.'

Butler returned the look of irritation with one of disdain. 'The reports are in the car.'

'What do they say – in brief? I'll read them later.'

Butler looked at him in silence for a moment, as though undecided as to whether to resist the demand. Then he sighed.

'Ollivier's officially on leave. There's a deputy in his chair at the moment, by name Georges Duveau.'

'SDP?'

Butler flicked a glance at Mitchell. 'We rather think so, yes. Ollivier's not in his flat, nor in his cottage in the Dordogne. But his car's gone.'

'Have you tried the Somme area?'

'That's where the pay-off is. Our men say there's a security readiness alert in four northern departments – Somme, Aisne, Pas-de-Calais and Nord. The Gendarmerie are thicker on the ground in the countryside than usual, there's a rumour that there's a Brigade Mobile squad in Amiens and one of our chaps spotted three old plainclothes friends of his from the Surveillance du Territoire killing time in Arras.'

'But no Ted Ollivier?'

Butler shook his head. 'No. But they're definitely watching the Channel traffic and the Belgian frontier more carefully too. Nothing too obvious, but they're there right enough. Sir Frederick says you were correct: there's something big happening, that's what it adds up to.'

'But he doesn't know what?'

'He doesn't. And he'd like to know how you produced your early warning too.'

'You can tell him my thumbs pricked. Has there been any untoward event in those four departments – say in the last week?'

'Yes. There was a car blown up in Amiens on Tuesday. Officially it was an electrical fault leading to a fire and a petrol explosion, that's what the local newspaper reported. But the unofficial word is that it was an explosion first, then a fire.'

'Yes?'

'That's all. The police were on the spot very quickly indeed – too quickly, you might say. So no one really knows for certain what happened.'

'Hmm . . .' Audley stared thoughtfully down at the village. 'And on the home front?'

Butler nodded at Mitchell. 'Your mother's cleaning woman, Mrs Johnson, she says an insurance salesman called yesterday while your mother was out. He asked some leading questions about you. I gather she gave him a number of useful answers, including the time of your train from London.'

So that was how he had been pinpointed – all too easily. But it was an incongruous thought that the garrulous and ever-helpful Mrs Johnson had very nearly talked him into the next world.

'The autopsy confirms the Emerson death cause,' went on Butler. 'One sharp blow, that's all. And there's nothing on that staircase which could have done it so neatly. It's straight murder.'

'A professional job, in fact – the killing? Unlike the fire, eh?'

'That's right.' Butler looked hard at Audley. 'The fire investigator says the papers were pulled from the files – like a bonfire, he says. Clumsy.'

'That figures.' Audley swung round, nodding to Mitchell. 'Like I said, they're accustomed to violence, these people, but not to covering things up. But none of this has been made public?'

'No, it's screwed down tight for the time being.'

Mitchell examined the two faces with conflicting feelings. Just as they had taken for granted a moment before that the French could suppress the news of some act of terrorism, so they both confidently assumed that they could do the same in England as it suited them. When Audley had done as much the night before he had been so battered and bemused by events that he had not seen further than his own interests, which seemed to be served by the suppression of the truth. But what had happened since – and what was happening now – was on a bigger scale. He knew it had nothing to do with him personally. He knew also what they would say if he asked them: *not in the public interest*, they would say.

He was mixed up, and mixed up inextricably, in an official secret. And more than mixed up – he was like the worm swallowed by the bird in the Don Marquis poem, his free will and individuality fast dissolving in the secret's powerful digestive juices: he was becoming part and parcel of the secret itself.

After chivvying them into the car like a nanny with two wayward children, Audley showed no immediate sign of wanting to disembark when they had actually reached Elthingham; instead he sat immovable in the back seat with his nose buried in one of

Butler's reports, leaving them standing beside the vehicle uselessly.

Not that the colonel seemed unduly put out by such cavalier treatment, or was at least no longer surprised by it. He stared round the little square with the air of a property developer, first examining the houses and shops on three of its sides and then homing in on the village war memorial at the entrance to the churchyard on the fourth side.

He examined it in silence for a minute.

'Typical,' he observed to Mitchell.

It certainly seemed typical, with its Sword of Sacrifice in bronze superimposed on the tall white cross, its list of names and regiments grouped year by year, first for the 1914–18 War, and then for the 1939–45 second round, and even with the familiar Laurence Binyon lines –

> *They shall not grow old, as we that are left grow old:*
> *Age shall not weary them, nor the years condemn,*
> *At the going down of the sun and in the morning*
> *We shall remember them.*

Hackneyed now, those sentiments were, though still moving. But only the first two lines were still true. Perhaps it would have been wiser to have chosen not these lines, which had in fact been written in 1914 when the war was hardly a month old, but the bitter truth which Siegfried Sassoon had foreseen in 1919 –

> *Have you forgotten yet? . . .*
> *Look up, and swear by the green of the spring that you'll*
> *   never forget.*

But that couldn't be what Butler had meant, he decided.

'Typical in what way?'

'Numerical ratio,' answered Butler shortly, pointing to the lists of names. 'Count them up – the '14–'18 ones are almost

67

exactly three times the '39–'45. It's surprising how accurate that ratio is across the country.'

Mitchell counted obediently, feeling somehow that his powers of observation were being put to the test. Well, he could maybe deal with that . . .

'Yes, perhaps you're right. And the graph of the annual loss is significant too, I'd guess.'

Butler looked at him curiously. 'What would you deduce from that?'

Mitchell in turn pointed to the names. 'Three dead in 1914, two in '15, eight in '16, nine in '17 and eight in '18 . . . and this is a good prosperous agricultural community – plenty of farms and a few big cities. A stable community, in fact.'

'You mean yeomen make prime soldiers?'

'Not exactly – I'm sure they do make good soldiers, but what I mean is that it shows there probably weren't many men from these parts who chose to wear the red coat before the war.'

'As regulars?'

'That's right.' Mitchell realised too late that Butler must be a regular soldier, but he was too far committed to his thesis to draw back. 'The army wasn't considered a suitable career for a decent man – the non-commissioned part, that is.'

Butler gave him an old-fashioned look. 'I joined up as an other rank.' His lips twitched and then drooped at one corner as he observed Mitchell's discomfort. 'But you're quite right – my father gave me hell when I told him I was making a career of it, and that was a long time after 1914. It was "the scum of the earth led by the fool of the family" then, I suppose. At least, that's what they thought.'

'It was also the best goddamn army in Europe in 1914,' amended Mitchell. 'The smallest but the best.'

'Aye . . .' Butler stared down at the names. 'Ironic, wasn't it? But go on. I'm still not sure what you're driving at.'

Mitchell pointed. 'Well . . . see how those casualties in the first two years came from the Grenadier Guards and the 8th Hussars and the RFA – I'll bet they were all regulars. The Kitchener volunteers of '14 didn't see much action in a big way until 1916 –

'On the Somme?'

'Right. Just look at those 1916 casualties – four from the county regiment.'

'But four from the Rifle Brigade. And that's a crack regular unit.'

Mitchell shook his head. 'They could still be Kitchener volunteers in one of the Brigade's service battalions, there were five or six of those on the Somme. But in any case I'll bet most of the names here from 1916 onwards are New Army men, because the old Regular Army was just about wiped out by then – Ypres and Neuve Chapelle and Loos and so on.'

'But these aren't the ones we're interested in,' came Audley's voice from behind them. 'If Paul's right, it's the old soldiers who haven't died or faded away that we want. So let's go and see if we can find any of them, gentlemen.'

The difference between the last two of the row of council houses was a commentary on the passions, ancient and modern, of the Englishman at home: Number Nine looked like nothing so much as the forecourt of a busy garage, with cars of varying ages and states of repair lining up on a narrow drive and spilling out onto the verge, their guts spread across the unkempt garden alongside them, while Number Ten's manicured flowerbeds were still ablaze with roses and chrysanthemums and dahlias thriving on the borrowed time of a mild autumn.

Audley bent down towards a pair of overalled legs which protruded from beneath a well-preserved Morris Traveller.

'Mr Hutchinson?'

The knees flexed and heels scrabbled for purchase as their owner eased himself out.

'Eh?'

'Mr Hutchinson?'

If this, beneath a layer of grease, was Mr Hutchinson then he dated from the wrong war, with only a frosting of grey in his hair. But that was very much what was to be expected.

'Ah, that's right. What is it, then?'

'Secretary of the Elthingham branch of the British Legion?'

'Ah, that's right.' Hutchinson sat up, wiping his hands on a rag. 'What can I do for you?'

'My name is Audley, Mr Hutchinson. And this is Colonel Butler – and Captain Lefevre . . . Could you spare us a moment?'

'Ah – ' This time the sound had a gravelly decisiveness to it ' – just a tick, then.' Hutchinson heaved himself stiffly to his feet, carefully erasing the dirty mark he made on the Traveller's re-cellulosed wing before turning to them. 'Now – you'd be from the County Headquarters, eh?'

'They directed us to you,' replied Audley cautiously, a slight frown creasing his forehead. 'Do you mean you were expecting someone from headquarters?'

Hutchinson peered down at the car's wing, absentmindedly polishing it as he did so. 'Not so soon, I wasn't – not if it's about George Davis, that is.'

If he was disconcerted about the unplanned direction the interview was taking Audley didn't show it.

'Chairman said he'd be phoning up about it,' Hutchinson stopped polishing abruptly. 'It's a tragedy. But it's also a bloody disgrace, that's what it is, Mr – ?'

'Audley.'

'Ah – Mr Audley.' Hutchinson squared his shoulders. 'We know old George wasn't very spry, and it's true he was half deaf too. *And* he'd been to the pub, we know that. But it doesn't make one bit of difference, 'cause we've been on at the council time and again about that stretch. They say the Ministry refuses point blank to put a limit on it and they won't put a sign up either, but we say that's just not good enough. We're the ones who live here, not the bloody Ministry, and we know better. And what's happened to old George just proves it – and there'll be others, you mark my words. So if the Legion can help us make a scandal of it – that's what it is, a scandal – to go through two world wars and then be knocked over like a stray dog by some little swine that shouldn't be let on the road – '

'Mr Hutchinson!' Audley seized the momentary pause in the rising spate of outrage. 'I'm sorry, but I think we're at cross-purposes. Or at least partially so.'

'Eh? How do you mean? You're not from headquarters?'

'We are concerned with your veteran members,' Audley ducked the question smoothly. 'Of whom Mr Davis was one, of course. But I believe one of our representatives may have been to see you already, just a few days ago – Professor Charles Emerson. Did he come to see you?'

This was the crunch. If Emerson had been running true to form – at least if he was in pursuit of a specific survivor – he invariably sought information first from the local Legion secretary to enable him to plan his questions precisely. Some of his success in recent years had stemmed from his remarkable ability to distinguish the tiny particles of pure golden truth in oral accounts which others had dismissed as being too adulterated by the passage of time and innocent self-deception.

Hutchinson frowned at Audley. 'There was a man earlier in the week came to see me at work . . .' He broke off, doubt growing in his voice '. . . but I don't see what that's got to do with what's happened to old George Davis.'

Mitchell came to life. 'A short man with thick grey hair – that would be Professor Emerson?'

'Aye, that's him. But – '

'And he inquired about your members who served in the 1914–18 War?'

'He did, that's right. He made a list of them.'

'Could you give us the same names? We've mislaid the list, you see.' The lie came easily and naturally.

'Well, yes – ' Hutchinson was puzzled rather than doubtful now ' – there aren't many of them, anyway.'

'Fine.' He sounded for all the world like Audley, who was regarding him with approval; the worm had become part of the bird beyond hope of recovery.

'Ah – well, just let's see . . . There's Ralph Owen and Joe Allen and Tom Brain – '

'Let me get them down.' Mitchell clicked his ballpoint pen. 'They all served in the army?'

'Tom did. With the RAMC at Gallipoli and later on in Palestine, he was.'

Mitchell put a line through Tom Brain.

'Ralph and Joe were in the Navy. Ralph was in the *Warspite* at Jutland and old Joe was three years with the Dover Patrol.'

A line through them also.

'And Air Vice-Marshal Howard, of course – he was in the Royal Flying Corps.'

A possible, because there were transfers from the infantry to the RFC. But doubtful because Emerson would have had quicker methods of checking on an air vice-marshal than through any Legion branch secretary.

'Then there's old Johnnie Pollard – he was in the army right enough. Won the DCM the first time he went over the top in 1918. And his twin brother Les – he was with him. That was on their eighteenth birthday, and at the end of the day they were the only two left out of their platoon, and not a scratch on either of 'em. The Lucky Pollards they used to call 'em.'

Lucky indeed. But if that was the first time then they couldn't have been at the Somme two years earlier, even if they'd lied about their age as so many youngsters had done in the first flush of patriotism. In 1914 they'd have been too young for that in any case.

'Yes?'

'That's the lot. Fred Foster died last year – he was in the Rifles – and Eddie Turner and Les Collins the year before. They were both with the county regiment, the Royals. That's the lot of them.'

Damn, damn, damn. Emerson had drawn a blank and so had they, thought Mitchell bitterly, looking at Audley.

'Except George Davis,' said Audley.

'Argh!' Hutchinson growled, recalled to his earlier anger instantly. 'And he was our oldest member. September 1st, 1914 he joined up – and it would have been August 4th he used to say, if the squire hadn't told him to wait for a bit – that was Sir Henry Bellamy. George was a keeper on his estate, so was Fred Foster. They joined up together in the Rifles and they were both wounded the same day in '16.'

1916: Mitchell felt a twinge of unease in his stomach, like the first onset of sea-sickness.

'On the Somme?'

'Ah, that's right, yes – ' Hutchinson broke off suddenly, staring at him as though the unease had transmitted itself. 'What you want to know all this for, then?' He looked hard at Mitchell. 'That's the same as the other one asked.'

The other one. And just like the other one, George Davis had met with an accident. Just like the other *two*.

Three accidents in one day.

'Hah-hmm!' Butler cleared his throat briskly. 'And you were in the army, Mr Hutchinson?'

Hutchinson turned towards his new questioner, frowning. 'Yes, I was.'

'What regiment?' Not even back in the lay-by on the hill above the village had Butler sounded so military.

'The 23rd Lancers, sir.' Hutchinson straightened up perceptibly. 'XXX Corps, attached to the Canadian First Army.'

'Normandy?'

'No, sir. I joined them just before the Reichswald offensive.'

'That's a coincidence – so did I. Royal East Lancs. That was a hard slog, the Reichswald.'

'Ah, it was. They said the Germans were beaten before we started, but it didn't look like it from inside a Cromwell.'

They were nodding at each other like old comrades sharing a private experience, the business in hand quite overshadowed by their memories.

'And you saw the finish of it, over the Rhine?'

'Yes, sir. Up beyond Hanover we were at the end.'

'Good.' Butler gave a final nod. 'Now – Professor Emerson asked you about Mr Davis, you say . . . And you told him what you've just told us.'

'Yes, sir.'

'I see. So you knew Mr Davis quite well?'

Hutchinson bobbed his head, grinning. 'Ah, that's right. He was head keeper on the estate when I was a boy – he larruped my backside properly once when he caught me in the woods after pheasants' eggs. And then when I joined the Home Guard as a lad in 1940 he was our lieutenant, and Fred Foster, he was platoon sergeant. Of course, he'd been a CSM in the Rifles when he was demobbed in 1919, George had. And he was chairman of our branch here after the war – our war – when I joined it.'

All thought of questioning them about their curiosity seemed to have been forgotten now. And that, thought Mitchell suddenly, had been the whole object of Colonel Butler's digression into the Second World War. He should have remembered that was how Audley and Butler operated, each one moving into the interrogation in support of the other, covering an exposed flank or putting down smoke as required. For all their obvious personal antipathy they functioned as a team when they were working.

'And now he's been the victim of a road accident, Mr Davis has, you say?' said Butler gruffly. 'How did that happen?'

'Nobody rightly knows, sir – it was bloody hit and run, that's what it was, hit and run.'

'Disgraceful!' Butler snapped. 'When?'

'Last night, sir. George always went for a drink about nine o'clock of a weekday – The Volunteer, that's the pub on the edge of the village, near the main road. That's where we want the speed limit moved to, because they come off the road like bloody maniacs into the lane and there's a blind corner just as you get to The Volunteer.'

'And that's where it happened?'

'So far as the police can tell, yes – about 9.45 it was.'

'But they have no idea who did it?'

'Not from what I heard this morning. I know they're pulling out all the stops, though – they don't like it no more than we do.'

'Of course,' Butler agreed vigorously. 'And you can rest assured we shall see they continue to do so, Mr Hutchinson. But in the meantime what about his next-of-kin? Was he married?'

'A widower, sir,' Hutchinson shook his head.

'Children?'

'Married daughter lives in Canada, sir. His son was killed in Burma in '44.'

'But he must have been getting on – who looked after him?'

'He looked after himself. He was very independent.'

Mitchell looked at Audley for signs of disappointment: it was a dead end – as dead as George Davis.

Audley's face was impassive, but the look seemed to galvanise him. 'Who's looking after the funeral, then?'

Hutchinson drew himself up. 'Why, we shall, of course. Unless General Leigh-Woodhouse wishes to – I'll be writing to him this evening.'

'General Leigh-Woodhouse?'

'Our County President,' said Hutchinson in the tones of one

surprised at such abysmal ignorance. 'He lives just over at Wellingbourne Lodge on the other side of the hill. He was George's old company commander.'

They were in business again.

7

J ack won't be long,' said Audley reassuringly.

'He'd better not be.'

'For General Leigh-Woodhouse's sake?' Audley acknowledged the point grimly. 'You could be right there, I agree. But we're only ten minutes from Wellingbourne. And we owe it to Mr Hutchinson to close up his mouth tight just in case anyone gets ideas about him too.'

Mitchell looked at him across the bonnet of the car, a little surprised. 'Is that what he's doing?'

'Applying the Official Secrets Act, yes – in a comradely sort of way. Jack has the right touch for Mr Hutchinson – they have the Reichswald in common.'

There was a patronising nuance in Audley's voice which niggled Mitchell, tempting him to needle the big man back. 'The right touch all round.'

'Very true – a shrewd fellow, as I said before, our Jack – ' The needle bounced off Audley's hide unnoticed ' – and you, too, Paul. For a first go you did remarkably well back there. Captain Lefevre to the life.'

'We were lucky to get Professor Emerson's contact man straight off.'

'Lucky?' Audley cocked his head thoughtfully. 'I don't know about that: you knew his methods, I'd say. What does surprise me is that he set so much store by oral evidence. Letters, yes –

though they're often too subjective to be any real use. But as for memories, I've always found them highly inaccurate even after a few hours, never mind half a century.'

'Yet you spend half your time talking to people.'

'And the other half cross-checking what they've told me.' Audley's attractive grin lit his face. 'I didn't say it was useless to me – I'm not a historian at this moment. In my business one good thumping lie can be worth more than a lot of mundane truth, and there are times when what a man doesn't say tells me more than what he actually does say . . . Come to that, there are times when questions are just as good as answers – I'd rather know the questions Emerson put to that poor old chap Davis than the answers he gave. He may not even have had any answers.'

Or they might have been different from the answers General Leigh-Woodhouse had in store for them, hopefully, thought Mitchell. And those in turn might be different from what Rifleman Fred Foster and the two long-dead riflemen whose names were inscribed on the war memorial might have told them.

He stared towards the memorial sadly. Although it didn't help, his flight of fancy for Butler's benefit had probably been accurate: those were almost certainly men from George Davis's battalion, killed on the Somme between July and November. One of them, he remembered now, had been a Bellamy, a relative – a son, even – of the 'squire' who had delayed Davis answering Lord Kitchener's appeal for volunteers. That had a positively feudal ring about it, the squire's son and two of his gamekeepers going to the war together, smacking more of Agincourt and Crecy than the Somme. But then those battlefields were all in the same bit of France, and schoolboys a thousand years hence would no doubt confuse them into the same war.

The squire's son and two gamekeepers!

'The Poachers!' exclaimed Mitchell triumphantly.

'I beg your pardon?' Audley's eyebrows lifted.

'The Poachers – that's the unit George Davis must have belonged to!' Mitchell clapped his hands together. 'I should have guessed it straightaway. It has to be them.'

'The Poachers?'

'They were gamekeepers, both of them. And the squire told them when to enlist – that clinches it, see?'

'My dear Paul, I don't see at all. Why should the gamekeepers turn into poachers?'

'Because that's what their nickname was – the 28th – no, it was the 29th – the 29th Service Battalion of the Rifle Brigade. They actually called themselves the Gamekeepers Rifles, but everyone called them The Poachers because they were supposed to be such terrible thieves, almost as bad as the Australians.'

Audley gazed at him tolerantly. 'They were all gamekeepers, you mean to say? All of them?'

'Well, not every single one. I believe they did enlist a few genuine poachers among others.'

'They?'

'The Landowners' Association. It was their executive committee who had the idea in the first place, when the Government called for half a million volunteers in 1914 – it was Lord – un – damn it, his name's on the tip of my tongue – Lord Horton, their president, who proposed it.'

'Simmer down, Paul, simmer down.' Audley was smiling at his excitement, little knowing its reason. 'So the Landowners enlisted their gamekeepers – and what did the War Office make of this remarkable gesture?'

'The War Office?'

'Well, did they welcome this private army?'

'Private – ?' Mitchell was surprised how ignorant Audley was of the war. It was amazing that so much had been forgotten about a great event still within the living memory of old men and women. And yet the fact was undeniable; even the Battle of

Britain in 1940 was history now, a finest hour which had ticked away before half of the present population was born. The Great War had not only been a generation before *that*, but it was the more obscured by the hideous memory of a million war dead – Butler's three-to-one ratio – like the scar of a wound too frightful to be displayed.

'It wasn't like that – it wasn't like 1939, when everyone knew how horrible war was. In 1914 everyone wanted to be in it – ' He was conscious that he was floundering, getting away from the vital fact.

Audley looked up suddenly. 'Ah, Jack – mission completed?'

'Aye. He understands the situation now, and I think we can rely on him. A sound chap,' Butler grunted. 'And now the sooner we see the General the better, I'd say.'

'Just one moment, Jack. Paul here seems to have something he wants to impart to us about the 1914 Volunteers.'

'Huh! Poor devils!' Butler swung towards Mitchell. 'I can tell you something about that. My dad joined up then with two-thirds of the men in his street – the Blackburn Industrials they called themselves. One of the Pals' Battalions of the Royal North-East Lancs they became.'

'The Blackburn Industrials – that's what I've been trying to say,' cut in Mitchell. 'They had so many volunteers the local people tried to join up in groups with their friends to form complete battalions. The Glasgow City Tramways formed a battalion – and the headmaster of a big grammar school up north enlisted all his old pupils. And there were the Tyne-side Irish and the Manchester Clerks' and Warehousemen's Battalion – '

'Joined together and died together,' Butler growled. 'After Beaumont Hamel half the wives in our street were widows.' He turned to Mitchell again. 'So what?'

'I know which unit George Davis was in, that's what. The 29th Special Battalion, Rifle Brigade.'

'The Poachers,' murmured Audley. 'Have you ever heard of them, Jack?'

'Eh?' Butler frowned.

'God! Don't you see?' Mitchell's patience snapped. 'I know more than that – I know where they served on the Somme. I can even guess why Charles Emerson was so excited if it was the Poachers he was after.'

'Why?' Audley came to life.

'It's one of the great feats of arms of the whole battle: how the Poachers took Bully Wood and the Prussian Redoubt. And it's also one of the greatest mysteries.'

'Why?'

'Let me show you in the Official History – I saw you've got Volume Two of 1916 in the car – '

'All right.' Audley held up his hand. 'You can brief me in the car on the way to the General. Come on.'

Mitchell thumbed through the familiar red-bound book to the index at the back. He ran his finger up the column: *Royal Scots, Royal Irish, Royal Fusiliers – Rifle Brigade* . . . 1st Bn, 4th Bn, 7th Bn, battalion after battalion – how many thousand riflemen had been engulfed by the Somme! – 18th Bn, 26th Bn – *29th*.

'Here we are.' He spread the pages open – *Hameau Ridge*, the name of the battle, on the top of the left hand one and *Capture of Prussian Redoubt* on the right, signifying the pages' contents.

'Wait.' Audley was shuffling the contents of one of Butler's files on his knee. 'I'm looking for a map.'

'There's one here.'

'Not the one I want – Bully Wood, you said?'

'Yes, but it'll be marked "Bouillet Wood", or maybe "Bois de Bouillet".' Mitchell craned his neck, looking curiously at the sheaf of papers in Audley's hands: they all seemed to resemble the photostated triangular fragment of the Beaumont Hamel map he had seen originally. 'What – ? These are German, though – '

'That's right. All from the map you so efficiently identified for us.'

'You mean, you had more bits of it – the French gave you more of it?'

'No, they gave us just the one bit. But it was obviously from a *folded* map, and once we'd traced a copy of the original map I thought it'd be interesting to see which bits they hadn't given us – our technical boys worked out from that how it was most likely folded. So here you are: take your pick.'

Mitchell examined the fragments in turn. One was near Grandcourt, on the Ancre, where the winter fighting had gone on remorselessly after the battle's end, half forgotten by the historians now, but in Emerson's view of decisive importance; another was south of Mametz, on the British start line of July 1st – too early for the Poachers – and another up the road to Bapaume, beyond the Butte de Warlencourt – in an area which hadn't fallen until the German retreat to the Hindenburg Line – that was much too late.

Hameau.

The name sprang at him. 'The deadly ruins of Hameau on the skyline' – Hameau, ground into the mud by ceaseless shellfire, but still vomiting up crews for its machine-guns from its cellars and dugouts every time the British infantry rose from their trenches.

'This is it,' he whispered. 'See where the ridge is – Hameau village there, then the sunken road and the open ground, then Wald von Bouillet and the Feste Preussen on the tip of the spur – this is it exactly. *Wald von Bouillet* is Bois de Bouillet – Bully Wood the soldiers called it – and *Feste Preussen* is the Prussian Redoubt of course.'

Butler's Rover slid to a standstill in the lay-by where they had left Audley's plebeian Morris.

'Do you want to collect your car now?' Butler turned to them. 'It'll save time later.'

'Yes.' Audley nodded. 'But more to the point, Jack, I've got work for you now. We'd better split up here. We'll take the General, Paul and I . . . you get on to the Department. Tell them about the old man, Davis – get to the police on that and see if they've turned up anything more on the Emerson killing. Get them to check Paul's insurance salesman against anyone who may have been here or at Farley Green – try the contract killers' file, this has a contract smell about it. And I want the latest report from France also, particularly if they've got a fix on Ted Ollivier.'

Butler glowered at him mutinously, presumably at the prospect of donkey-work to be done by him while Audley enjoyed himself.

'But most of all I want you to dig up all there is on the Poachers – the 29th Battalion of the Rifles. Find out how many of 'em are still alive, where they live and so on. And then dig up the records on – what would it be under, Paul – the Bully Wood-Prussian Redoubt business?'

'The battle of Hameau Ridge – September–October 1916.

Audley nodded. 'On that, Jack.'

'There are some good air photographs of it in the Imperial War Museum,' said Mitchell.

'Air photos – now there's a thought,' exclaimed Audley. 'We should have thought of that before. Get them to hire a light aircraft – Hugh Roskill's fit to fly now and he can take the man Steele, the photographic genius – get them to fly over the Somme area and pick up anything interesting. But especially the Hameau Ridge – get that from all angles.'

'That's going to take time,' Butler demurred.

'Not much. From London to the Somme as the crow flies must be about the same distance as London to York – if Dick Turpin could do that in a day on horseback, Hugh Roskill can be there and back by plane before tea.'

'And the French?'

'What's it got to do with them? Tell Hugh to fly on to Paris and have tea *there* – and then change his mind and fly home again. It's practically on the direct route.'

'And if Sir Frederick queries it?'

'Tell him we've got one murder, one likely murder and one attempted murder already. Remind him Ted Ollivier's mixed up in it, and my thumbs are still pricking. And tell him I've got Mitchell with me, and everything's shaping up nicely.'

They watched Butler disappear in a shower of disapproving gravel and with an angry engine roar. Yet there was a lesson he'd left behind him – that with Audley disapproval didn't mean disobedience.

'I don't think your shares stand very high at the moment,' said Mitchell.

'Oh, Jack doesn't like me very much,' replied Audley airily. 'He doesn't approve of the *homo Audliensis* in general, it figures too many angles for him to regard it favourably. Like why our boss will give me everything I want just at the moment, for instance, whether it's a uniform for you or a spy-plane for me.'

'And why is that?'

'Ah, that would be telling! But let's say now the British and the French are in the European Community together we're not above doing them a good turn ... And as for our Jack – if you think his not liking me influences him in any way, then you mistake your man. Jack sees himself in some sense as my nursemaid – which in some ways is what he is – and consequently he becomes uneasy when I'm out of his sight. The nursemaid may not love the Little Master, but she doesn't let him reach through the bars and prod the lions and tigers all the same. And she expects him to play the game too –

> *Always keep tight hold of Nurse,*
> *For fear of finding something worse.'*

It occurred to Mitchell that simply by doing the driving himself Colonel Butler could go a long way towards preserving the Little Master from life's perils. But he didn't know Audley well enough yet to criticise his car-handling without giving offence; that was an action as foolhardy as finding fault with a woman's cooking, to be undertaken only when death was the alternative.

'And naturally the Little Master can't resist prodding lions.'

'Only to wake them up a bit.' Audley grinned at him, drifting into the centre of the road as he did so. 'But I don't mean just me. Butler's like that with everyone – if there's a risk to be taken he can't bear to let anyone else take it.'

There was something rather 1914–18 about Jack Butler. He was like Feilding, the Coldstream Guardsman who had commanded the Connaught Rangers at Ginchy, who could never bear sending out a subordinate on any dangerous duty and always contrived to do the job himself.

'And are we going to prod a lion now?'

'General Leigh-Woodhouse? I hardly think so, Paul. A very old lion, he'll be – and on our side of the bars.' Audley paused. 'It's the snakes in the grass we've to watch for . . . But you were going to read me that passage about Hameau Ridge from the Official History. You've been holding on to the book as though your life depended on it. I can't wait to hear your mystery story.'

'Oh – yes – ' Mitchell looked down guiltily at the red volume which he'd been holding in front of him like a buffer, his finger still thrust in the Prussian Redoubt page. 'Well – yes, of course . . . It was all part of the XX Corps night attack on Hameau – '

'Night attack? I thought they only raided each other at night.'

'Yes, well strictly speaking it was a dawn attack, the main one, like Rawlinson's successful attack on July 4th, remember – '

'Remember?' cut in Audley testily. 'I can't remember what I never knew. It'd be better if you remembered you only spoke generally about the Somme last night. I'm not an expert.'

'Sorry. The idea was for the assault brigades to form up during the night, when they couldn't be seen, and then go in just before first light. But before that they needed to capture Bouillet Wood on the right flank of the attack, or at least keep the Germans busy there while the main attack went in to the west.'

'The main attack being on Hameau village?'

'That's right. You've got to imagine this ridge lying parallel to the British line – Guyencourt on the left, then Cemetery Cross-roads, then Hameau village, with the sunken road leading up to Bouilletcourt Farm, then open country and finally Bouillet Wood – Bully Wood. The key objective was Hameau in the centre.'

'And what about the Prussian Redoubt?'

'That was on the very edge of the ridge east of Bully Wood."

'Where did that figure in the attack?'

'It didn't. It was too strong to be attacked, they reckoned: it was built into the ruins of the Château de Bouillet, with ravines north and south – Cobra was parallel to the British lines, just behind the German front line, and the north one, Rattlesnake, was where their reserves used to mass, because it was safe from everything except plunging fire.'

'So they were just going to leave it?'

'They hoped to outflank it eventually, after they'd taken Hameau. But that was to be in the exploitation phase.'

Audley nodded. 'I see. And where did the Poachers come into all this?'

'They were in the second wave of the Bully Wood attack, part of the 291st Brigade. The North Berkshire Fusiliers went in first, but they were wiped out. They overshot the mark and no one really knows what happened to them.'

Audley peered to his left, slowing down to a crawl, then coming to a standstill.

'Sorry, Paul, but I think we're here. I'm afraid the Poachers' great feat of arms will have to wait – that sign says Wellingbourne Lodge – or it once did, unless I'm very much mistaken.'

Mitchell followed the pointing finger, just making out the words 'Private Road' on a sign so streaked with green mould from the ancient yew tree overhanging it that the original white and black paint was scarcely visible. Below it, equally green and in addition half obscured by a trailing spray of yew, was the two-line legend 'Welling Lod', which put him in mind irresistibly of Piglet's 'Trespassers W' in *Winnie-the-Pooh*.

'Well, here we go,' murmured Audley as he swung the car into the narrow opening. 'The General evidently values his privacy.'

The same thought was crossing Mitchell's mind: the yew at the entrance was the forward sentry of a whole avenue of them, their branches often interlaced above. It was like travelling down a tunnel with air shafts revealing grey sky at irregular intervals; and they were very old, these trees, their twisted trunks thick and hairy with shredded bark. If the General ever decided to raise a regiment of archers there was enough wood here for a thousand longbows.

But now there was light ahead at the end of the tunnel, and a stretch of lawn which seemed vivid emerald after the sombre driveway. It was strange how the yew tree, which in death provided such warm, golden wood for furniture, was so dark and funereal in life, with its poisonous foliage and deadly red berries.

'Good lord!' Audley said suddenly. 'What a beauty!'

Wellingbourne Lodge lay at right angles to them, long, low, and as ancient as the oaks which framed it. It seemed, indeed, to grow out of the grass as naturally as the trees themselves, its stonework and brick chimneys weathered into the setting, if anything more restrained than the yellows and golds of the autumn trees. The only dabs of contrasting colour were the blooms of the huge old rose clinging to it, seemingly independent of the ground: just as the house grew out of the grass, so the roses appeared to spring out of the stonework.

'Wonders will never cease,' murmured Audley. 'Early Tudor – practically untouched, probably a hunting lodge. And on the site of something very much older – see that dimpled line there to the right of it, by the – it must be a mulberry – and where it turns across the front of the house? That's the remains of a moat for sure: there was a castle here once upon a time. Or at least a fortified manor. The ground never lies, you can't put a spade in it without leaving a mark, you know.' He shook his head wisely. 'It's astonishing how many of these old places there are. Once I thought I knew every one south of the Thames, but new ones are always turning up – usually when some stupid bastard wants to put a motorway through it.'

He turned, grimacing horribly, then did a double-take as he saw Mitchell's face. 'What's the matter?'

Aware too late that he had betrayed himself, Mitchell was at once in two minds about explaining truthfully – or even trying to explain – the sense of unreality which had assailed him, or shrugging it off and allowing himself to be led like a donkey along any strange path Audley chose.

'What's the matter, Paul?' Audley repeated. 'Does it surprise you that I should be interested in old buildings?'

'A little.' Mitchell tried to buy time with a partially false explanation: with two dead men behind them and last evening's nightmare a recurrent and fearful memory, anything normal was not so much surprising as incongruous. Even the khaki sleeve on his lap was a reminder of his divorce from the real world. It was his arm in that sleeve, his body in the uniform; but he wasn't Paul Mitchell any more. This morning Paul Mitchell would have eaten his cornflakes and read his *Guardian* in the train, and then caught his usual bus to the Institute for another slow, quiet day's research.

Now he was someone else, not even someone real, but an imaginary creation of the man beside him, existing in a world as shadowy as the driveway behind them. Captain Lefevre hadn't read a paper this morning or listened to the radio; he knew nothing about art or politics or religion, and cared less.

So naturally Captain Lefevre wasn't interested in Tudor hunting lodges and motorways. Only real people were interested in such things.

'What would happen to Paul Mitchell if anything happened to me?'

Before he had finished asking the question its answer flashed into his mind: Paul Mitchell was already catered for, already missing in the real world. He would simply stay missing.

'Why should anything happen to you?' Audley frowned.

'Something happened to Charles Emerson – and George Davis.' But he knew he couldn't expect the real answer from Audley, and now that he'd answered it himself that hardly mattered. 'What are we really doing?'

Audley blinked, obviously perplexed by the question. 'We're going to see General Leigh-Woodhouse.'

'But why? How can anything that happened in 1916 – and anything that happened on Hameau Ridge – have anything to do with what's happening *now*? It's crazy.'

'Crazy?' Audley sat back, suddenly more relaxed. 'No, it's not crazy. Intriguing, certainly – maybe even remarkable. But not crazy.'

'It's crazy to think anyone would kill someone because of what happened so long ago – that certainly doesn't make any sense.'

'Very unlikely, I agree. But the past is always waiting to revenge itself on the present. Take buried treasure, for instance: that's a killer for you.'

'Well, there's no goddamn treasure buried on the Somme. Just a million dud shells and half a million dead soldiers.'

'Again – I agree. But the past has a way of catching up on us, as a historian you should agree with that. You wouldn't be here now if the past hadn't caught up with you, and that's a fact you can't argue with.'

'But – '

'No! Now listen, Paul.' As Audley spoke the last vestige of flippancy left his voice. 'There are too many facts relating to each other here for coincidence. Ted Ollivier's bit of Somme map, and Emerson's visit to the Somme before he was killed – and his visit to George Davis. And your visit to him and what happened to you afterwards.'

'But you said the French – the SDP – are mixed up in it. And Colonel Butler said the French security were out in force. That's quite different from trying to find out what happened in 1916 – that's happening now.'

'Of course it is. And you don't think I really care what happened in 1916, do you?' Audley stopped suddenly, smiling. 'Actually I am rather interested – you've aroused my curiosity with your Poachers. But they aren't important.'

'So what is?'

'What is? Well we don't know yet. But I'm guessing that your Charles Emerson saw something, or someone, that he shouldn't have done. And I'd guess he saw them somewhere in a place which interested him for a quite different reason – a pure 1916 reason, you might say.'

'But he didn't really know what he'd seen?'

'In 1916 terms he knew – and it excited him so much he started digging here in England immediately, and planned to go back to France as soon as he could. Which was why he had to die, I'm betting.'

'And you want me to spot the same thing?'

'That's exactly it. Because whatever it is, it won't mean a thing to me, but it will to you. And I'm betting it will excite you just as much.'

'And then?'

Audley shrugged. 'That'll be the moment of truth, I'm hoping. Because when you see what he saw I think I'll see what he missed.'

8

The first thing Mitchell noticed about General Leigh-Woodhouse was that his head was like a billiard ball, so shiny that it caught the light from the standard lamp behind his high-backed chair.

The second thing was that the General's aura of kindly good humour shone as brightly as his bald head and that his almost toothless smile of welcome had an authenticity which went beyond conventional good manners.

And the third thing, and the least surprising one, was that the General was as courteous as he was decrepit: although he required two sticks and a great deal of exertion to rise from the chair – the parchment-thin skin was drawn tight over the knuckles, conveying the hidden effort behind that simple action – rise he nevertheless did.

'Dr Audley and Captain Lefevre? Come in, gentlemen – take a pew.' He waited patiently until they were seated before subsiding back himself.

'Now what can it be that you want to see me about?' The implication was clear that as far as the General was concerned it was both a pleasure and a surprise that anyone should want to see him about anything. 'But first you must have a drink – sherry or whisky? Will you see to it, Captain?' The slender, bony figure pointed towards a small table bearing decanters and glasses. 'You will excuse me if I don't join you. I am rationed to one glass a day, and I do prefer to take that in the evening, but do please help yourselves – ' he chuckled ' – and I shall content myself with the vicarious pleasure of watching you drink.'

'Thank you, General,' said Audley. 'Whisky, Paul – not too much.'

'Thank you, sir,' echoed Paul. Somehow he felt more disgracefully a fraud than ever in the General's presence.

'Good.' Worse still, the General was examining him carefully now. 'The Royal Tank Regiment, eh?'

'Yes, sir.'

'Where stationed?'

'Germany, sir.'

'Leave, eh? Or duty?' The bright old eyes twinkled behind the spectacles.

'Duty,' said Audley. 'Special duty.'

'Special duty?' The twinkle faded a little. 'And what special duty brings you both to me, of all people?'

'Do – did you by any chance know a Professor Charles Emerson?'

'Charles Emerson?' General Leigh-Woodhouse's eyebrows lifted above his spectacles. 'Why, yes – I know Charles Emerson. That is to say I knew him.' The frail hand patted a creased copy of *The Times* which lay on the top of a pile of books beside him. 'I was reading about his death just a few minutes ago – a shocking tragedy. Why do you want to know?'

'You knew him well?'

'Not well. He came to see me last year about a book he was writing. Asked me some questions and then went away again. He struck me as having his head screwed on the right way – they were sensible questions.'

'What about?'

'A bit about the Somme – I was wounded in Bouillet Wood there. And some more about the fighting up the Ancre in '17. He certainly knew his stuff, there wasn't much I could tell him he didn't know better already.' He chuckled modestly. It was certainly true, thought Mitchell, that Emerson really did know more about the battles on that front than those who had actually taken part in them. What was more unusual was that here was someone – and a general at that – who accepted the fact without rancour.

'But has he come to see you more recently? As recently as last week?'

'Ah – now, he did try to – ' the General wagged a finger ' – you're quite right there. But I was away in Oxford staying with my daughter – no, not my daughter, my granddaughter.' He smiled broadly. 'And now you'll be thinking I'm getting ga-ga – which may be true, but not for that reason. It's just that my granddaughter is the image of my daughter at that age. Married to some sort of biologist, she is – a decent type all the same . . . Let me see, now – I only got back here the day before yesterday, and my housekeeper told me he'd called and that he said he'd be coming back to see me again, poor fellow. I was rather looking forward to it, too. He understood about the First war, did Emerson – fought in Italy himself during the last lot, and some of that wasn't unlike the First war, you know. The Anzio fighting, for instance.' He paused suddenly. 'But that's funny – you're the second person I've told this to. Practically the self-same questions. And certainly the same answers – only yesterday.'

For once Audley didn't come back directly. Perhaps for once, thought Mitchell, Audley was moved by the same conflicting emotions as he himself was feeling, disappointment swallowed up by relief.

General Leigh-Woodhouse had been saved by his granddaugh-ter in Oxford and her decent biologist husband just as surely as if they had plucked him out of the path of a runaway bus. Maybe after killing twice – three times including himself – the enemy had grown more cautious before increasing their score without first checking on the necessity for it . . . Maybe they'd checked on George Davis just like this, but had found that unlike the General he knew too much ... And maybe they had balanced the risk of leaving the General alive against the risk of killing someone as distinguished in his way as Charles Emerson, unlike the humble old soldier and the unknown researcher whose deaths would never make headlines.

No matter. For whatever reason this kindly old gentleman, who would have been as easy to kill as a kitten, had been spared. And that was something to be glad about.

'What was he like?' Audley had recovered his wits.

'Charles Emerson?'

'The man who came and asked you about him?'

General Leigh-Woodhouse considered Audley in silence for a few moments. 'First, you tell me a thing or two, Dr Audley. I am beginning to become a little curious about my sudden popularity with strangers –' he took the edge off the words by adding a smile to them '– delighted as I am to see you both, because I don't get many visitors these days.'

This would have been the point where Colonel Butler thundered to their rescue, but for the life of him Mitchell couldn't think of anything to say that might divert the General from his curiosity. And since the General outranked him possibly Butler might not have attempted a rescue this time, anyway.

'Well, I'll tell you, General,' said Audley. 'It's altogether possible that your visitor killed two innocent people yesterday, tried to kill a third – and thought he'd succeeded – and contemplated killing a fourth. Would that be sufficient reason to want to know about him?'

'Killed – ?' Shock was succeeded quickly by disbelief on the General's face. 'You're not serious?'

Audley seemed somewhat surprised by the reaction. 'What makes you think I'm not, General?'

'Well, there are a lot of cranks around these days. Had a

young couple round last week trying to make a Christian of me.'
The General continued to scrutinise Audley as though checking
him for signs of eccentricity. 'And if there was a mass-murderer
loose and he'd come calling on me – well, you're not a policeman, I'm certain about that, whatever you are – ' the eyes
switched to Mitchell, disconcertingly shrewd and hard now
' – and you're certainly not a policeman either, Captain. So what
are you, eh?'

Mitchell could see that the wind had been quite comically
taken from Audley's sails. He was accustomed to people turning
awkward, but not to being taken for a crank.

The General leaned forward. 'Hmm! I see you are perfectly
serious. God bless my soul!'

Audley drew a deep breath, reaching into his breast pocket for
the magic folder. 'Perfectly serious. We're from the Ministry of
Defence.'

'*That* lot?' Leigh-Woodhouse held the folder at arm's length.
His gaze shifted again from Audley to Mitchell as if he was about
to question what a nice clean-cut lad was up to in such doubtful
company.

'I was the third target, sir,' said Mitchell quickly. 'The one
that got away.'

'And you were very nearly the fourth, General,' said Audley
harshly. 'You've had a lucky escape.'

'I have?' The General sat back, resting his hands on the arms
of his chair. 'Well, I won't ask you how or why, because you'd
only tell me a pack of lies of course. What is it you want to
know? What the man was like, eh?'

'For a start, yes.'

'For a start . . .' The General smoothed his bald head thoughtfully. 'Well, he said his name was Craig – James Craig – and
that he was a freelance journalist. He said he was doing a series
of articles on the Great War and Charles Emerson had recom-

mended me to him. Said maybe Emerson had mentioned him when he came to see me just recently – and of course I told him that Emerson hadn't yet seen me, just as I've told you.'

'Can you describe him?'

'Nothing unusual about him. Medium height, darkish hair, horn-rimmed spectacles . . . youngish – about thirty-five, I'd say, but his hair was rather long and I find it hard to guess a man's age when he wears his hair long. A London accent. Not a very remarkable person.'

'And he asked you about the war?'

The General nodded. 'That's right – and nothing very remarkable there, either. He didn't seem to know a great deal about it for a man who was going to write on the subject. But then he was only a journalist, so I don't suppose that would worry him too much.'

'He asked you about the Somme?'

'Yes, that's right. How did you know?'

'What did you tell him?'

'What did I tell him?' The General stared at them. 'Well, nothing very startling, certainly . . . but I suppose it's no good my asking what possible use to you anything I say will be, eh?'

'I'm afraid we don't really know ourselves,' said Audley disarmingly. 'But if we know the questions he asked and the answers you gave, that'll be a start anyway.'

'Well, you know best – ' The General shook his head ' – but I fear it'll be of little use to you. Which was what I told him, in fact. You'll learn far more from what Miles wrote in the Official History – it's in the shelf over there, Captain, down by your elbow – that's it.'

The General's collected volumes were faded and thumbed, unlike the pristine copy in the car, and Mitchell could see that the Somme one had been heavily annotated long ago in thin spidery handwriting, full of tail loops and curlicues, in violet ink.

'You find the place, Captain. It's in the battle of Hameau,

about three-quarters of the way through. I think there's a marker in it.'

A marker there was: the menu of the Christmas dinner of 'C' Company, the 29th Battalion of the Rifles, December 27th, 1915.

Mitchell examined the card, fascinated.

'SOUPE "ROLE RENVERSE" (It is usually we who are in it – TURKEY & SAUSAGES ("Made" in France) – CHOUX DE BRUXELLES (Further refugees) – POMMES DE TERRE "DUG-OUT" – PLUM PUDDING (An excellent opportunity of getting a little of your own back) – CHINESE "QUICK-MARCH" – RATION BISCUITS – DESSERT (Nobody wants to. Much too risky in war time) – CAFE (Not yet out of bounds) – SPIRITS – LIQUEURS (Not for the youngsters).'

He turned the card over. There were five officers, including a 2nd Lieut. D. W. Leigh-Woodhouse, and well over a hundred NCOs and other ranks – nearer 150 including a dozen or more machine-gun instructors who had shared the feast. He ran his eye down the printed names. If Leigh-Woodhouse had eventually been George Davis's company commander it didn't follow that they'd been in the same company at the start of the battle. But it would be useful to know, nevertheless.

Acting Corpl. Davis G.

It was the Rifle Brigade, of course, and there was no such thing as a Lance Corporal in it – they were always called Acting Corporals. Obviously this battalion of civilians had taken over all the jealously-guarded Rifle Brigade customs and usages, lock, stock and barrel.

'Have you found it?' said the General rather querulously. 'The 291st Brigade attack, you want.'

The 291st Brigade moved forward at 4.30 a.m. when the guns lifted their fire to form a barrage beyond . . .'

'Yes, sir. Where do you want me to start?' Mitchell could see that the violet ink marks didn't start for a long paragraph after the lifting of the barrage.

'With the Berkshires, boy – they were just ahead of us. Our "D" Company supported them, poor devils.'

'*The 9/North Berks Fusiliers –* '

'That's it. Go on from there.'

'*The 9/North Berkshire Fusiliers lost heavily by enfilade machine-gun fire, direct and indirect, from Bouilletcourt Farm and Bouillet Wood as it approached Hope Trench and came to a halt in shell-holes some distance short of their objective. By then Lieut. Colonel H. P. T. Challener had been mortally wounded and every officer except one hit.*'

'Go on a few paragraphs, Captain.'

'Yes, sir . . . *Following them, the rest of the 29/Rifle Brigade also suffered from enfilade fire, but it was at this point that the crew of the second tank broken down in the sunken road behind Honey Trench succeeded in restarting their machine –* '

Mitchell looked at the General. 'You've written "Euclid" in the margin, here, sir?'

'That's right. Euclid was the name of the tank. It was commanded by a lieutenant with a classical education, we went back in the same ambulance together. He was a schoolmaster from Yorkshire, and he insisted on telling me why he was there. It seems they'd come round asking for volunteers who understood the working of the internal combustion engine. He assumed it was for the Army Service Corps, so he naturally volunteered – he maintained he was a tank commander under false pretences. I told him he should have known better than to have volunteered . . . He'd called his tank "Euclid" anyway. We were supposed to have two tanks that morning – it was only the second time I'd ever seen the wretched things.' He acknowledged Mitchell's badges with an apologetic chuckle. 'I'm sorry, my boy, but they *were* wretched things in those days; they were frightfully slow and they were always breaking down. And the poor fellows inside were practically asphyxiated by the carbon monoxide from the engines, I believe – not at all what you're used to.'

Mitchell smiled back uneasily. It was ironical that in reality the only tanks he knew anything about at all were the General's 'wretched things', which he had studied at length. Indeed, the old man's memories of them came as no surprise at all, they tallied with other first-hand accounts he had received from survivors of Flers and Bullecourt; only the armchair strategists of a later generation confused Haig's tanks with Rommel's panzers.

'Anyway, both our tanks broke down. One broke its tail on the way up – those wheels at the back, you know.'

'The hydraulic stabiliser.'

'That's it. And the other one, the schoolmaster's tank, was stopped in a sunken road just behind our front line, so the poor old Berkshires attacked without it, for all the good it might have done them. But go on, Captain, go on.'

' – *succeeded in restarting their machine. Veering to the right –* '

'That was the only direction it could veer,' murmured the General. 'There was something wrong with its steering – that was how it got into the sunken road in the first place, I think.'

Mitchell stole a side-glance at Audley and was surprised to find an expression of rapt attention. Either the big man was a fine actor or he was genuinely interested.

But the General was looking at him, expectantly.

'*Veering to the right, this tank dealt with a machine-gun in Harrow Trench and successfully engaged the strongpoint on the edge of Bouillet Wood –* '

'Huh!' snorted the General, matching a violet exclamation mark in the margin. 'Go on, go on!'

' – *and enabling the surviving members of the flank company to enter the southern tip of the wood –* '

'Successfully engaged?' The bald head shook vehemently. '"Successfully engaged the attention" was more like it. It did that at least, so I suppose it's fair enough, that last bit. But our chaps were the ones who dealt with that strongpoint, as I remember, because that was when it got ditched for good and all. Go on, then.'

' – *before breaking down again. Although tangled undergrowth made movement difficult, the Riflemen skirmished through the wood with skill and determination, being joined by the rest of the battalion and a party from the 9/North Berkshires (consisting of one sergeant and twenty-four men). As the light increased the Riflemen and Fusiliers fought their way through the southern part of the wood, suffering more casualties (including Lieut. Colonel Lord St Blaizey, killed by a sniper) but extinguishing all resistance by Germans belonging to the 450th Reserve Regiment –* '

'Bavarians. Good soldiers – died hard.' The General regarded Mitchell benignly. 'One of them saved my life.'

'Saved your life?'

'Oh, he didn't mean to. He meant to do exactly the opposite – he shot me. Just here – ' The General tapped his shoulder ' – bullet went clean through, made a big hole in the back. What we used to call "a nice blighty one"; sent me back to England.'

'And that saved your life?' said Audley.

'Undoubtedly, yes. I was the senior subaltern left by then, the company commander had been killed, so I was leading the company. The chap who took over from me – a friend of mine named Dickie Dyson, a very nice boy, very brave – much braver than me, I was a timid fellow – he came up to take over from me. I remember I was lying in a shell-hole between the roots of a tree, there were still quite a lot of trees standing in the wood at that time, unlike later on, and I could see first light through them, so I knew we were near the edge of the wood . . . we seemed to have been going through it for hours . . .'

The General fell silent, staring at a point in space just above him.

'It's really quite a small wood, Bouillet Wood,' said Mitchell, gently jogging him forward.

'Is it now? You know it then?'

Mitchell nodded. 'I was there in 1971. It's grown up again and there's quite a large house in it.'

'Is there indeed? And you say it's small?' The General nodded politely. 'Well, you see – it does seem very large when you can't get out of it ... and I was absolutely convinced I was dying and that I was there for good. In fact, I said to him – quite stupidly – "They've done for me, Dickie." And I told him to push on to the edge of the wood and dig in there.' He paused again, looking candidly at Mitchell. 'You see, what I was afraid of was that the Germans would counter-attack from the Prussian Redoubt and I should be left alone in there. But then I remembered the man who'd just shot me, and I said "Watch out for the sniper, Dickie – it's almost morning now" – by which I meant that he could see us properly. And he said "Well then, Woody, I expect I'll be saying 'Good morning, God' in a moment or two" ... and *crack* – the moment he put his head up over the edge of the hole the sniper got him too. Killed him straight off, just like that – *crack!*'

He spoke quite without rancour or sadness; it had all happened so long ago and in another country, and a million other Dickie Dysons and snipers had died since then, too many to allow even a particle of feeling to be expended on them.

'And what happened then?'

'Ah, well strictly speaking I can't tell you, because I passed out as he tumbled back on top of me, poor chap. And the next thing I remember was lying in Battalion Aid Post, next to the schoolmaster from the tank. But they told me what happened ... You see, there was one of my acting corporals with me, George Davis, who was my sergeant-major at Ypres the next year ... and as Dickie fell back into the hole he dropped his shotgun.'

'His shotgun?' said Audley.

'Yes, one or two of our chaps – the officers, that is – went into action with them. Harry Bellamy of "D" Company had a silver-chased one, a real beauty. He claimed it made the war more of a sporting occasion, though I believe the Germans regarded shotguns as *un*sporting. Actually, except for the need to keep reloading they were quite sensible weapons for close fighting . . . Anyway, when Dickie dropped his, Corporal Davis snatched it up quick as lighting and shot the German with it – he was only a few yards away, and Davis had seen the flash.'

And Davis, being an ex-gamekeeper, would have probably been more deadly with his own type of weapon than with a rifle, reflected Mitchell.

'But that's only what they told me, of course. I didn't see it with my own eyes. In fact I missed the really remarkable part of the whole show.'

Audley cocked his head on one side. 'Remarkable?'

The General looked to Mitchell for confirmation. 'I don't think that's too strong a word for it. It always seemed like that to me when I heard about it afterwards, anyway.'

Audley also turned to Mitchell. 'And is this your mystery, Paul?'

Mitchell had an uneasy feeling that after waiting so long for it, Audley would find the climax of the Poachers' achievement something of an anti-climax.

He bent his attention to the Official History again.

'*All the oficers and senior NCOs of the feeding companies now being killed or wounded, parties of Riflemen nevertheless debouched from the eastern side of Bouillet Wood. Although for the most part leaderless, but still in good heart, they pressed down Scrub and Scarab Trenches towards the Prussian Redoubt, negotiating several makeshift bomb-stops which had been hastily constructed by men of the German 155th Reserve Grenadiers. Machine-gun fire from the Redoubt now began to slacken, the whole area having been under heavy shellfire (though whether from British or German artillery is by no means clear).*

'*Entering the Redoubt, the surviving Riflemen found that the garrison had been almost wiped out by the bombardment and that every dugout had been blown in. Although the handful of German soldiers remaining resisted with great gallantry, fighting to the last man, the position was effectively in British hands by 7.30 a.m.'*

He raised his eyes to meet Audley's. 'Well, that's it.'

'That's . . . it?' Audley looked puzzled.

'As far as the Poachers are concerned. There were two or three NCOs left and about sixty-five riflemen. Out of about three hundred who went into the wood, plus a handful of Berkshires.'

'Seventy-nine all told,' said the General.

'There were two Australian brigades who came up in support immediately after – ' Mitchell tailed off as he saw the disappointment in the big man's expression. 'Jesus Christ! They took the Prussian Redoubt, don't you see?'

Audley nodded slowly. 'Yes. A great feat of arms, you said. I see that.'

'They weren't meant to – '

'Hah! And we weren't even meant to think of trying,' the General observed. 'In the unlikely event of getting through the wood we were supposed to dig in at once on the edge.'

Audley stared from one to the other of them. 'Yes, I understand that too. But where's the – ah – the mystery?'

'The mystery?' The General sat back, contemplating the word. 'Well, perhaps "mystery" is a trifle strong. But the Germans did behave in a most extraordinary manner, no doubt about that.'

'The Germans?' Audley repeated in surprise. 'I thought we were talking about the Poachers.'

'Good gracious me – no!' The General laughed. 'Our chaps behaved foolishly, even suicidally. But that was quite understandable, perfectly understandable.'

'Understandable?' Audley said in the controlled tone of one determined to hide his bewilderment.

'Why, of course. You see, I don't think they had the slightest idea where they were. We're talking blithely about woods and villages and front lines and redoubts, but it wasn't like that at all . . . My dear fellow, I remember arriving on the Somme – that's one thing I shall never forget, never . . .'

Audley started to speak, then stopped as though some instinct had warned him off.

'It was like nothing I'd ever expected,' said the General. 'You see I imagined, as most people did, that there'd be a sort of drill trench . . . trench, wire, no-man's-land, enemy wire, enemy trench and so on, but it wasn't like that at all. To me it looked all like no-man's-land, you could hardly tell the line from what wasn't the line. It was just a mass of shell-holes . . . And, you know, you talk of attacking a redoubt – the Prussian Redoubt was built into the ruins of an old château, I believe – but it wasn't visible, it all looked alike. You didn't know when you were in your line or theirs, except for the smell. The difference was the smell: dead Germans didn't smell like dead British – I don't know what they ate or drank . . .'

He focused on Audley, nodding his head as though suddenly aware that he was digressing. 'I'm sorry – but you see there we were, in our first battle, and only a handful of us had seen the maps and none of us had ever seen the top of that ridge . . . That was what was so wonderful about them, our men – they just went on and on, even after three-quarters or more had been killed and wounded, and they hadn't any idea where they were. Maybe that's a mystery, if you like, eh? Or maybe you think we were all soft in the head – that's what my grandson maintains.'

Soft in the head. And that was what father had maintained, thought Mitchell. Grandfather victoriously dead at twenty-seven in the hole he'd punched in the Hindenburg Line and father getting up at daybreak to milk the cows, with another world war going on around him. They couldn't both be sane, that was the only certain thing, not both of them.

'But it was the Germans who behaved – well, out of character, to put it mildly.'

'How out of character?'

'They made such a hash of it, and that wasn't like them, you know.'

'Well, no one's perfect all the time,' Audley chided him mildly, 'not even the German Army.'

'My dear fellow – ' The General leaned forward in his chair ' – they were the old German Army, the old German Field Army – '

The old German Field Army. This might have been Charles Emerson talking now: if the British dead on the Somme had been the cream of the nation, irreplaceable as men, the German dead, equally numerous, had been the cream of the army, irreplaceable as soldiers.

' – and they were damn good. Dug like moles and fought like tigers . . . blow a mine under them, and they'd be back in the crater before we could get there; take a trench, and they'd come back at you before you could blow your nose – wouldn't give an inch back in '16.

'But *that* morning it was different.' The General raised a thin finger. 'They should have counter-attacked us in the wood – but they didn't. And they should have reinforced the redoubt as soon as we were in the wood – but they didn't . . . What did they do? They shelled the redoubt before we got there, knocked the blazes out of it . . . Bad enough to be shelled by the enemy, but to be shelled by your own side as well – !'

Audley started to shrug, then stopped as though unwilling to show the extent of his disappointment any further. 'Hardly the first time that's happened. But presumably they were simply taken by surprise.'

'Surprise?' The General grunted comically. 'Then we were surprised as much as they were. It was a godsend we had those Australian Brigades to hand, even though we'd done all the hard work. We'd have lost the lot if it hadn't been for them, I tell you.'

'I mean, surprised at the direction of the attack,' said Audley patiently. He turned to Mitchell. 'You said the main attack was on Hameau village – the Prussian Redoubt was an accident.'

He was sharp, thought Mitchell. That had been the generally accepted explanation for the whole extraordinary affair, which had been almost as embarrassing for the British as the Germans. For while the main thrust towards Hameau had been a disastrous failure, the Australians had gone on to take the two much-feared ravines, which had fallen into their hands like ripe plums once the redoubt had fallen. While the main part of the Corps was battering at the door, the Poachers and the Australians had lifted the whole thing off its hinges.

'How did they explain it?' Audley pursued him relentlessly.

'No one really knows. The Hameau attack pulled most of their reserves westwards, it's true. And there was a garbled message sent back to their divisional headquarters quite early on, about 6 a.m., that we were in the Redoubt – '

'Which was absolute poppycock – as I told Emerson when he came to see me last year,' said the General. 'I can vouch for that of my own knowledge, because I was right up front as we went through the wood towards the end, and I wasn't hit until after six. Which means we weren't even out of the wood then.'

This time Audley did shrug. ' "The fog of war",' he murmured. 'And it was a garbled message, you said, Paul. It could account for their shelling their own men, anyway.'

There was no mystery in Audley's mind about the taking of the Prussian Redoubt, Mitchell saw that with all the bitterness of a man who sees a favourite anecdote devalued to a minor and rather esoteric footnote. Obviously nothing short of the Angels of Mons qualified as mysterious to Audley.

'I don't agree,' he said obstinately.

Audley looked at him lazily. 'It doesn't matter, actually.'

'It doesn't – ?' Mitchell's hackles rose. 'So we're just wasting our time?'

The lazy look was transformed into a mischievous grin. 'Not at all! I mean what I think doesn't matter, not what you think, Paul. If you reckon it's a mystery that's good enough for me.'

'Eh?'

'Because Emerson will have thought the same, and that's the line we need to follow.'

Mitchell's rising irritation was blotted out by the realisation that he had been had again, had like the very tiro he was: Audley had laid down the rules of the game less than half an hour earlier, and he had clean forgotten them.

'Is there anything you could tell Emerson now that you didn't tell him last year?' Audley addressed the General. 'Is there anything fresh you've remembered?'

'Anything fresh?' The General's lip curled. 'My dear fellow, at my age you don't remember things, you forget them. And half of what I do recall, I wonder if it ever happened, or if I haven't read it somewhere. In fact I'd forgotten half of what I've told you until Emerson dredged it out of my memory . . . It's all a very long time ago, you know, a very long time.'

A very long time ago, that it was; nearer sixty years than fifty. Working so closely with it, reading the letters and the despatches, the memoirs and the communiqués, scrutinising the maps and the photographs, Mitchell knew that he sometimes fell into the trap of losing those long years between. It was difficult to appreciate that Hameau Ridge was ancient history when there were still men alive who remembered it; it was even more difficult to accept that other men had been born, had fought in another great war, had raised families and had died in those years since Second Lieutenant Leigh-Woodhouse had climbed out of his trench in the darkness and had set out for Bully Wood.

'And in any case you couldn't have told him about the Prussian Redoubt,' mused Audley to himself aloud. 'So what could you have told him that he didn't know already?'

They stared at each other in silence.

'If it's the Prussian Redoubt you want to know about, then you should ask my old sergeant-major – at least, he was my sergeant-major the next year at Ypres. He was an acting corporal then. The man who shot the sniper with Dicky Dyson's shotgun – George Davis. Lives over the hill at Elthingham. And his memory's much better than mine, for a fact.'

Damn, damn, damn.

And yet George Davis couldn't have answered every question, otherwise Emerson wouldn't have wanted to speak with Leigh-Woodhouse also. Indeed, he might not have answered any question at all . . .

'George Davis,' Audley repeated the name. 'And failing him, who else? Are there any other Poachers still alive? Men who might remember?'

Men you might have recommended to Professor Emerson, General Leigh-Woodhouse – Audley had put his finger on the possibility an instant ahead of him: it was not what the General knew, but who he knew.

'One or two – not many of us now, you know,' the General said. 'But George Davis is your man, you know. Besides, you can see him straight away, and you won't be able to talk to the others until next Thursday at the earliest.'

'Why not?'

'Because they're over there at the moment, that's why. First week in October every year – the 191st Division Old Comrades' Association goes back to the battlefields.'

Part two

Death's Kingdom

1

He had expected the terminal to be less crowded than on a working weekday, but it was as busy as ever. Yet the people eddying around him seemed to provide no protection: he felt exposed and obvious, and as lonely as a small child on his way to a new boarding school. Under Audley's protection he had almost become accustomed to sailing under false colours, but here and alone that veneer of confidence vanished utterly, leaving him naked.

'Captain Lefevre?'

There was something odd about the voice, but the oddity was overshadowed by the screaming pink-panther blazer which the speaker wore over an equally pink polo-necked sweater. At Henley Regatta it might have blended with the other rainbow colours, but here among the drab browns and greys the plump little Frenchman was like an exotic bird in a cage full of sparrows.

'It is Captain Lefevre – Captain Paul Lefevre?' Doubt creased the little man's face. 'It must be.'

It wasn't a French accent at all – it was broad Yorkshire, almost a stage 'Ah coom fra' Bradford' accent – that was what was odd about the voice. Allied to the pink blazer it almost took Mitchell's breath away.

'Er – yes,' he admitted.

'By heck, am I glad to see you, Captain!' The doubt was

replaced by profound relief. 'Here, give us your case, then. Car's just a few steps away round corner.'

Before Mitchell could stop him the little man had grabbed his suitcase.

'Lefevre is it? I thought I might have it wrong when they phoned me up last night, you know.'

'It's pronounced "Lefever",' Mitchell rallied.

'Oh, aye?' The little man beamed. 'Well, Lefevre or Lefever, you're the answer to a maiden's prayer, that's what you are, Captain – Bob Whitton's the name, that's me – Cords Coaches' Continental Manager by title – did they tell you? – and old Bert Cord's nephew by misfortune of birth, and interpreter, garage mechanic, relief driver and bloody head cook and bottle-washer by night and day to every coach-load of trouble that comes 'cross Channel, and that's the truth . . . And don't be put off by blazer, lad, I'm not queer, it's badge of servitude, that's what it is. Cord's does everything in pink – old bugger'd have me drawers in pink if 'e thought I'd lose me trousers. If it breathes, get its money – if it doesn't breathe, paint it pink, that's the motto. Come on, then – '

Before Mitchell could say anything the broad pink back was presented to him and Whitton had cleared a space ahead by flailing out with the suitcase.

'Did you 'ave a good flight?' Whitton shouted over his shoulder.

'I – ah – '

'I only say that out of 'abit because it's in book of rules. Calling it "flight" is supposed to turn bloody hovercraft into Jumbo jet. Don't like the things, meself – might as well travel in tube-train on Underground.'

That was true enough, thought Mitchell. The hovercraft was fast and convenient, but it took all the atmosphere out of the Channel crossing, the spray blanking out everything but a few blurred yards of sea from which by some optical illusion there had seemed to rise wisps of steamy mist. It had reminded him of the canal, and he hadn't liked the reminder.

Whitton stopped without warning, as suddenly as he had started off, so that Mitchell nearly collided with him as he turned round.

'No, I can't do it to you.' Whitton dumped the case on the tarmac decisively.

'Do what?'

'I've got a coach broken down in Amiens – got to go there first, and leave you to it. Maybe if I could go along with you I wouldn't feel so bad. But you look a nice lad – I'd expected one of your haw-haw la-di-da sort, you see, but you're not, so I can't do it to you. I 'aven't the 'eart.'

'The heart to do what?' Mitchell was bemused as much by the manner as the words. They seemed to have missed a whole stage in their relationship, progressing from introduction to intimacy without the interim of acquaintance.

'I wanted to see look on your face,' Whitton winked at him, 'but there you are, I'll just 'ave to imagine it. The Frogs 'ave taken finger out at last – we've been on to them for ages just like we've been on to your lot – taken it out with a vengeance, by gum! But I've got to love you and leave you at Amiens – leave you with Ministry of Tourism to look after you. Got to get that bloody coach back on road.'

Mitchell stared at him helplessly, stupefied by stampeding words.

'But I'll leave you car, lad. You can always strap yourself in if you feel scared. Maybe you won't, though – ' Whitton studied him for a moment 'Do you speak French at all?'

'Tolerably,' replied Mitchell with caution.

'Well, you don't need to worry about that.' Whitton ignored the answer. 'You've got an interpreter.'

'I don't need one,' snapped Mitchell. The last thing he needed was a goddamn Frenchman dogging his footsteps. 'This isn't the first time I've been over here.'

'Oh, aye?' Whitton's voice hardened, as though he was disappointed by such intransigence in a nice lad. 'Well, if I were you I wouldn't make up my mind straight off like that. I'm only warning you – don't say you 'aven't been warned.' He picked up the suitcase again. 'Come on, then.'

It was on the tip of Mitchell's tongue to protest that he hadn't really been warned at all, or so imprecisely that the warning was of little use. But the little Yorkshireman had disappeared round the corner ahead of him before he had time to formulate the complaint. And in any case, after Bob Whitton himself nothing could take him by surprise, he felt.

But it could.

There was no mistaking the car belonging to the Cords Coaches' continental manager: it was a Ford Capri soaked in the same shade of pink as the blazer, so that it stood out from the cars around it as horribly as Whitton had done from the crowd in the terminal.

Only Mitchell hardly noticed it – it was seen and forgotten in the same instant.

'May I introduce Captain Paul Lefevre – pronounced Lefever – ' Whitton began ponderously ' – Mademoiselle Nicole MacMahon.'

He was watching Mitchell with unconcealed curiosity now, and Mitchell had no doubt that the expression on his face would be rewarding, no matter how hard he fought to control it.

He was aware of colour first, rather than features: Mademoiselle MacMahon had burnished auburn hair and incredible green eyes, the greenest he had ever seen – it was those eyes which assured him that the coppery-red of the hair was genetic rather than artificial. And then the pale skin, which made the pink of the car a crime against humanity; and finally the striking green trouser suit, matching the hair and eyes . . . hair and eyes and skin and suit added up to a girl to take one's breath away – the sort of girl he associated with advertisements in colour supplements . . . not a real girl at all.

'How do you do, Captain?' She extended a hand.

Mitchell looked down at the small hand stupidly. There was a smudge of dirt on the knuckle of the index finger. Come to that, the trouser suit was creased from sitting in the car and there were tendrils of hair which had fallen loose from the pinned-up coils.

'Mademoiselle.' The small hand was cold.

A real girl. No different from Valerie in essentials, or from any other girl. An interpreter with the Ministry of Tourism, probably as nervous at meeting the strange English captain as the English captain was surprised at meeting her.

Whitton looked at his watch ostentatiously. 'Come on then, both of you. Goin' to 'ave plenty of time to get to know each other, you are. And I've to be in Amiens before three, or I'll not 'ave that coach of mine back on road before Christmas – Sunday double-time rates and I still don't know whether they're mechanics or statues, they move so slow. So into car with you, lass – back seat for you this time.'

The French girl shot the Yorkshireman a look of such undisguised distaste that Mitchell instinctively reached for the door-handle himself.

'Whoa, lad! You go up front.' Whitton was utterly unmoved by the look. 'Your legs are longer, and there's plenty of room for a slip of a girl in back. So come on, Mademoiselle – let's be 'avin' you, then.'

Mitchell decided he was already tired of the 'Coom on' exhortation himself, but the girl moved before he could make an issue of the matter.

Whitton took his arm. 'I don't hold with any of this women's liberation nonsense. Nor does any Frenchman neither, I'll say that for 'em,' he observed loudly. 'But truth is, lad, she doesn't approve of England, doesn't that young lady. "Bloody British", that's what we are, I reckon – ' he squeezed Mitchell's arm familiarly ' – though whether you may count as exception with your name I can't say. You may be in luck, you never know, eh? But me – I've 'ad a basin-full.'

Mitchell wondered as they moved off whether Mademoiselle MacMahon's disapproval of things English dated before or after her exposure to Bob Whitton, and if the latter whether it was because Whitton was a believer in the ancient British misapprehension about French morals which rendered all French girls fair game, or simply because his bluff familiarity had been misconstrued. More likely it was the latter, plus a bit of male chauvinism, because no continental tours manager could survive long here without learning the real score.

'Did you volunteer for this lot, then, eh? Or did they give you your marching orders?' began Whitton directly.

Mitchell tensed as the car swept into the town, trying to adjust himself to sitting in the driver's seat without anything to hold on to.

'I was ordered to join the tour,' he said cautiously.

'Aye, that's what I thought. Only a madman 'ud volunteer and you know better than that, eh?' Whitton gave a short laugh. 'That's Army for you . . . But mind you, I won't have a word said against 'em today, by gum – not a word. Even though you could 'uv downed me with a feather when Old Man phoned to say you were coming. Don't even answer our letters – too thick to see publicity value – and then give us VIP treatment when it's almost too late. Getting a full colonel up at Ypres, the old buggers 'ave, full-fledged colonel. And now you down on Somme. Have half the British Army helping out Cords Coaches 'fore we're finished, I shouldn't wonder.'

So Colonel Butler had agreed to join the veterans' coach tour – that was good news indeed.

''Course, they took their time, your lot,' Whitton quickly qualified his praise. 'Missed half the Ypres part – Pilckem, Passchendaele and Hooge for sure. Have to pick 'em up around Wytschaete and Messines, or Ploegsteert, maybe, that colonel of yours will have to. Then come across the frontier with 'em at Armentières.'

That had been Audley's plan, Mitchell remembered. Butler to become an established fixture by the time the coaches left Belgium, during which part of the tour no special knowledge of the battlefields was required.

It was eerie, all the same, to hear the little man reel off those doom-laden names, to which so many thousands had taken one-way tour tickets.

'You just run these tours for the veterans, or do other people want to see the battlefields?'

'Other people?' Whitton echoed him incredulously. 'No one else wants to see Flanders and Picardy – there isn't anything to see. 'Tisn't like Normandy – we run a lot of summer tours there. Lovely country and good food in Normandy, and beaches – *and* a battlefield, if that's what turns you on. Me, I stick to the other things. Cathedrals, castles and such like, there's something to see. Battlefields, they're just a piece of ground, just a field – unless someone's built a housing estate or a factory on it. Morbid too, to my way of thinking.'

'Morbid?' The word came out involuntarily. Someone else had said that – it had been Butler, that first time in the Institute.

'Not those old boys, they're different – they fought there. That gives them right to go back if they've a mind to.' Whitton paused, then shot him a quick glance. 'And I don't mean you neither, lad; you're in same profession, and you've got your orders too, come to that. And of course there's some as 'ave got relatives buried there in the cemeteries – that's really all there is to see, cemeteries, dozens and dozens of 'em.' He sighed, looking sidelong at Mitchell. 'To be honest, I'm glad we don't make a profit out of 'em – did you know we don't make a penny on these tours?'

'Indeed?' But just yesterday General Leigh-Woodhouse had put it another way, Mitchell remembered: the cut-price expeditions Cords Coaches had clinched with several old comrades' associations enabled the firm to keep all their vehicles busy in the off-season, breaking even after the holiday business had tailed off. Whitton was simply trying to create a good impression for the Army's benefit now: official recognition was no doubt well worth having.

But he needed more information. 'How long does it last, the tour?'

'A week from door to door. Three days in Flanders and two in France. And you've got easiest bit, too – most of 'em are a bit knackered after first two or three days. Go to bed earlier, and that.'

'You always take them to the same places?'

'Oh, no.' The negative shake of the head was vigorous. 'We take 'em where they want to go, it's all agreed in advance. Depends on what they were in, you see. Ypres and the Somme are the regular stops, most want to go there. Last year I took one lot up and down Messines ridge for hours – miners they were. Another lot'll want to see the St Quentin Canal or Cambrai. It all depends where they were.'

Mitchell felt he had arrived at the vital point in the dialogue in a sufficiently roundabout manner. 'And this group of mine, where are they going?'

'Ypres and the Somme, same as most of 'em.'

'But where on the Somme?'

Whitton pointed. 'There's a bit of paper in compartment

there, I guessed you'd want to know so I wrote it down for you.'

Mitchell unfolded the paper, which not only bore the Cords Coaches superscription but was also hideously and distinctively pink into the bargain.

Vimy Ridge –

'They're going to Vimy first?'

'Aye. To see the Memorial, and that. You meet up with them there. Then Bapaume for the night.'

Bapaume, Le Sars, Guyencourt, Hameau No. 1 Cemetery, the Glory Hole, the Ulster Tower, Prussian Redoubt Cemetery, the Serre Road Cemeteries, High Wood, Pozières Church, Thiepval Memorial, Newfoundland Park, Albert . . .

There was one name missing.

'Is this the lot?'

'The lot? They won't even manage all those, lad, I can tell you. They're not spring lambs any more, you 'ave to let 'em take their time. You rush 'em and you'll 'ave one drop dead on you, mark my words,' Whitton admonished him gravely. It was obvious that sudden death among his elderly charges was one of his biggest nightmares.

'I don't mean that. But you've left out Bouillet Wood, haven't you?'

'No lad, that's private, that is.'

'I know. But Monsieur Regnier always lets you in if you ask.'

Whitton gave him a quick glance, frowning. 'Monsieur Regnier? How d'you come to know Monsieur Regnier?'

Mitchell was aware too late that in his eagerness he had maybe gone too far in showing such interest in Bouillet Wood and, in doing so, by revealing an unexpected degree of special knowledge. Also too late he remembered Audley's parting advice to accept nobody on his face value . . . and because on face value nobody could be more innocent than Bob Whitton he had immediately forgotten every syllable of that advice.

Talk your way out of this, Captain Lefevre!

'I t-told you, I've been over here before, t-to France, I mean,' he stuttered.

Too quick ... Why would Captain Lefevre have met old Amaury Prosper Regnier? Think, Captain Lefevre: why would Bully Wood interest you?

Euclid!

'My regiment – ' Mitchell slowed his voice to a drawl ' – we used tanks for the first time on the Somme, Mr Whitton. One of them was used in the attack on Bouillet Wood. When I was over here in '71 I visited all the locations of early tank actions – Flers and Coucelette, Morval, Gueudecourt, High Wood and Bouillet Wood, Saucourt l'Abbaye – '

Whitton cut him off with a grunt; running battlefield tours had clearly not aroused his interest in the battles themselves – he had already indicated as much.

'Aye – well, he's dead now, Regnier is,' he said.

'Dead?' Mitchell repeated sharply. 'How?'

'How?' Whitton sounded as surprised by the question as Mitchell had been by the information. 'Well, old age for a start, lad – 'e was eighty if 'e was a day. And 'e had a bad chest, too. Bronchitis, I think it was. Just about a year since.'

Mitchell relaxed. A year ago ruled out the same foul play that had carried off Charles Emerson and George Davis, and the bronchitis rang true. As a liaison officer with the British Regnier had taken a lung-full of chlorine at Ypres in the first gas attack in 1915.

'But you're right,' Whitton conceded. ''E always let us into wood. But new man won't. His agent says wood's private property, and that's that. Won't even let us use track past it to cemetery, the blighter.'

'The Prussian Redoubt Cemetery?'

'Aye. We've to use the road on t'other side, which means 'alf a mile walk up the ridge.'

Mitchell lapsed into silence, letting his brain slip into top gear. He was sure he had something valuable to give Audley now, something that justified his earlier error. It could well be that the new owner of Bouillet Wood was as keen on breeding pheasants there as Amaury Regnier had been, yet not so much of an Anglophile as to be willing for them to be disturbed. But there was absolutely no reason why he shouldn't let a couple of dozen old Englishmen walk along the track at its side and across the open ridge to the war cemetery, where the Poachers lay in rows beside their Berkshire and Australian comrades in the centre of what had once been the Prussian Redoubt. Even an Anglophobe Frenchman would think twice before doing anything like that: it was ungracious in a peculiarly unGallic way, and therefore suspiciously ungracious.

He sensed a movement at his shoulder and in the same instant was conscious of the French girl's perfume; after the impact of that first sight of her the fact that he could so quickly forget her presence struck him as rather disturbing. He was not himself in more ways than one, that was for sure.

He swivelled sideways in his seat. 'I'm sorry – we must be boring you, mademoiselle.'

'Not at all. You are a student of military history, naturally.'

She had an enchantingly husky voice, a positively come-hither voice. If that had led Whitton on to make a tactical error, then maybe the error was excusable.

'Regimental history, anyway,' he smiled at her, secure in his uniform for the very first time. Whatever the defects of his disguise might be, he had nothing to fear from a French girl.

'And you are of a tank regiment?'

'The Royal Tank Regiment,' Mitchell nodded. He pointed to his badge, 'That's a portrait of the world's first tank, mademoiselle.'

Mademoiselle MacMahon examined the badge politely. 'Yes, Captain.' The green eyes surveyed him. 'But it is true, is it not, that France also produced tanks at the same time as the British – independently?'

Mitchell's jaw dropped and he was forced to cover his confusion with an unintelligible sound. 'Er – ah – ' For God's sake, a French girl who knew about tanks – it wasn't possible! 'Well, yes – that is to say – yes.'

'The Schneider and the St Charmond,' added Mademoiselle MacMahon sweetly. 'And later the Renault.'

Whitton gave an amused grunt. 'She's got you there, lad,' he observed in the satisfied tones of one whose warning had passed unheeded. 'I knew she'd 'ave you one way or t'other.'

And more cruelly than the Yorkshireman could possibly know, fumed Mitchell. The Schneider had proved incapable of crossing wide trenches and the St Charmond hadn't appeared in significant numbers until well into 1917. But how could he possibly say so, short of a formal declaration of war?

He compromised. 'They weren't actually used until 1917 – ' he began.

Mademoiselle MacMahon had no such scruples. 'The British used them prematurely,' she said accusingly. 'There were at the Somme but a handful – perhaps fifty, yes? And half of them broke down before they reached the front line.'

That was exactly the sort of facile popular half-truth Charles Emerson had been engaged in demolishing, Mitchell thought bitterly, beginning himself to feel like one of the tanks which had come so painfully and secretly all the way from England, only to run into an unexpected and unfair obstacle in the last mile . . . No wonder Whitton had come unstuck with this beautiful opinionated blue-stocking.

But this time he was determined not to behave like a beginner: defeating her arguments presented no problem at all, and ordinarily it would have been a labour of love. But that would be the action of Paul Mitchell, whereas Paul Lefevre had been raised on the Maintenance of the Objective as the first principle of war and had bigger fish to fry than young Frenchwomen.

Paul Lefevre found it very much easier to swallow his irritation and smile charmingly. 'I think we'd better argue that one when we know each other better, Mademoiselle MacMahon,' he said. 'But if you'll allow me to change the subject – "MacMahon" is a most unusual French name.'

'Aye. Sounds Scottish to me,' chipped in Whitton. 'Are you a Highland lass in disguise, Mademoiselle, eh?'

The girl paused before replying, as though disappointed that the British tanks were moving out of her range.

'In fact it is an Irish name,' she said finally.

'Of course!' Whitton nodded at the road ahead wisely. 'I should 'ave realised. You've got proper Irish colouring, and that's a fact.' He half turned towards her. 'And did your father come from Ireland, then?'

Again there was a slight pause. 'No, Mr Whitton,' she said. 'It was the great-grandfather of my great-grandfather's grandfather.'

'And 'e emigrated to France – all those years since?'

'No, Mr Whitton. He did not emigrate, he fled from the persecution of the English, like many thousand other Irishmen. And he came to France to join the Irish Brigade in the French Army – to fight the English with twenty thousand other good Irishmen.' She threw Mitchell a cool glance. 'It is an unusual name, Captain. But there are plenty of others like it – Maguires and Dillons and O'Reillys. I think you might be surprised how many there are.'

They had jumped out of the frying pan into the fire – and a fierce Irish fire, too, which had evidently not cooled in two and a half centuries or more.

'Have you served in Ireland recently, Captain?'

And there, of course, was the fresh fuel for the old fire.

'No, mademoiselle. Happily not.'

She nodded. 'But naturally! The English have not yet used tanks in Ireland. Armoured cars are sufficient for civilians.'

But there was a limit even to what Captain Lefevre could take. Particularly Captain Lefevre, in fact.

'But we do have something in common, you and I, mademoiselle. Very much in common.'

'Indeed?'

'Oh, yes. You see my ancestors fled from persecution also, but in the opposite direction. They fled to England from French persecution.' He grinned. 'In fact that's how the word "refugee" came into the English language – that's what my French protestant ancestors were called. And, mademoiselle, the ironic thing is that our refugee regiments helped the English drive your ancestors out of Ireland. Tit for tat, in fact.'

It was going to be a bumpy ride up the line to the Somme.

2

A million men had marched down the old Roman road into Albert, staring up at the great golden statue of the Virgin hanging precariously at right angles from the highest pinnacle of the shattered cathedral, but Mitchell had never heard the echo of a single footfall.

Only now there was a new ghost at his back to remind him of what lay beyond the town. For it had always been here, on the slope just beyond the high-water mark of the last German offensive of 1918, that Charles Emerson had stopped the car as though to draw breath before going on through the little town to the start lines of the 1916 British advance.

Obediently he slowed the car down and pulled in to the roadside, staring across the drab roofs at the second Golden Virgin, the replacement for that finally lost without a trace during the war's closing convulsion. When the Virgin fell, the war would end – that superstition at least had been not far off the mark.

Abruptly he reached for the starter, conscious of the girl beside him.

'I'm sorry. I suppose we'd better get on,' he apologised.

'There's no hurry. Our rooms in Arras are booked, so if you want to stop and look at anything, I do not mind – I quite understand,' she said.

'Understand?' He turned and looked at her questioningly. 'Understand – what?'

'Why – that you might want to stop and look,' she replied, meeting his gaze candidly. 'If there is a piece of France that is English it is here. If I were an Englishman I would not drive quickly past it. I would wish to see.'

Some corner of a foreign field . . .

'Thank you, mademoiselle.'

She had mellowed appreciably during the past few miles, he decided. During the drive to Amiens they had fought to a Franco-Irish-Anglo-French stalemate, over a two-hundred-year battlefield stretching from the banks of the Boyne to the Suez Canal in 1956. But once Bob Whitton had left them to attend his ailing coach the fire had seemed to go out of their antipathy and they had moved from hostilities to truce, and from truce to armistice; it was as though the Yorkshireman's presence itself had set them at each other's throat.

'My friends call me Nikki, Captain.'

And now from armistice to honourable peace? The change in her mood was quite startling now ... but also undeniably gratifying, opening up most delectable possibilities, Walter Mitty dreams which until this moment had been too far removed from reality for serious consideration –

> *The next thing we'll pray for –*
> *We'll pray for a wench:*
> *O Lord, may we have one,*
> *And may she be French!*

Except that was a Bob Whitton prayer, unworthy of an officer and a gentleman, even a bogus one – and particularly a bogus one with other things to think about. He dare not forget that for one moment.

But friendship, platonic friendship, innocent and uncomplicated, might lend Captain Lefevre a little extra substance. Certainly, no one would look twice at him when they could look once at Mademoiselle MacMahon, and it would be worth seeing Audley's face when he turned up with her on his arm.

'And my friends call me Paul.' He grinned at her: how very easy it was to live a lie when there was no alternative! It was positively habit-forming. 'And we can agree to differ on past history?'

'We can invoke the Entente Cordiale, can we not?' She returned the grin, and then her face grew serious again. 'You wish to see the battlefield – Paul?'

'Why not?' No time like the present. 'We can see a piece of it before it gets dark, anyway. Is there anything you'd particularly like to see?'

'I don't know what there is to see.' She gave a small shrug. 'To tell the complete truth, I do not really know very much about your battle, Paul.'

'But I thought you were an expert – all that stuff about tanks you fed me – where did that come from?'

She grimaced. 'From a book. Monsieur Whitton told me on the phone an officer from the British Tank Corps was coming to join his party, so I tried to do my homework.' She paused. 'But it was a very terrible battle, that I know – as Verdun was for France.'

If anywhere had been the British Verdun, it had been Ypres, thought Mitchell. But there was no point in quibbling about it, it was relief enough to discover that she wasn't such a bluestocking after all, and that he wouldn't have to re-fight every inch of the Somme with her. The important thing now was to get a look at Bouillet Wood as soon as possible without being too obvious about it.

'Terrible – yes, it was that sure enough,' he nodded. Only terrible wasn't the half of it: if there was a word in the English language for the loss of fifty-seven thousand men in a few hours that first day, he'd never been able to find one. He'd always felt the same inadequacy at this precise point on the road out of

Albert – the town had passed like a phantom – on the last rise before the German lines came into view ahead. But he mustn't think of that now.

'So where shall we go?' She spoke softly now, as though she sensed his sombre mood.

Hameau Ridge without being too obvious.

'La Boiselle's just ahead – ' he thought for a moment ' – this is where the Tynesiders attacked – the Tyneside Scottish and the Tyneside Irish. And that's the beginning of Sausage Valley on the right there – ' He pointed.

'Valley?' She peered along his finger. 'Where?'

It was the identical question he had put to Emerson when they had first come this way: the awful Sausage Valley, in which wave after wave of the Geordies had passed through machine-gun fire on three sides of them, had loomed in his imagination like the Valley of Death at Balaclava. But when he had come face to face with it he had found that a thousand men had fallen in a few yards of gently dipping fields of sugar beet.

He remembered General Leigh-Woodhouse's memory of Bouillet Wood: '*And you say it's very small? But it does seem large when you can't get out of it . . .*'

He swung the car to the right just at the edge of the village, ploughing alongside a narrow, crazily-humped wilderness of grass.

'There you are, Nikki: the Glory Hole. Guaranteed untouched by human hand since 1916.'

'The – what?'

'The Glory Hole. It's an original piece of no-man's land – the trenches were so close here they could bomb each other all the time without artificial aids. But don't ask me why it's been left, I don't know why.'

Nikki craned her neck at the Glory Hole. 'There's a sign saying "For Sale" on it.'

'Is there?' He drove on slowly. 'Well, I don't think I'll put in a bid. With all the unexploded shells and grenades still in the ground there it doesn't strike me as a desirable property.'

'Unexploded?' She twisted in her seat to look back. 'Do you mean they could still go off?'

'I do indeed! And if we go walking across any ploughed fields or through any woods I wouldn't go kicking any clods of earth or odd-looking piles of leaves, either. They've been known to go off bang.'

'After all these years?'

'Oh, sure. I kid not at all, mademoiselle: they last one hell of a long time, and just because they didn't go off when they were meant to doesn't mean they can't ever go off. Not a year goes by without someone getting killed out here.'

'Killed?'

'Too right. A couple of children were blown up just before I was here last time – they were trying to take the brass nose-cone off one of our howitzer shells. And the year before that there were four farm workers.'

'Dead?'

'Very dead. You see, the shells that went deep are working their way to the surface all the time. Every ploughing helps to bring them up.'

'Even after fifty years – they still come up?'

Mitchell drew the car off the road on to the edge of a recently harvested beet field. 'Not so many now, maybe.' There was no point in frightening her unnecessarily, but if she was busy watching her feet she'd be less likely to notice any particular curiosity he might display on the ridge. 'But you can figure it out for yourself mathematically: we fired two hundred million shells, give or take a few million. And so did the Germans. Say ten per cent were dud – and on the Somme it was more like twenty per cent.' He gestured at the landscape. 'This whole place is planted with high explosive. When they drove the motorway through the old Hindenburg Line near Arras the construction gangs were paid special danger money.'

That ought to do it – indeed, from the way she looked from the rolling farmland back to him, eyes wide, and then back again to the open, peaceful scene ahead it had already done it. Anything more would be over-kill now, except for the final masterstroke.

'But it wasn't all dud.' He opened the car door. 'If you come with me now I'll show you.'

He climbed out and stretched himself gratefully. The weather had improved steadily during the afternoon, so that now the sky was almost cloudless, with the first touch of evening pink in it. The next day would be fine and possibly even warm; only the suggestion of a chill in the air and the ploughed fields on the horizon towards Fricourt and Mametz betrayed the autumn. He could see very clearly the white stain of chalk mixed with the clay topsoil zigzagging across the freshly-turned earth, the tell-tale marks of the German trenches from which Sausage Valley had once been enfiladed. Fifty ploughings and fifty harvests had failed to erase those marks, so maybe they were etched into the land for all time, just like the spadework of the ancient peoples which the archaeologists studied with such fervour.

As he came round the front of the car he noticed that Nikki was still inside.

'It's perfectly safe here,' he reassured her. 'It's only the places that haven't ever been touched, or the newly ploughed places you have to keep an eye open. Come on.'

She emerged gingerly, following him off the road as though the ground under her feet was uncomfortably warm.

'Quite safe,' he repeated. 'All you're likely to find here is – ' he bent down, staring at the line of pulverised earth left at the edge of the field by the harrow ' – *this.*'

As he stretched his hand out to pick up the object beside her foot she came to an abrupt halt.

'What?'

He dropped his find into her hand. 'Do you know what it is?'

She stared at the little round ball, weighing it as she did so. 'It's heavy . . . but it's not a bullet. What is it?'

'A shrapnel ball. You don't see so many of them now, but after the war they picked them up by the basketful – it was a job they gave to the unemployed.' He bent down again. 'Here's another one – we're in luck. First time I came out here it took me a whole day to find one of these. I suppose yesterday's rain washed these to the top. Both British, these little chaps – probably from the 18-pounder shells they tried to cut the wire with. Not very efficiently, I should think. Later on they developed a special fuse for the job, the 106. Cut barbed wire up a treat. But on July 1st there was a lot of uncut wire.' He pointed to the line of straggly bushes on the turf humps ahead. 'Not here, though. There was not much wire left here – not much anything in fact.'

She followed him to the edge of the Lochnager Crater.

'That's what sixty thousand pounds of ammonal does when you explode it underground: you get a big hole,' he said casually.

'A big hole,' she repeated mechanically.

'When they first blew it – 7.28 a.m. on July 1st – it was 450 feet deep and 450 feet across. This is where the Schwaben Hohe strongpoint was – not to be confused with the Schwaben Redoubt up Thiepval way . . . it's not so deep as it was originally, but it's the best one on the Somme. The Y Sap crater on the other side of the village is partly filled in, the Hawthorn Redoubt crater's full of trees and bushes, and the High Wood ones are full of water. This is the best one to see.'

She continued to stare down into the stupendous crater, pale-faced.

'The 10th Lincolns took it – the Grimsby Chums Battalion. They started out in 1914 as a volunteer company raised by a grammar school headmaster from his old boys. This is as far as they got.'

She raised her eyes at last, examining him with a hint of distaste. 'How can you be so cold-blooded about it?'

'Cold-blooded?' he frowned.

'Doesn't it mean anything to you? Don't you feel anything when you come here?' She held out the shrapnel ball. 'You just pick up – souvenirs?'

He met her green eyes steadily. 'What should I feel?'

She lifted her shoulders in a gesture of helplessness. 'The pity of it ... But I suppose soldiers aren't allowed to feel pity for other soldiers.'

Mitchell wasn't at all sure what his answer – Captain Lefevre's answer – ought to be to that one.

Suddenly she shook her head. 'Not a fair question, I guess. *Mort pour la patrie* – that's how we justify it in France – *mort sur le champ d'honneur*. One minute it is a field of cabbage, but with a machine-gun you can turn it into a field of honour with a single burst.'

He sensed that the old argumentative Mademoiselle Mac-Mahon was still too close to the surface for comfort, and that it had been largely his own fault she was showing through now: his sombre silence before Albert had aroused her sympathy, but his behaviour since had struck the wrong note again.

'Would you rather go straight on to Arras now?'

'Not if there is somewhere else you wish to visit.'

'Well – ' he shrugged ' – I thought we might have a look at Bouillet Wood.'

'Bouillet Wood? But is not that the place from which Monsieur Whitton was turned away?'

'That's right. But it's one place our old soldiers will want to see all the same. They'll be very disappointed if they can't.'

'And you think you will succeed where Monsieur Whitton failed?' She regarded him quizzically.

'I'm not Monsieur Whitton.'

She half smiled. 'And you think the British Army will be more persuasive than Cords Coaches?'

'It'll be better-mannered, certainly.' He carefully didn't return the half-smile; she might take as too flippant any reminder that other occupiers of Bouillet Wood had tried without success to keep the British Army out of it.

But as they drove slowly on again he felt those unanswered questions of hers lying between them, inhibiting them both from further conversation. One way or another they had to be tackled, and perhaps in this at least he might allow Mitchell to speak for Lefevre.

'You asked me what I felt,' he began cautiously, 'about this countryside.'

'That was – I do not know the word for it – but none of my business, anyway.' She stared directly ahead. 'Would you say "presumptuous", maybe? You are here because you were told to come here.'

'But I have been here before, and that's why I'm here now.'

She looked at him. 'So?'

'So maybe you deserve an answer.'

'No, I – ' She stopped.

'But you may not understand it, I'm afraid.' He paused. 'I feel nothing.'

'Nothing?' That wasn't the answer she'd been expecting. '*Nothing?*'

'When I'm here – nothing . . .'

The Hameau turning would be at the bottom of this road, on the left.

'. . . I know what happened, and where it happened. And very often why it happened as well. Before I came here the first time I thought I would be choked up with emotion. But I wasn't at all. I was just surprised how ordinary everything was – and how small everything was.'

She said nothing to break the silence.

'I should have known better. There was an Englishman who wrote a book about the battlefield just after the battle – he was a poet, actually, and a good one . . . He knew – he said it would all go back to the farmers and you'd not be able to recognise it in a few years. I didn't believe him, so I was surprised, even a bit disappointed when I first saw it.'

Hameau 2 km

And an Imperial War Graves sign: *Hameau No. 1 Cemetery, Hameau No. 2 Cemetery, Bouilletcourt Farm Cemetery.*

'It wasn't until I'd been back in England two or three weeks, and I went for a walk in the country not far from my home. And it was all there, every bit of it; there was a little stream just like the Ancre – it's a little stream, the Ancre, not a river – with watermeadows and willows, and there was a wooded hillside with a country house on the top, just like Thiepval – or like the old Bouillet château. And there was a ridge – Christ! you could pick up the whole of the Somme and put it down in a dozen different places in England, and not know the difference. And the only difference is that half a million men killed each other there – and if you look carefully you can pick up the odd shrapnel ball, or maybe a bullet or two.'

He stopped abruptly, aware that this might be where the views of Mitchell and Lefevre diverged, and that he was now climbing to the crest of Hameau ridge.

'We're just about on the German front line now – we turn right at the crossroads here. That's Bouilletcourt Farm just ahead, on the right. Big German strongpoint there, taken on the first hour of the Hameau battle. It was the only place the main attack did take, though.'

He swung the car sharp right, past fields thickly spread with the chalk spoil from the deep German dugouts which the British had methodically blown in, one by one, during the savage fighting of that first day. Bouillet Wood lay directly ahead now, across four hundred yards of open country.

But no longer open: there was a high wire fence – it must be all of ten foot high – cutting across the open plateau maybe a quarter of that distance from the edge of the wood; an ugly, obtrusive thing, planted along a scar of bare earth. Where the narrow metalled drive bisected the wire there was a tall double-gateway, as tall as the fence itself and strongly braced, with a black and yellow sentry-box just inside.

Mitchell felt his heart sinking within him. The whole thing had a 'No Admittance' look about it, like some top security secret government compound dedicated to guided missiles, poison gas and germ warfare. Only the big red warning notice-boards were absent, nothing else was needed to stop travellers dead in their tracks.

'This is all new,' he growled. 'I wonder what the hell they're playing at?'

'It does not look welcoming,' agreed Nikki. 'Whoever lives in the wood, he does not wish to receive visitors, that is very clear, Paul.'

As they drew up in front of the gate a dark-suited man emerged from the sentry box.

'M'sieur?' The man made no attempt to open the gate.

Mitchell could think of nothing but to go on with the plan he had originally decided on to gain entry to the house hidden behind the thick screen of trees. He wound down the car window fully and leaned out. 'I am a friend of Monsieur Regnier's. I wish to see him.'

The man looked at him stolidly. 'Monsieur Regnier does not live here,' he said finally.

'He no longer lives in the house?' Mitchell feigned a mixture of surprise and annoyance. 'Then who does?'

The stolid look remained in position. 'Monsieur Regnier does not live here,' the man repeated.

'Then who does?' Mitchell said patiently. 'I wish to speak to the owner of this property.'

'It is private.'

'I can see that it is private. I wish to go to the house and speak to the owner.'

'It is private, m'sieur. There is no entry.'

'Who is the owner?'

No reply this time. Mitchell felt the blood go to his cheeks. 'God damn!' he muttered.

'Paul – ' Nikki put her hand on his arm. 'He is an idiot. You'll get nothing out of him.'

'We'll see about that!' Mitchell clicked the door open and jumped out. *Shoulders back, chin up, he heard Butler snap. It's the man inside the uniform who is the soldier.*

He marched to the gateway. 'I am a British officer and I wish to see the British war cemetery, which is the property of the Imperial War Graves Commission. Kindly open this gate at once!' he ordered.

The result was not in the least gratifying. The gatekeeper simply pointed back towards Hameau. 'The war cemeteries are beside the village,' he said politely but firmly.

'I don't wish to see those cemeteries. I wish to see the Prussian Redoubt Cemetery – over there – ' He pointed decisively through the wire. 'I also wish to see Bouillet Wood.'

The gate-keeper shook his head. 'I'm sorry, *mon capitaine*, the wood is private property. For the cemetery on the far side you must return to the public highway and drive round to the far side. There is a path from the road to the cemetery. It is the only way.'

That had been exactly what Mitchell had feared he would say from the start: the reply that Whitton had received. And of course that was the official route to the Prussian Redoubt Cemetery. The short cut had been a kindly gesture on Regnier's part, never a right-of-way.

There was nothing for it but to admit defeat – for the time being the new defences of Bouillet Wood were too strong, its wire uncut – and retreat in good order, with dignity. He stared longingly through the fence at the trees, noticing for the first time that there was a second fence, of similar height and design, on their margins.

But this wasn't the time or the place to examine either of them, under the gate-keeper's eye; he could do that at his leisure from the other side.

'Very well,' he snapped. 'Nevertheless, I wish to know the name of the new owner so that I may address a letter of complaint to him. I shall point out to him that in Monsieur Regnier's time visitors to the cemetery were permitted to use this driveway. His name, if you please.'

'I regret, but that is not possible,' the Frenchman replied coolly.

'Not possible?' This time he didn't have to pretend outrage. 'What do you mean – not possible?'

'I have my orders. The wood is private. Entry is by invitation only.' The gate-keeper shook his head emphatically, and then retired towards his sentry-box before Mitchell had time to react.

Nikki raised her shoulders sympathetically as he turned back to the car. 'No good?'

'Tchah!' Mitchell grunted angrily. The exchange had been humiliating, and he was glad now that he hadn't boasted in advance too confidently about his ability to succeed where Whitton had failed. But it was more than humiliating, it was decidedly suspicious, and the sooner Audley heard about it the better: if Charles Emerson had penetrated those fences where he had failed, the thing that he had seen with such fatal results might be concealed among the trees. There was certainly something there that somebody was prepared to spend a good deal of money to keep hidden, that was for sure.

'So what do we do now?' asked Nikki.

'Hah!' Mitchell remembered who he was suddenly. A proper mixture of irritation, suspicion and determination wouldn't be out of place in Captain Lefevre. 'The whole thing's very queer – I don't know what they're playing at. The man wouldn't even say who he was working for, never mind why he wouldn't let us in.'

'Well, short of charging the gate I don't see what we can do, Paul. And even then – you're not in one of your tanks now, remember.'

Mitchell stared morosely at the wire. The irony of it was that this must be almost the exact spot where the tank *Euclid* had gone into action, hosing down the edge of the wood with machine-gun fire in preparation for the Poachers' attack.

'There's something strange going on in there,' he repeated. 'I've a good mind to get on to the local police and see what they have to say.'

'The police?' Nikki looked askance at him, as he hoped she would. 'Oh, Paul – I wouldn't do that!'

'Why not?'

'Well, for a start it's probably perfectly innocent – probably some tycoon who wants to be alone,' she began breathlessly. 'And our police aren't like your cosy English ones – they'd probably arrest you for causing trouble. And we'd be stuck in some horrible police station for hours even if they didn't. Honestly, I wouldn't do that.'

That was the typically French reaction he'd been banking on – a resigned 'them-and-us' suspicion of the forces of law and order which he had noticed even among his most respectable French friends. Although in some sense a Government servant, Nikki ran true to form.

'Hmm . . .' he pretended to consider her plea. 'All right. But I'm darned well going to have a closer look at the place from the other side.'

'The other side?'

'The Prussian Redoubt Cemetery is on the other side of the wood, Nikki – that's what we came here to see. It's on the very end of the ridge. We can get to it from the road, Whitton said so. Then I can – I can make a reconnaissance of my own there.' He nodded at her judiciously: Captain Lefevre salving his injured military dignity by trying to create a mystery where there was none. That word 'reconnaissance' was a good touch, too; he had decided at the last moment not to abbreviate it to the more authentic 'recce' on the ground that she might not understand him. As it was, she regarded him doubtfully, as if she found his curiosity disturbing . . . It was either that, or maybe the prospect of visiting the cemetery upset her.

Well, if the latter was the case she might as well get used to the prospect now as later: the trenches might have gone, the sandbags long since rotted, the millions of miles of barbed wire grubbed up and the tens of thousands of guns and tanks hauled away to be beaten into the next generation's ploughshares, but the British had left one enduring reminder of their occupation of this narrow strip of France: they had left their dead.

3

The sign pointed directly up the bare hillside, along a tractor-beaten track which was edged on each side with the merest wisps of grass; it was only the rarity of hedges that made this farmland different from England, and with it the relative absence of birds, as though the thrifty Frenchmen were determined to use every square inch of field-space, sharing it as little as possible with wild creatures.

But he would have known the place without a signpost, even though he had never before approached the eastern tip of the ridge from this direction: with Bouillet Wood in view on the skyline all the time it was impossible to become disorientated.

And that in itself was strange, for on his previous visit to this section of the front he had never been so aware of the wood's commanding position. Now that it was closed to him, and maybe hostile too, he saw not only how it dominated the landscape but also began for the first time to understand why the men of 1916 had written about it with such loathing. They had been like ants, vulnerable under the eyes of the enemy above them, and if the defences of the redoubt under the demolished château had been far more formidable, those had been virtually out of sight: it was because they could always see the wood that they knew the Germans in the wood could always see them.

He thought – and the thought came to him so quickly and suddenly that it stopped him in his tracks as though it created a physical barrier – *maybe someone up there is watching me now, another rash ant unwisely straying into forbidden territory to be squashed without compunction.*

But that was ridiculous. He was just another Englishman doing what dozens of others must have done before him: he had gone to the other entrance and had stated his intention without equivocation – and had even made a fuss when he had been turned away. Now he was only doing what he had been told to do, and there was nothing suspicious in his action; it would surely have been more suspicious to have done anything else, or even to have done nothing else.

He lifted his field-glasses, sweeping the far distance to the south and west. There, just visible in the slightly fading light above its belt of surrounding trees, was the top of the huge redbrick Thiepval Memorial; there, peeping over the top of the Tara-Usna ridge, was the Golden Virgin herself . . . and there, much closer, was Bouillet Wood – Bois de Bouillet, Wald von Bouillet, Bully Wood.

He focused on the inner fence, against the dark background of trees and bushes. His first impression, that they were pressing against it, imprisoned by the wire mesh, was wrong: there was maybe a yard or two of open ground between the fence and the vegetation. Beyond that he could see nothing and could only try to recall what lay within.

The house had been built about two hundred yards in from the southern edge, long and low, with an inner courtyard; full of rooms for unborn Regnier grandchildren – unborn and never to be born . . . There were lawns round it, and straight geometrically-driven avenues cutting through the wood.

Just to the north, or north-west, of the house there had been a single tiny field of sweet corn, he remembered; between the rows, lying on the sticky rain-washed clay, unused British and German ammunition had been scattered thickly, green with age and damp, but still live enough when dried out.

Apart from the lawns and the avenues and that field there had not been a square yard of level ground in the wood; the trees had been allowed to re-establish themselves naturally among the craters and crude trenches which were themselves formed of interlinked craters, all fallen in now and softened by the fallen leaves of half a century. Perhaps in the bright sunshine of a summer's day it might have passed for any piece of rough woodland, anywhere. But he had seen it first on a dark, rainy autumn day when it had been ugly and depressing.

He stopped his sweep along the wire as his eyes caught a tiny brief movement, a momentary shivering of the leaves which could not be accounted for in the surrounding stillness.

'Can you see anything?' said Nikki.

He lowered the field-glasses.

'No. Just the fence. It's the same as on the far side – it obviously goes right the way round.'

It was true: he could see nothing, the patch of undergrowth was motionless. But it had moved, of that he was certain.

'And that's the cemetery?' She pointed to the low wall of dark grey bricks ahead to the left.

'That's right. See how thick the chalk is in the fields here – and there are bits of brick in it. This is where the old Château de Bouillet was, and then the Prussian Redoubt.'

And now and for all time the Prussian Redoubt Cemetery.

He pointed suddenly to the right of the arched gateway. 'There! I said you'd see one – and there's more than one. That's from the recent ploughing.'

Stacked neatly beside the gateway were three very rusty shells.

'Two British 18-pounders and a German 5.9 – or they could be two German whizz-bangs, I don't know.'

'What are they going to do with them?' She stared at the shells fixedly. 'They're not going to just leave them there?'

Mitchell laughed. 'Oh, no. The army comes round and picks them up from time to time.'

'But aren't they dangerous?'

'Not unless you take gross liberties with them. There's Hindenburg Line blockhouse I know, just over the Sensee at Fontaine-les-Croiselles – '

He looked back down the slope towards the way they had come, where he had left the car by the roadside. Without remarking on it he had heard the sound of a motor-cycle a few moments earlier, but now he was aware that the sound had not passed on into the distance, but had stopped abruptly at the bottom of the hill.

'Yes?'

Two motor-cyclists.

'Er – Fontaine-les-Croiselles, just near Arras,' he repeated. In another moment they would start up again. 'I trod on an unexploded 18-pounder lying in the grass there, a beauty – '

They had not started up. One rider had climbed off his machine and was sniffing round the car. The other stared up the slope, pointing with a black-gauntleted hand.

He raised his field-glasses, but the close-up only confirmed what he knew already. 'We've got company.'

Nikki folowed his gaze. 'Oh – ' Her shoulders sagged. 'Oh, no. The police!'

'So what?' He injected a confidence he didn't feel into his tone. 'For God's sake, we haven't done anything. At least, I haven't – have you?'

'Me?' The squeak of protest was cut off by the renewed roar of the powerful engines. The rider who had examined the car circled his machine in the road expertly and swerved sharply into the track to the cemetery. An instant later his colleague kicked his own engine into life and turned to follow him.

Mitchell watched them with a sick certainty that he was their objective: on the road they had been disturbing enough in their black uniforms, helmeted and goggled to match; on the track, heading straight towards him, they were as malevolent as Cocteau's outriders of Death.

But now he was letting the girl's police-phobia get the better of him, he told himself. Butler had warned that the security forces were out in force in Picardy, and it was impossible that they could yet suspect him of being here under false pretences. So this was just a piece of routine checking, routine curiosity, routine officiousness. He only had to stand his ground and be what he was supposed to be, with little to fear except his own fear.

Unfortunately that was enough, and more than enough, to expose his false courage to his own contempt. If he owed nothing to Audley, he had a score to settle on Charles Emerson's behalf and his own, not to mention the poor old man, George Davis. He even had a responsibility of some sort to the girl beside him to put on a brave face and bluff it out.

'Now, whatever can they want?' he heard himself say. The voice was Captain Lefevre's, full of insular confidence.

'Well, whatever it is, please give it to them – don't argue with them, Paul. They aren't like your "coppers", these animals.'

'So you keep telling me – you'll have me scared stiff in a minute.' He managed a grin to match the words, a grin not wholly forced as the irony of the situation took hold on him. It was surely a sign of the times that the pure in heart no longer had the strength of ten, and this girl's clear conscience was no more comfort than his own bad one. Indeed, with a bad conscience one did at least know what to worry about, he decided, remembering the fear and confusion of his meeting with Constable Bell. 'Stop worrying, Nikki. They're just policemen.'

'Policemen?' She gave him a pitying look. 'Have you ever seen our policemen handle a riot?'

The black figures were closing on them now in a rising

crescendo of noise. 'We're not a riot. And I gather your rioters aren't exactly boy scouts, either, are they?'

The pity was transformed into displeasure. 'I was forgetting you wear a uniform too,' she shouted.

Perhaps it was just as well there was no more time for this argument to develop, since it was clearly heading straight for Northern Ireland. But with a final burst of sound the motorcyclists drew up alongside them, one on each side.

For a moment both sides took stock of one another in a sudden silence almost as crashing as the noise which had preceded it. Then the nearest policeman raised his goggles and climbed stiff-legged off his motor-cycle.

By that time Mitchell had abandoned any idea of opening the dialogue, for with their machine-pistols slung across their chests and holstered guns at their waists these two characters were a world away from Constable Bell and his notebook and pencil. Artillery like that explained Nikki's sense of anxiety all too well, drying up any thought of argument on his own part: where Bell, unarmed, had been the arm of the law, what faced him now was the fist of the state with a weapon clenched in it, to be defied at one's peril.

The policeman looked him up and down once more, as though to confirm his goggle-eyed view, and then raised his hand in a salute.

'M'sieur. Vos papiers, s'il vous plaît.'

The salute had caught Mitchell by surprise, his own hand already halfway to his pocket. He was glad Colonel Butler wasn't present to witness his belated acknowledgment of the unexpected courtesy, which fell far short even of the standard required by the Cambridge University OTC.

Not that such slovenliness seemed to matter to the Frenchman: he removed one gauntlet and examined the documents with methodical care, his lips spelling out the words silently. But he could go on reading them until doomsday for all the good it would do him, thought Mitchell, drawing strength from Audley's assurance on their authenticity: there was nothing wrong with the bill of goods, it was the real thing. Only the goods themselves were counterfeit.

Finally the man looked up at him again. 'Capitaine Lefevre?'

'Yes – oui.'

'You are on 'oliday?' The policemen had evidently decided to try out his English. 'On leave from your regiment?'

'No. I am here on official business. I have been asked to meet a party of old soldiers – anciens combattants de la bataille de la Somme – who will be visiting this place in a day or two. I am looking over the battlefield in preparation for that – ah – that duty.'

The policeman took a moment or two to assimilate the information. Then he gestured to Nikki. 'And this is madame, your wife?'

'Oh, no,' Mitchell smiled. 'This is Mademoiselle MacMahon of your Ministry of Tourism who has been assigned to help me. Mademoiselle's presence here is a token of Anglo-French friendship for which we are very grateful.'

The policeman's eyes flicked over Nikki and then returned to Mitchell, the eyebrows lifting for a fraction of a second to suggest a certain envy. It was like a shutter opening, revealing a human face for an instant, and then snapping shut again.

'Vos papiers, s'il vous plaît, Mademoiselle.'

Nikki's credentials received the same thorough inspection, with the same eventual result.

'Merci, mon capitaine – mademoiselle.' The hand came up in salute again. Mon Capitaine had passed another test.

But success was something to build on, not to sit on.

'Un moment – ' No. Better to keep it in English, which was more flattering to the man's ego. ' – I wonder – could you tell me one thing, officer.'

'M'sieur?'

'When I was last here, two years ago, Monsieur Amaury Regnier lived in the house in the wood.' He pointed towards the fence. 'Could you tell me who lives there now?'

The Frenchman frowned. 'Why do you wish to know?'

That wasn't the answer he had hoped for – it was no answer at all – but this time he was ready for it. 'Some of the men I am to meet captured that wood from the Germans in 1916. Most of their comrades are buried here, in this cemetery. I had hoped we might visit the wood, but I have been unable to discover who owns it now.'

'I am afraid I cannot help you,' the policeman shrugged. Then he looked at Mitchell sidelong. 'But perhaps – you are resting nearby tonight?'

Mitchell turned to Nikki. 'Where are we staying?'

God! That was the wrong way to put it, he realised too late as he saw her face change. 'I m-mean, which hotel in Arras have you booked me into?'

'La Belle Etoile in the Place Lloyd George, Captain Lefevre,' she replied icily.

The policeman coughed politely – in fact so damn politely, that it was clear that he had formed his own interpretation of the nature of this example of Anglo-French friendship. 'Very well – La Belle Etoile. If I am able to find out the answer to your question I will telephone the 'otel.'

Mitchell watched them ride away, relief and embarrassment cancelling each other out within him. With an effort he turned again to meet the astonishing green eyes.

'I'm – ah – sorry for putting my foot in my mouth.'

But the eyes were no longer arctic green, and she shook her head at him with an expression of half-amused resignation. 'You're all-British now, Paul – there's no doubt about that.'

Mitchell was agonisingly aware that he was blushing.

'But . . .' She laughed out loud, gently, as though she was doing her best to save his feelings from total demolition '. . . but at least you know how to disarm French policemen – which is more than most Frenchmen are able to do.'

If that was the case, maybe there was consolation to be derived from his very gaucheness, humiliating though it might be: only the innocent should be so – so innocent. Perhaps that was what Audley was reckoning on.

Then the amusement in her face was gone, just as suddenly as it had appeared. 'But now I will see your cemetery, Paul. And then it will be time to go, because it will be getting dark very soon – and I don't think I will like it here very much then.'

She was quite wrong, of course – wrong to feel disquieted in this place, in these places, of all places.

Where the long rows of white headstones were, lined meticulously on their weed-free strips of tilled soil, carved just as meticulously – number, rank, name, regiment, age and day of death, regimental crest – there was no menace, only melancholy. Maybe outside, in the busy fields and roads, there were ghosts and unspent passions unable to rest because continuing life mocked them. But in the war cemeteries on the battlefields the dead had finally conquered the land and had no call to contest it with anyone. Nothing would stir here until the last trump, and even then there would be no fuss or jostling for position, but only a quiet, well-ordered reunion.

Nikki pointed. 'Look – poppies.'

Poppies, sure enough. A few late roses, dark red, blossomed between the stones, but some inspired gardener had carefully left the true flowers of the battlefield, the flowers of remembrance and forgetfulness, while removing every other weed.

'I thought it was in Flanders that all the poppies grew,' she added.

In Flanders fields the poppies blow ... So she must have read that poem, or at least encountered it while doing her hurried official homework.

'They grow wherever the topsoil is disturbed. Maybe they like the chalk, I don't know.'

'It's very chalky here.'

He tore his gaze away from the name on the stone behind the poppies: 2103113 Rifleman A. SMITH RIFLE BRIGADE AGED 20.

One of the Poachers. So was the next one, and the next – and as far down the line as he could see. Somewhere along here, as likely as not, there'd be SECOND LIEUT. R. DYSON, General Leigh-Woodhouse's friend.

I expect I'll be saying 'Good morning, God' in a moment or two . . .

'Chalky?' He repeated vaguely.

When he finally focused on her he saw that she was regarding him sympathetically now, as though she could read his face.

'Forget it – it's not important, Paul.'

Beneath the provocative female – and the prickly Franco-Irish nationalist – there was a human being, and a rather nice one too, decided Mitchell, decisively shelving the last vestige of his plans for an amorous evening. They probably wouldn't have worked out anyway, at that, particularly when he ought to be keeping his mind on a very different sort of objective.

'Chalky, yes.' The decision was like a burden lifted from his shoulders. 'We're right on top of the redoubt now. Do you see where those headstones have been laid flat over there?' He pointed to the centre of the cemetery.

'They are graves?' She peered over the standing stones to where a whole group had been arranged horizontally. 'I thought that was a pavement.'

'No. They were like all the rest once, but they wouldn't stand up straight – they kept sinking and falling over. So in the end they laid them flat. They had to do exactly the same thing at the Mill Road Cemetery, which is built on top of the Schwaben Redoubt.'

'Why?'

'Because of the German dugouts underneath. They're gradually falling in.'

'Underneath?' She looked at him, puzzled. 'You mean the dugouts are still there?'

'Oh, sure. The one here must be quite close to the surface, actually.'

'But didn't they fill them in – after the war?'

'And during. But the Germans used to dig deep, thirty or forty feet, and even more than that. Under the Butte de Warlencourt the galleries went down maybe six levels into the chalk. They had two years to get dug into the Somme, remember. They didn't just sit on their backsides waiting for us – they put in all the comforts of home, heating, electric light, air pumps, kitchens, the lot. And we didn't have guns big enough to reach any of it, which is one reason why we lost such a hell of a lot of men in '16. They stayed snug while we shelled them, and then popped up in time to catch us in the open when we attacked. Or they waited until we'd moved on, and then hit us from behind.'

'So all the dugouts are still down underneath us?' She repeated the question disbelievingly.

'Ah well, we did learn in the end – ' Mitchell began to feel that he was doing the British Army less than justice. 'We underestimated them because we never dug so deep ourselves – because we didn't intend to live here for the rest of the war. They became an army of defence and we became an army of attack. Which is why we won the war in the end.'

Nikki stared around her at the long lines of white stones. 'It doesn't look like a victory monument to me. Where are the losers?'

The jibe stung. 'Under the victors,' snapped Mitchell. 'Every dugout entrance on this whole ridge was blown in the moment we reached it. There are more Germans under Hameau Ridge than – '

A sudden sharp explosion – a concussive crump which made him duck instinctively – cut off the end of the sentence.

'What – ?'

The echo reverberated for a second or two, and then was lost in the sound of panic-stricken birds, disturbed from their evening roosts, trying to get airborne.

'From there!' The girl pointed northwards, across the downward slope of the field, to where the tops of the trees in Rattlesnake Ravine appeared over the edge of the dead ground, a hundred and fifty yards away.

Mitchell saw a hint of smoke – dirty grey – and as he watched it rolled upwards, not in the growing column of a fire bursting into life, but like a signal hidden under a blanket and then released in a single concentrated mushroom cloud with a fading stalk. All along the tree-line of the ravine the birds rose, heavy-winged, screeching and chattering and falling away to the left and right of the smoke.

'What is it?' She took up his unfinished question. 'Is it a shell?'

He watched, hypnotised, as the smoke thinned in the still air. It wasn't possible – he had been talking gaily about it, but it still wasn't possible. It was simply a cautionary tale.

'Was it a shell?'

'A shell?' Damn it, she'd jumped to the conclusion because he'd prepared her for just such an event, as though it happened all the time. 'I – I don't think it's that – '

'Well, what is it?' She frowned at him.

What was it?

One thing was sure: whatever it was, he didn't want to find out.

'Tree-blasting?' He stared at the last wisps of smoke. 'I don't know.'

'Tree-blasting?'

He wilted inwardly, knowing what she was about to say, what she wanted him to do – and what she expected him to do.

And, of course, what Captain Lefevre would *have* to do!

'I'll go and have a look.' He swallowed. 'You stay here.'

It was odd how his knees didn't seem to bend the way they should, as though his legs were stiff.

It had been a potato field: there was dozens of tiny greeny-brown potatoes lying on the surface, like shrapnel balls.

It was a shell, sure enough. It couldn't really be anything else. But that wasn't what was scaring him.

The edge of Rattlesnake Ravine was humpy and uneven, like all the unploughed ground of the Somme, where the grass had grown on the untouched battlefield for half a century . . . This was where the Australians had come that day, very angrily too, because a prisoner had killed two of them with a hidden grenade. So *we'd had a belly-full of mercy that day* and there hadn't been a single prisoner taken in the whole ravine.

A cart track at the bottom now, grass between the wheelruts, all very peaceful . . . It was more a very deep sunken road than a true ravine . . .

Acrid smell.

Tall bank of stinging nettles, partly beaten down.

Sweet-rotten smell – cow-dung smell –

'Can you see anything, Paul?'

'Go back!'

A boot, a dirty boot with steel studs on –

'What's the matter?'

A dirty boot with steel studs and a foot in it, with a spike of pink bone and tendons and a long flap of brownish skin with black hair bristling on it – God!

The sound of motor-cycles in the distance.

4

The car must have been waiting for him, parked in the darkness just up the road from the Belle Etoile, because he had to wait no more than a minute before it came sliding alongside the kerb abreast of him.

The driver leaned across to the window. 'Lefevre?'

'Roskill?'

'Jump in.' The voice was casual and decidedly public school. 'You're a couple of minutes late. Everything okay?'

'I was just getting into bed when you shoved the note under my door. I had to dress.' Mitchell paused, undecided as to which of the two questions uppermost in his mind he wanted to ask first. 'Where are we going?'

'Not far.'

'How did you know where to find me?'

'Oh, we're bloody good at "hide and seek" – didn't you know?' The over-casualness of the man's voice began to jar on Mitchell when he suddenly remembered he'd clean forgotten the most important question of all – the one which meant everything and nothing at all.

' "If one told thee all was betrayed, what wouldst thou do?" ' he quoted hurriedly, grateful that the darkness of the car spared his embarrassment at the gaffe.

'Heaven be praised – I was beginning to get nervous,' said Roskill with evident relief. "I would run away. It might be true."

And that's what I would do too, by damn! David's sense of humour certainly hasn't improved since I last worked for him, I'll say that.' He gave Mitchell a quick nod of sympathy. 'We're just driving about to make sure no one's tailing you, and we got your address from the tours manager – the coach company fellow – what's his name – ?'

'Whitton.'

'That's the man. Got the War Department to phone him up at Amiens. Satisfied?'

It was as easy as that – ridiculously easy.

'And we didn't phone you or come barging into your room because the French are terrible fellows for tapping and bugging, far worse than we are. Journalist pal of mine in Paris always says hullo twice when anyone phones him, just to be polite to the other chap on his line.'

Mitchell digested the precautions, recalling his warm, comfortable room in the Belle Etoile and the innocently empty boulevards outside the hotel with immediate and fearful suspicion. He had let his tired mind relax back there for a moment, and now he had been forcibly reminded that such weakness was not permitted.

'But nobody's on to me?'

Roskill glanced into the driving mirror. 'Nobody's following us, that's true. So you may be right. Better to be careful than sorry though, eh?' He glanced at Mitchell again. 'Tell me, are you another of David's bright ideas?'

Mitchell was not so much surprised at the accurate guess about his amateur status, which his fumbling use of the recognition phrase must have rendered apparent, as by the fact that Roskill clearly wasn't in Audley's confidence. That being the case he could hardly give a straight answer, but an instinct warned him not to stop the question dead in its tracks without finding out what lay behind it.

'Does it matter?'

'Not to me it doesn't, old boy – I'm just passing through, thank God. But to you . . .' Roskill's voice trailed off. 'Half conscript, half volunteer, that'd be my guess.'

Again it was an uncomfortably accurate guess. 'What makes you think so?'

Roskill shrugged. 'Well . . . let's say I don't know you, but I do know David Audley very well. So I'll give you a piece of advice, Lefevre – absolutely free: get back to your regiment as quickly as you can, even if it's on its tenth tour in darkest Ulster. Get the hell out while you still can.'

He was being warned off again, this time half-flippantly in a very different style from Colonel Butler's explosive disapproval, but nonetheless sincerely. And yet although the warning appealed to him as plain common sense he felt a perverse reluctance to accept it, even after the horror of this evening. It went beyond the original mixture of self-preservation and revenge now, and he suddenly felt an overriding need to pin it down in his mind.

It wasn't simply curiosity, the need to know – the same insatiable need to answer questions in his mind, a drive which he had recognised but never quite understood . . .

'Huh!' Roskill broke the silence. 'You're hooked! I don't know how he does it, but he does it: one look at you and he bloody knows where to fix it so you don't even know he's done it – '

'Audley?' Mitchell tried to sort out the mixture of regret, admiration and dislike in the man's voice into some order of precedence.

'Dr David L. Audley, MBE, MA, PhD – you'll find out soon enough if you haven't already. He's quite a guy for getting results – he's famous for it. But he solves trouble by making trouble, and someone always has to pick up the bill. This time it could be you.'

The bitterness was personal as well as professional, Mitchell was certain. But without knowing anything about Roskill he couldn't gauge its justification.

Except that he did know one thing about Roskill: *Get them to hire a light aircraft – Hugh Roskill's fit to fly again . . .*

'Did you manage to fly over Hameau Ridge, Roskill?'

Roskill stretched and shifted his position, leaving the final 'Don't say I didn't warn you' admonition unsaid. 'No. I didn't get to fly anywhere. Because over-flying the Somme is *verboten*.'

'Forbidden? As of when?'

'As of now. Light aircraft, private aircraft – nothing flies off the airline corridor or under their operational ceiling. The whole area's under military control.'

'They give a reason?'

'Military exercises. Only there aren't any military exercises: all we can pick up on our radar is a few choppers buzzing around. Someone's conning us, looks like.'

Not conning, thought Mitchell. Or not deliberately conning. This was just the aerial version of the situation Butler had reported on the ground: something was happening in the Channel departments. Even the presence of those motorcycle police, and the speed with which they had summoned men to Rattlesnake Ravine, only confirmed that. The French security services were obviously –

Christ! He'd been dim! The explanation or at least one part of it – had been staring him in the face for hours now, and he'd looked right through it.

Even as the implications of the idea began to spread like ripples he felt the car slow down. Looking around he saw that they were in an anonymous side-street, with the lights of a main thoroughfare some fifty yards ahead.

'This is where we part,' said Roskill. 'David's waiting for you in Number 17, just across the street – Flat Four. The front door's on the latch, you can go straight up.'

Mitchell looked up and down the street. 'Are you coming back for me?'

'Not likely! It's Paris for me now. Straight on to the motorway just outside town, and I'll be there before midnight – the place'll just be hotting up. Knocks Arras into a cocked hat for late night enjoyment, Paris does, you know.'

The interior of the car was striped with bars of light and darkness thrown through the venetian blinds of a window in the house beside them. One bar told him that Roskill was grinning happily, like a soldier ordered back to base on the eve of an enemy attack, but as the man moved his head Mitchell saw that the happiness didn't extend upwards to his eyes.

'How do I get back to my hotel, then?'

'Get back? Down to the bottom of the street, turn left three hundred yards and you're back in Place Lloyd George.'

Mitchell regarded him with astonishment. 'Three hundred – then why the blazes have we been driving all over the place?'

'I told you – to see if you've got a tail. And then to slip it if you had.'

'But I still don't see why I should have a tail – I haven't done anything, and nobody could possibly know me.'

At least, nobody could know Captain Lefevre anyway: he'd only been born the day before. Except that after this evening even that cry had a hollow ring about it.

'Well, you're a lucky fellow to have such a clear conscience – and such touching confidence too,' Roskill chuckled grimly. 'But don't ask me for whys and wherefores. I'm just the taximan this time, thank God.' He took a final look up and down the street. 'You're in the clear at this moment, certainly: you tell David that from me. On which happy note I must bid you adieu, old boy.'

Mitchell fumbled for the door handle. 'Thanks for the ride . . . old boy.'

Roskill's teeth glinted in the bar of light across his mouth. 'Think nothing of it. Just one final thought though, Lefevre. You wanted me to take a look at Hameau Ridge – the old battlefield, wasn't it?'

'That's right.'

'Who was that cartoonist chap – Bruce someone – who drew all the old trench jokes?'

'Bairnsfather.'

'That's the chap. Always drew the same soldier. Little man with a walrus moustache?'

'"Old Bill".'

'Right. And he was the one who was in this shell crater full of mud and water during a bombardment and turned to his mate and said "If you know a better hole, go to it." And that's pretty damn good advice; it seems to me – as far as you're concerned.'

Roskill had entirely misunderstood Old Bill's advice, Mitchell reflected as he closed the door of the flat behind him. The whole analogy was off the point. And yet the warning was plain enough all the same, echoing Butler's doubts of the previous day about the advisability of sending forth a sheep dressed in wolf's clothing.

Only in a crazy way he had nevertheless been enjoying himself. Even the moments of fear in retrospect had a quality of excitement which made them exhilarating.

But this was no time for self-analysis; Audley was talking to him –

' – and not followed at all? That's good, Paul – because if Hugh Roskill says you weren't, then we can rely on it. He's a first-rate operative, is Hugh.'

That somehow made it worse, thought Mitchell: whatever Roskill thought of Audley, the big man had no lack of confidence in his subordinate. The relationship betrayed a defect in each of them: if the younger man was bitter to the very edge of disloyalty, the older one was totally unaware of his disaffection. And if that cut them both down to human size it wasn't exactly reassuring.

Audley regarded him solicitously. 'You look tired, Paul. But that's only to be expected, the first time on your own – here, sit down – have a cognac.' He pointed to the bottle on the table.

Mitchell shook his head.

'You look as if you've got something for me, too,' said Audley. 'You've seen something?'

'Yes.'

'What?'

'A – fence.' That was strange: he'd wanted to say 'A foot', but the word had refused to be said at the last moment.

'A fence? What sort of fence? Where?'

'On Hameau Ridge. There's a double wire fence round Bouillet Wood. No trespassers.'

Audley frowned. 'But you said you knew the man who lives there?'

'He died last year. There's a new owner now.'

'Who owns it now?'

'The man on the gate wouldn't say. Nor would the police.'

'The police?' Audley took the information well, with controlled interest untainted by the least sign of worry. 'How did you run into them?'

His coolness rekindled Mitchell's confidence in him. 'They ran into us. It was when we went to have a look at the wood from the Prussian Redoubt side.'

'We?' Audley pounced on the pronoun. 'The interpreter was with you?'

'You know about her?'

'Her?' Audley cocked his head questioningly. 'The tours man told Hugh over the phone you'd be supplied with an interpreter – he didn't say it was a female one.'

That sounded like Whitton right enough, though it was impossible to say whether he'd omitted that additional fact because of his quirky sense of humour or because he unselfishly wanted to give 'a nice lad' a clear run with a pretty girl.

Audley listened to his portrait of Nikki MacMahon with good-humoured interest. 'Delightful. And a most accurate description too – go on, though.'

'What with – the police or the fence?'

'Whichever you like. It's your story. Tell it your way.'

It would be logical to be chronological, thought Mitchell: to progress from the fence to the police, by way of Bouillet Wood. But the appalling image of the foot was overprinted on every other memory, becoming clearer every second while everything else faded.

'We've got another body.'

'Another – ?' This time Audley reacted sharply. 'You mean a dead man?'

'They don't come any deader. He was spread all over Rattlesnake Ravine. I think I found the largest piece of him. It was his – foot.'

'His foot? What do you mean – he was cut up?'

'Not cut up – blown up. Blown to bits – '

It tumbled out now, the foot, the ravine, the police. What he couldn't paint in words was the unreality of the scene as darkness had fallen and the powerful headlights of the police cars had blazed up the cutting, illuminating the trees and bushes with unnatural sharpness against their own black shadows . . . and he'd kept on thinking, the knowledge going round and round in his brain, that this horror was a small thing compared with what once had happened here –

We'd had a belly-full of mercy that day . . .

Audley listened in silence, right to the end, asking no questions this time, only nodding. Finally he looked up at Mitchell thoughtfully.

'But you don't believe him?'

'The police inspector?'

'He said it was an accident, but you evidently don't believe him. Why not?' Audley was studying him closely: it was as though he was being questioned and tested at the same time.

'Well, two reasons. F-first – ' Mitchell broke off for a moment in order to marshal his thoughts, warned by the return of that tell-tale nervous stutter. Whatever the man Roskill said, Audley wasn't likely to carry a dumb passenger with him as the pace grew hotter. If his instinct about the nature of these questions was right then his continued presence in France might depend on his performance in the next few minutes.

'It was a shell right enough. The smoke was right and the smell was – was how I've heard it described.' Steady now. 'It could be an accident, people do get blown up on the Somme now and then. In fact everyone loves to tell stories about the danger – I was telling Nikki – Mademoiselle MacMahon – just before this one went up. But . . .'

'Yes?'

'It could have been an accident – there wasn't enough left of the poor devil to prove otherwise. But that isn't the point.'

'Which is – ?'

'Wherever we go there are accidents. If someone hadn't spotted the fire in time Charles Emerson would have been an accident – and George Davis would have been just another hit-and-run case.'

'And Paul Mitchell would have been just another suicide?' Audley had no scruples about mentioning the unmentionable. 'If you're right, then no one could accuse them of being unimaginative. But you've still only got a working hypothesis in this case.'

'That's all we've ever had – a hypothesis that Charles Emerson saw something out here. But maybe he didn't see anything – maybe someone showed him something, or told him something. Someone who's just had an accident, maybe.'

'While on the way to see the next Englishman who started sniffing around Bouillet Wood?' Audley stared at him over his glasses. 'And meanwhile the police are happy with their accident?'

'That was just for my benefit, I'll swear. They wanted me out of their hair, that's what – they don't like strangers on Hameau Ridge, alive or dead. That's the point.'

'The police?'

'The gate-keeper wouldn't tell me who lived there – five minutes later the police were checking our papers. They spoke the same language – I'm damn sure the gate-keeper was a policeman . . . and that fence has "official" stamped all over it, I knew it when I saw it, but for some reason it didn't register . . .'

'Go on.'

'The motor-cycle police weren't following us, they were directed to us, I'm damn sure of that too. And they didn't just clear off after they'd checked us, because they reached the ravine only a second or two after I did – and the place was crawling with police within ten minutes, not only uniformed ones but chaps in plainclothes. They were there too quickly, far too many of them. Police-dogs too, and they were setting up a portable generator as we left.'

Audley nodded slowly. 'All for – an accident.'

'That's exactly it! The inspector who questioned me went out of his way to tell me it was an accident – told me how people were always tampering with old shells as though it happens all the time – '

'Which it doesn't?'

'Well, hardly. Children maybe, but the locals know the score by now – you've got to be crazy to try getting a brass nose-cone off, for a few pounds it's not worth the risk. But it all adds up to the same thing: whatever's happening in Bouillet Wood, it's official not private.'

Audley was looking at him with that irritating abstracted expression again, not so much looking at him as through him. Only now that he could well understand the reason for the abstraction, and knew himself to be the cause of it, it seemed much less irritating – it was pleasing even.

'And the French aren't letting anyone overfly the ridge,' he added, popping the cherry on top of the cake. 'Roskill said – '

'I've already heard what Roskill has to say,' Audley interrupted him smoothly, still gazing through him but otherwise apparently unruffled. The hand he had raised to check Mitchell pointed vaguely towards the table nearby: 'Got something for you on there – a special little present.'

Apart from the brandy bottle and glasses the only thing on the table was a book, an oldish-looking red volume with a sun-faded spine.

'The book,' Audley murmured as Mitchell hesitated. 'Have a look at the pictures, they're rather good.'

A special little present? Mitchell picked it up gingerly, frowning: *With the Tanks at Cambrai: The War Diary of Sergeant Frank Briggs* . . .

His eye was caught by the inscription on the fly-leaf: *Paul Lefevre, 16 August 1966 with love from Mother* . . . someone had taken a lot of trouble with the special little present – even the ink had been skilfully faded.

Look at the pictures.

They were in a group in the middle, a very typical selection for this type of war memoir, which had begun to appear about a decade after the war's end, as time had started to blur the horror: first the customary Edwardian family group, Father Briggs moustachioed and watch-chained, staring sternly out of the picture; Mother in her leg-of-mutton sleeves, the obligatory baby on her lap, two little girls in pinafore dresses and black stockings, and young Frank himself, his sturdy body buttoned up in a best suit already one size too small for him . . . a portrait not only of a family, but of old Imperial Britain, safe and solid behind the largest navy in the world and the empire on which the sun never set, blissfully unaware of barbed wire and mustard gas and Flanders mud.

Over the page history had trapped Frank Briggs, first in a group of identical young men posed against a patriotic background of allied flags, the *Prince Albert Street volunteers of 1914*, and then proud and innocent in his new ill-fitting khaki uniform.

Next page, the reality: *Café Belge, near Dicksbusch* – only the

café was a crumpled nissen hut in a hideous wilderness ...
Shrapnel Corner – and judging by the eagerness of the passing
field battery, plus the wreckage beside the road, the Germans had
the range to the last inch ...

Now the tank pictures: a Mark I in Chimpanzee Valley, a
male tank with its long naval six-pounders ... tanks single and
tanks massed; tanks whole, surrounded by curious infantrymen,
and tanks bogged and shattered, sinking like dead dinosaurs in
ancient swamps.

More group pictures. Somewhere here there would be a
gaunter, wiser Frank Briggs –

That was odd –

In fact it was downright impossible.

Mitchell bent over the picture, checked the caption – *In billets
before the battle* – checked the faces again and the names below
them.

Corporal J. Manson and Sergeant 'Jocko' Ogilvie.

'Well?' Audley was very much with him again, watching his
bewilderment with unconcealed interest.

Mitchell lifted the book. 'I don't understand it.'

'Don't understand what?'

'This picture. There are two men here ...' he trailed off,
unwilling to hear himself finish the sentence.

'Two men – what?'

Mitchell squinted at the photograph once more, stripping the
crumpled uniforms and sandbagged background away. For once
his memory had to be playing him false.

'I could swear I've seen two of these men.'

'When?'

That was the sticking point. Faces must logically recur with
the same mathematical certainty which rolled golf balls into holes
in one stroke. But this coincidence was altogether too great.

He nerved himself to the word. 'Today.'

'Which two?'

Mitchell stared at Audley questioningly. What was almost as surprising as this impossible identification was that the big man was not the least surprised by the impossible.

'Which two?' Audley repeated. 'Show me.'

Mitchell surrendered the book, speechlessly.

'*In billets before the battle?*'

'Yes.' Mitchell nodded. 'Top left, standing – he was on the gate at Bouillet Wood.'

'Corporal J. Manson?' read Audley equably. 'And the other one?'

Mitchell swallowed. 'Bottom row, second from the right. Sergeant Ogilvie.'

'Sergeant Jocko Ogilvie?' The corner of Audley's mouth lifted. 'And where did you see Sergeant Jocko Ogilvie?'

'Obviously I didn't see him. But I saw his double.'

'Where?'

'In Rattlesnake Ravine this evening. When the inspector questioned me he – his double – came over and listened. He didn't say anything, he just listened. I thought he was some sort of official, a sort of Home Office observer type.'

'I see . . .' Audley nodded. 'You've got a remarkable memory for faces.'

'I thought I had.'

'But you have. A nearly photographic memory to spot those two, to pick them out like that. It's a very useful gift.'

The picture and Audley were equally incomprehensible, so there was no point in asking any fatuous questions: if they were still alive, Corporal Manson and Sergeant Ogilvie were white-haired eighty-year-olds, and the possibility that they had facially identical grandsons serving in the French security forces was too remote to be worth considering. He could only wait for enlightenment.

Audley grinned. 'I told you it was a special present. I had our photographic section put it together for you – they took out the original pictures and reprocessed them with some trick photography of their own. Anyone who goes through your belongings wouldn't give it a second glance, and I reckoned you might like to carry it round with you. I didn't think it'd pay off so quickly though.'

Mitchell looked down at the picture again. It showed, some smiling, some serious, nine very ordinary British soldiers, vintage 1917. The faces were a little drawn and wary, older and more mature than the Prince Albert Street volunteers of the earlier page, but that was only to be expected. Veterans of two years' trench warfare never looked young, no matter what age they were.

'You are looking at an artificially assembled gallery of nine known members of the Service de Documentation Présidentielle – the nine men we know, that is,' said Audley. 'If you care to turn over you'll find another equally worthy group.'

Mitchell turned the page, to find a chorus line in old time music hall dress, their costumes clearly makeshift.

'*The Divisional Christmas Party – 1917?*'

'That's the one – someone in photographic has a warped sense of humour. Have you seen any of them?'

Mitchell ran his eye along the line, several of whom were gazing out of the picture at slightly awkward angles.

'No.'

'I'm relieved to hear it. Those are the eight faces in our files who most resemble the man who called on General Leigh-Woodhouse – minus the long hair and the phony spectacles. Men who in our opinion would undertake contract killing if the price was right.' Audley paused. 'They matter less, but it could be one of them put you in the river, my lad.'

Mitchell examined the fancy-dressed line again, though this time with a sudden chill between his shoulders as though the memory of the freezing water still was able to produce a physical reaction. The original faces on this picture had also belonged to killers; tank crewmen who had crushed their way through the Hindenburg Line. But they had killed for King and Country and a shilling a day; these men, working on their own account, would be much more expensive. He was disappointed to see how very ordinary they were. Except that ordinariness must be an essential attribute of their calling, another simple application of the Darwinian law of natural selection.

He shook his head. 'No, I've never seen any of them.'

'No matter.' Audley gave a small shrug. 'Just keep the book with you and your eyes open. If you spot anyone you think you've seen, let me know double-quick.'

Mitchell's heart gave an extra thump: whatever the test had been, he had passed it – his first solo flight had not been a failure. He hadn't disgraced himself.

'How will I keep in touch with you?'

'That won't be any problem. We can work together again now.' Audley smiled. 'The wraps are off now.'

'The wraps – ?' Mitchell felt a sense of dismay. 'You mean they know about us?'

'Oh, sure. They know about us – and they want us to know – the SDP, that is. You told me so yourself just now. They want us to make contact.'

'*I* told you so?'

'Indirectly. When Sergeant Ogilvie carefully showed you his face he was serving notice to me that he wanted us to come out of the bushes. He expected you to report straight back to me, as you have – he was relying on you. That's why they didn't bother to follow you from the hotel. No point in frightening the messenger.'

The card-house of Mitchell's confidence was in ruins, his pride flattened. The French had known: all the while he had been congratulating himself on his cleverness, they had known. But how – ?

'How do you know?'

'Because I know how Sergeant Ogilvie's mind works – and he knows how mine works,' said Audley disarmingly.

'Sergeant Ogilvie? Who – ?'

But he knew even before Audley replied.

'Alias Edouard Ollivier. I wasn't absolutely sure he was in charge of this operation, of course – which is why I let things move at their own pace. But he was obviously expecting me – ' Audley stopped suddenly, as though he had noticed Mitchell's dismay at last. 'Don't look so sad, Paul. You've done splendidly – not put a foot wrong. No one could have done better.'

The force of Roskill's warning was more evident now: he had underestimated the French and Audley alike. But, far more serious, he had started to overestimate himself.

Yet Audley was regarding him sympathetically. 'I mean that, Paul. And in case you think I don't I'll prove it to you here and now. If you want a job with us when this is over, then you've got it. You can finish your book and then come to us, and you can have sabbaticals for other books. Don't answer me now, just think about it.'

Mitchell was taken flat aback, but before he could grapple with the offer – a job with us? With who? With what? – Audley drew himself up decisively.

'But now – we make contact with Ollivier.'

Mitchell pushed the job offer to the back of his mind with an effort.

'How?'

'You can do it very easily. Just look at the last picture in that book of yours.'

Mitchell thumbed through the photographs. The Briggs family, the 1914 volunteers, Café Belge, the tanks, the SDP men in billets, the line of killers –

Blighty: No. 8 Military Hospital at Rouen –

The nurse in the picture was unmistakably Nikki MacMahon.

5

'So that's the famous Butte de Warlencourt.' Audley craned his neck sideways, his large body obviously uncomfortable in the low-slung car seat. 'The tomb of a Gallic chieftain slain by Caesar, according to Charles Edmonds – am I right?'

'I don't know about Gallic chieftains,' replied Mitchell. 'But there are a hell of a lot of Durham Light Infantry buried hereabouts.'

'And Germans – and Dutch and Spaniards, I shouldn't wonder,' murmured Audley.

Mitchell heard a rustle of silk behind him. 'Dutch and Spaniards, Dr Audley?'

Audley looked over his shoulder at Nikki MacMahon. 'It's your frontier, mademoiselle – you've been fighting here for a long time, long before Germany was re-invented by old Bismarck. I don't know much about the Hindenburg Line, but I remember your Marshal Villars drew his 'Ne Plus Ultra' Lines through this place back in 1711, and our Marlborough broke through them near Vimy Ridge. And we fought the Germans at Arras again in 1940, come to that. And came through Amiens again in '44 – if blood makes the corn grow it should stand shoulder-high in these fields.'

It was the longest speech Audley had addressed to her since they had met just after breakfast. In fact until now he had been so nearly monosyllabic that Mitchell had been unable to decide whether this was the correct attitude to be maintained between professionals in the field, or whether the man was rather shy of attractive young women. But then Nikki had been just as formal with him too since their midnight telephone conversation, with no more prickly Franco-Irish nationalism to put him off his guard.

'We must be getting close to Hameau Ridge,' said Audley.

'We're almost on it. The turn-off is just ahead, but we're approaching from the German side and the rise in the land isn't so obvious from the north.'

Audley nodded. 'I see – it's rather like Monte Cassino. When you come down the autostrada from Rome it isn't nearly so obvious either. But going north you can't miss it, it's looking down on you for miles and miles. You can understand why our people hated it.'

There was a moment of silence, and then Nikki spoke.

'I don't quite understand – ' she paused diffidently ' – what is so terrible in being looked down on . . . if the man on the hill can see you, you can also see him – he is stuck on the hill for all to see.'

Audley grunted. 'Yes, but stuck on his hill in a dugout with a telephone. And when he sees you move he simply murmurs a map reference into the phone and a battery of guns miles behind the line opens up on you.'

Or whistles up a couple of police motor-cyclists, thought Mitchell, she certainly ought to understand *that*. And maybe that was still part of Bouillet Wood's virtue, whatever was going on there now.

Which, with any luck, they were about to discover at last.

'It was an artilleryman's war, Nikki,' he said, slipping into Captain Lefevre's character instinctively. 'If their gunnery spotters could see you and your own spotters couldn't see you – then you were dead. In 1917 two whole battalions disappeared that way up at Monchy – just vanished off the face of the earth.'

'Vanished?' She spoke incredulously.

The first straggling houses of Hameau village were just ahead now, squat and ugly, with peeling brown paint. He could see a tractor towing a trailer-load of sugar beet in a field away to his left. Somewhere not far from where the beet had been planted, grown and harvested – maybe on the very ground – the greater part of the 9th North Berks Fusiliers had all vanished just as completely. They had passed over the crest of the ridge just ahead of the Poachers in the half-light, out of sight and out of recorded history. Only a lucky few of the handful who had lost their way and had joined the Poachers in the assault on the wood had survived.

She didn't really believe him, or she thought he was exaggerating, and he no longer had the heart to argue the point. It had all happened a long time ago, and the Fusiliers were part of the same clay as Marlborough's dragoons and grenadiers.

He drove on in silence through the village, past a trio of police motor-cyclists standing beside their machines at the crossroads outside the church – the lovingly rebuilt replica of the monstrosity which the British gunners had pulverised in 1916 – and turned on to the straight road which ran along the axis of the ridge.

Audley leant forward intently. 'This would be the German line.'

Mitchell turned the wheel slightly to avoid two black-clad grandmothers shuffling along, fresh loaves cradled in their arms. 'That's right.'

'And Bouilletcourt Farm is just ahead, then.'

As the high banks of the road sank away on each side of them the blank brick walls of the farm appeared on the left: a fortress below ground in 1916, it had been rebuilt like a fortress above ground, inward-looking except for a gateway fronting the road – in which another two motor-cyclists sat astride their machines. The arm of the state was much more evident this peaceful morning than it had been the previous evening.

Then they were on the open ground again, with the lower ridges rolling away to the south, the land a jigsaw of green and pale brown fields, autumn woods and little clustered villages, very tranquil in the sunlight.

Mitchell was disappointed to see that the unhelpful SDP man of the day before, alias Corporal Manson, was no longer on duty; small-mindedly, he had been looking forward to witnessing Captain Lefevre's entrance as an invited guest. Not that even invited guests were allowed to enter without precautions: after the gates had been opened by the new man – a character out of the same mould as his predecessor, but not one of the gallery in the Cambrai tank book, Mitchell noted – the car was instantly checked by red and white bars like a miniature railway crossing barrier, the existence of which he had overlooked the day before and which penned them in effectively until their credentials had been checked. Even then the gate was locked behind them before the barrier lifted, triggered apparently by the gatelocking mechanism.

Audley eyed the fences with undisguised interest before turning to Nikki.

'A double fence . . . I take it there are dogs loose in no-man's-land at night – or is it sown with nasty little mines?' he asked.

'I'm afraid I haven't the least idea, Dr Audley.'

'Hmm . . .' Audley stuck his head out of the car and scrutinised the roadside as they moved forward. 'Dogs for choice, I'd guess – ' Something caught his eye and he sniffed with distaste ' – in fact dogs for sure. Large and unfriendly dogs with eyes as big as soup-plates, radio-bleepers in their collars and murder in their hearts.'

Suddenly Audley had become quite talkative, quite jovial even, as he had been the night before after the decisive phone call had been made. But Mitchell found it difficult to concentrate on what he was saying as they drew closer to the wood: the vague tangle of greens and browns and black, resolving itself into distinct trees and bushes, dragged his attention from the words.

He could see clearly now that the fence erected beyond the furthest overhang of the trees had tubular metal uprights that were crowned with downward shaded lights. He saw too that there were no wires visible, so the electric cables must be buried underground, running up the hollow of the uprights. Altogether, with the fences and the lights, the men and the dogs – and heaven only knew what other invisible devices – Bouillet Wood had once again become a heavily defended strongpoint.

He drove slowly along the edge of the wood to where, as he remembered from the old days, the entrance had been. That also was gated now, and had another dark-suited keeper. But the gate was open and the keeper waved them inside.

The curving drive within was much as it had been, the gravel better weeded and the grass somewhat trimmer. In the gaps between the trees he could see the unevenness of the wood itself, not much changed in surface outline from when Leigh-Wood-house had led his Poachers through it, for nothing but time itself had happened to the ground since then. Twice afterwards the war had swept over the ridge, first the Germans pushing south in their March offensive, then the British pursuing them northwards again; but neither side had attempted to stand on this bloody strip – each had maybe had enough of it in 1916.

They were getting near the house now, the open clearing in front of it lightening the woodland ahead. He caught a momentary ripple of white façade between the trees –

'Stop the car,' said Audley.

Obediently Mitchell pulled the car to the left, into the mouth of one of the rides which cut at right angles through the undergrowth. As he did so he caught a flash of movement out of the corner of his eye.

As the movement registered on his brain his foot went down harder on the brake pedal in an involuntary reaction, so that they were all jerked forward. Sergeant Ogilvie was in conversation with Corporal Manson a dozen yards down the ride from them.

'Ted – good to see you again.'

'My David. Always the early bird!'

They shook hands with all the warmth of old friendship. Ollivier's gaze shifted directly to Mitchell, candid and appraising. 'And Captain Lefevre – good morning to you.'

The hand was cold and firm.

'Monsieur Ollivier.' *A better morning than the night before, Monsieur Ollivier.*

'Shall we go on up to the house, my David? I was on my way to receive you there.'

Audley looked around him. 'If it's all the same to you, Ted, I'd prefer to stretch my legs. I've been so cooped up these last few weeks a bit of your country air would do me a power of good.'

Ollivier smiled. 'But of course! Not enough exercise is the curse of our age – and *our* age particularly.' He struck his stomach with his fist. 'All that rugger-playing muscle wishes to retire and turns itself into fat, it betrays us both.' He nodded to Corporal Manson. 'Tell them we shall make our way in at our leisure, Pierre.'

'M'sieur.'

'And perhaps Mademoiselle will chaperone me,' went on Ollivier, acknowledging Nikki MacMahon's presence at Mitchell's shoulder. 'And so we will walk . . . undisturbed.'

'Undisturbed is right,' murmured Audley. 'You've got yourself a fine and private place, Ted.'

They fell into step, four abreast.

'We like it – we like it.'

'A rare thing these days, privacy.'

'A jewel beyond price.'

'Which someone now wants to steal from you.'

Ollivier gave Audley a side-glance. 'You think so?'

'Not think – know.'

'What makes you so sure?'

'Because there are too many damn bodies around for comfort, for one thing. We've got three – '

'*Three!* Ollivier stopped abruptly. 'Who?'

'The man you wanted us to talk to, Emerson. And his research assistant, a young man named Mitchell. And an old soldier.' Audley faced Ollivier squarely, all the friendship draining out of his voice. 'Three innocent men, Ted. Your privacy's too expensive for us. We can't afford it.'

'*Three!* Ollivier blew his cheeks out. 'Why didn't you tell me before?'

'Tell you? You gave us a bit of map and a name – man, you haven't been exactly open and above board with us. What the devil do you expect?'

'Did you talk to Emerson?'

'Talk to him?' Audley gave a derisive grunt. 'Everyone we want to talk to has an accident before we reach him. You want to watch out, you're the first living person we've met who's got any answers. You've got your dogs and your infrared scanners – '

Infra-red scanners? Mitchell switched back to the fences. As always, he had seen but not seen everything.

'I'm sorry, David.' Ollivier cut the big man short. 'I have erred – '

'Damn right, you've erred. You've got trouble. You wanted me and you've got me. But I need some answers first.'

'Give me the questions.'

'This is a neutral house – right?'

'Yes.'

'Who's due to meet here?'

Mitchell woke up with a start. *A neutral house?*

'I can't tell you, David. That's absolutely classified. I don't even know myself, I promise you.'

A neutral house?

'My men start to hand over today – this afternoon,' said Ollivier urgently. 'You know the rules.'

Audley knew – had known from the start – just what was happening in Bouillet Wood.

'What is a neutral house?' said Mitchell.

'Stay out of this, Paul,' Audley snapped.

It was the moment of truth and decision.

'No.'

'That's an order.'

'There aren't any orders for me. You asked me a question last night. Now you can choose your answer.'

Audley turned towards him. There was a strange blank look on his face for an instant. Then it softened into something Mitchell couldn't place. It seemed almost as though they were meeting again after having met long before and learnt to know each other, and now were meeting again at last.

Then he smiled. 'All right, Paul . . . It's quite simple, really . . . if the chairmen of two big companies, say, have got a mutual problem, something that's going to put a lot of people on the breadline if they don't handle it quickly, it doesn't always do for one to march straight up to the other. Because too many other people have big ears and big eyes – not just their rivals and competitors, and not just the wheeler-dealers on the stock exchanges, but on their own side maybe. What they need is somewhere safe and private, where they can slip in and out with nobody the wiser.

'It's the same with countries. You have a summit meeting in public, with the TV cameras and the political commentators, and too many people want to know why – and who won ... That's the curse of open diplomacy – one side's got to be seen to win or lose, and if neither does then it's just as bad. So the first thing they came up with was the hot line, which was a big step in the right direction. Except that when it's a matter of life and death nothing beats face-to-face talking.'

It was very quiet in the wood, with not a sound from its thousands of dead soldiers, British and German.

'So then they set up the neutral houses. If two countries have a problem, they just approach any third party for the key to a neutral house. No publicity, no TV, no questions asked – permanent top security guaranteed at head-of-state level. All the latest anti-bugging devices and experts from all sides can spot-check them at any time as a matter of routine. They've been in operation for five years now without a hitch.'

'They?'

'No names, no pack-drill, Paul. There are a dozen safe houses in half a dozen countries – maybe.'

'How long have you known?'

'That this was a neutral house? For sure, not until a moment ago. It's a new one on me.'

'But you guessed?'

Audley flashed a glance at Ollivier, then shrugged. 'France is a popular country for meetings – got a reputation for fair dealing, I can't think why. Maybe because the cops have got things screwed down tight. But Americans met the North Vietnamese here – maybe right here – long before the Paris talks started. They've met the Russians too, and the Chinese. The Israelis have met the Egyptians three times in France to my certain knowledge ... And the specification fitted like a glove.'

'Specification?'

'The place is just right. Biggish house, but not too big. Screened from direct sight. Impossible to approach without being seen. Off the beaten track – strangers in these villages stand out like sore thumbs, and there's no tourist traffic – but not too far off. Close to the Paris motorway, and the major junction with the Brussels-Liège-Aachen motorway is just south of Bapaume. Close enough to the Channel! And I'd guess there's a helicopter pad behind the house somewhere. Made for the job, the whole place.'

There was that little field in the middle of the wood just north of the house, where he had once found all the British and German cartridges, Mitchell remembered, his mind staggering under the implications of the situation. Because he still didn't know what Audley and Butler did – although he now seemed to have joined them, for God's sake! – he hadn't known what to expect. They had always seemed more like cops than robbers, defenders of the peace and security of the realm, but what he had never suspected was the rarified level at which they operated: the ultimate level of secret summit meetings.

He realised he was staring at Audley – and clear through him – just the way Audley had in the past stared at him.

'I understand – more or less.'

'Good.' Audley swung towards Ollivier. 'You've got a meeting here and the security angle's going sour on you – is that it?'

'We think something's up – ' Ollivier began cautiously.

'Oh, come on, Ted – how many bodies do I have to produce to make you talk? What about last night, come to that? Was that an accident, then?'

Ollivier smiled wryly. 'Oddly enough, David, it looks very much as if it *was* an accident.'

'To whom?'

'A Spanish farm worker. They employ them on the farms hereabouts, have done for years. This man was a – a scavenger of old war material. He sold what he found. His employer had warned him before that he was living on borrowed time, but it seems he was foolish.'

'You'd vetted him?'

'We have vetted everyone who was not born and bred on the ridge – and some of those who were, also.' There was an edge of exasperation in Ollivier's tone. 'Do you want to teach us our business, eh?'

Audley rubbed his chin, staring at the tall Frenchman in silence. 'But you called me in, Ted. Why did you do that?'

'Because you I can trust, my friend,' replied Ollivier simply. 'I know you will not go shooting your mouth off – I know you will keep your counsel, and mine if need be . . . I trust you.'

'I'm touched,' Audley murmured. 'Relatively touched, anyway.'

'Relatively?'

'Relatively . . . Gensoul insisted you made contact with Perfidious Albion about Emerson, and I was your best bet. That's fair enough – so relatively touched, yes.'

'As a matter of fact, you were all my own idea.'

'Indeed!' Audley missed his step, scuffing his shoes in the carpet of fallen leaves. 'Then you really must be in a hole, Ted.'

'Not a hole. Maybe a quandary – an impasse.'

'Sounds like a hole to me.'

The silence was broken suddenly by distant barking. The dogs with eyes as big as soup-plates were hungry, probably.

'A few days since – ago – one of our agents, a man of the Surveillance du Territoire, spotted someone he knew . . . not far from here. A known terrorist.'

'Someone I know?' asked Audley.

Ollivier shook his head. 'I would think not. The man is a former Pied-Noir known as Turco. But you would know the type very well, I've no doubt – you have them in Ireland now.'

That was one for Nikki, thought Mitchell, keeping his eyes down.

'Political? Or non-political?'

'Non-political.'

Mitchell looked at Audley. 'Is there such a thing as a non-political Irishman?'

Audley returned the look, unsmiling. 'What he means is an old-fashioned psychopath. When the going gets nasty and most of the genuine patriots have been killed or captured – or had enough – the scum comes into its own. They don't find the dirty jobs unpleasant, the psychos don't. They like 'em.' He turned back to Ollivier. 'A hit man?'

The Frenchman nodded.

'Then you've got trouble. What did your agent do?'

'It was in a village near Amiens – Querrieu – they were both in cars. Our man turned round and followed him, but Turco's no fool and he must have been on the look-out – '

'Which clinches it. So the following turned into chasing?' Audley cocked his head on one side. 'And – let me guess – someone's car got itself blown up, maybe?'

Ollivier gave an exasperated grunt, squaring up to Audley. 'The devil with it! How much do you really know?'

'Unfortunately just that. Whose car was it?'

'Turco's – he ran out of road on the edge of town.'

'So Turco is no longer with us?'

'Regrettably – most regrettably – he is.' Ollivier spread his hands eloquently. 'Our agent was approaching the car when it exploded – another few metres and he would have been caught by it himself. He was disconcerted – '

'Disconcerted? I don't wonder!'

Ollivier shrugged. 'Well . . . he assumed Turco was still inside. By the time he learned otherwise it was too late.'

'Hmm . .' Audley nodded to himself. 'What sort of explosion was it – bomb or petrol?'

'Our experts say there were explosives in the car. The explosion set off the petrol.'

Audley's head continued to bob. 'I see . . . so Turco crashed his car and then blew it up, resourceful fellow – two birds with one grenade, so to speak.'

'Two birds?'

'That's right. He caused a diversion to cover his escape and he reckoned on destroying whatever was in the car, which he didn't have time to take with him. Right, Ted?'

Ollivier regarded Audley with a suspicious frown. 'You still aren't being straight with me, my friend, are you? Just how much do you know?'

'Only what you've told me – and I'm having to work damned hard for that.'

The frown graduated to a scowl which creased Ollivier's face into crumpled brown wrapping paper. 'Come on, my David – *perfide Albion* is right! – I didn't say there was anything in the car. You said it.'

Audley stared back at his friend with one eyebrow insultingly raised. 'But you didn't say I had to act stupid – I know you prefer *stupide Albion*, but we can't always oblige you, no matter how much we try.' The eyebrow came down and the voice levelled. 'Man – you sent us a charred map of the Somme battlefield. A German map, but Lefevre identified it in five seconds flat. A map we captured in 1916, and I give you one bottle of fine cognac to a pint of lukewarm beer that it had "Charles Emerson" on it and you got it out of Turco's car . . . and if you trust me, how about damn well showing it, eh?'

Mitchell caught a glimpse of Nikki's face beyond the Frenchman's, and wondered whether his own bore the same look of fascinated and inadequately concealed amusement. Obviously Audley and Ollivier were men out the same mould, and nobody, superiors or inferiors, treated them with the same outspokenness as that with which they treated each other. They were probing each other and playing to their little gallery at the same time, and vastly enjoying themselves into the bargain: big, clever children entranced with their game because short of war it was the most exciting game of all.

The barking in the distance reached an angry crescendo, then cracked into frightening yelping and trailed off through whimpering into silence.

'The map, of course!' Ollivier's face uncreased. 'It is I who am getting slow in my old age.'

'Too suspicious, certainly. If you'd just come clean for one minute we could do business.'

'Business?' Ollivier seemed surprised by the word. 'What business has your country got in this?'

'I told you – three dead bodies. Dead Englishmen, and killed in England too – they make it our business, Ted. We'd like to balance our books with a dead Frenchman or two, maybe.'

'A somewhat . . . insular viewpoint under the circumstances, if I may say so.'

'You may say so. But screw your circumstances, *mon ami*,' said Audley lightly. 'The map was in the car, but Turco could have taken it with him without much sweat I should have thought. So was there something else he couldn't take, then?'

'The map was in the trunk – how do you say it in English, the boot? – in the boot of the car, and it was blown clear. But you are right, there was something else in there. A weapon.'

'Surprise, surprise.'

'An unusual weapon.'

'Let me guess again. Something to knock down a visiting helicopter, like our Rapier and Blowtorch – or a Redeye – ?'

'Nothing like that.'

'Not that new Czech sniper's SLR?'

Ollivier shook his head. 'You'll never guess, not in a million years. Does the names Charles Lancaster mean anything to you?'

'Charles – Lancaster? Who – ?'

'Who and what. You are not devotee of *la chasse*, clearly.' The Frenchman lifted an imaginary rifle, traversing it at the undergrowth just ahead. 'Pouf! Pouf! Two pheasants for the pot – '

'A shotgun.'

'A shotgun exactly. But not just any shotgun. The Rolls-Royce of shotguns. And this was a most special of the most special.'

'A custom-built job.'

Ollivier nodded. 'We took it to a gunsmith in Paris. It was only slightly damaged in the explosion, and still he almost wept. He said the English guns were the finest in the world, and a Charles Lancaster was the best of the finest, better than Purdey or anyone.'

'He identified it?'

'Identified? He knew it straight away – it seems there was a Lancaster patent trigger, single action – the recoil from the right barrel cocks for the left – '

'I'm sorry. I meant did he know whose gun it was – you said "special of the special".'

'Ah, I see what you mean. He could not, no, but it was a gun made for one man, one of a pair of guns. It had the initials "H.J.V.B." in silver on the stock and it was numbered "Two" on the top of the barrel flat.'

'And valuable, I suppose?'

Mitchell circled unobtrusively to get a better view of Audley's face, warned equally by the shallowness of the question – it was a useless, fatuous question, utterly extraordinary under the circumstances – as by the lack of excitement in the voice. And the big man's expression only confirmed his suspicion: the one thing he wasn't going to admit here and now was that officers of the 29th Rifles had carried shotguns into battle.

Ollivier shrugged. 'A matched pair of them now, in good condition – not less than 30,000 francs, possibly a lot more. It is hard to be precise with such things.'

Audley went through an elaborate process of mental arithmetic, staring casually at Mitchell as he did so. 'That would be, say, £2,500 in real money . . . was it brand new?'

'No, it was not. The gunsmith dated it to the turn of this century. About 1903 he estimated.

'Practically a museum piece,' said Audley. 'Not that it matters either way. The obvious thing to do now is to cancel the meeting here. It doesn't matter who's coming – get them to some other neutral house of yours.'

'Impossible.'

'Nonsense! If somebody's got something planned for this place it's the only sensible thing to do.'

'And admit that we cannot guarantee security in the heart of our own country? That we can spend tens of millions on the latest equipment, and one glimpse of one piece of scum throws us into a panic?' Ollivier's tone hardened. 'If we did that just once there would be no neutral houses – anywhere.'

'So you ignore Turco?'

'No. The wasps buzz round the jampot – naturally. So we seal down the lid tighter while we look for the wasps' nest.'

'We?'

Ollivier wagged his finger at Audley. 'You didn't come over here just to talk to me, my David. You had your plan of action too.'

'True. And naturally you want to know what it is.'

'Naturally I *must* know what it is. Without that you can have no plan any more, only the next boat from Calais.'

'Well that's laying it on the line, certainly.' Audley eyed the Frenchman dispassionately. 'We tell all or we get the bum's rush, eh?'

'Most regrettably – yes.' Ollivier smiled. 'I cannot have you stirring the wasps' nest upon your own – we might both get stung. But I might be prepared to let you help me look for it.'

Audley considered the proposition, slowly nodding to himself.

'Fair enough, Ted. You've got yourself a deal,' he said decisively.

'So?'

'So we find out for you why Charles Emerson had to die. And in return you make sure his killers are paid in full?'

'*D'accord.*' Ollivier held out his hand. 'You and Captain Lefevre will report to me, and to me only, through Mademoiselle MacMahon. Trust nobody else – your side or mine. We trust only each other.'

'*D'accord*,' said Audley.

Like hell, thought Mitchell.

6

The old men straggled up the pathway from the coach park in twos and threes, making their slow way towards the notice-boards which marked out the old British front line.

While they had gathered beside the huge pink coach they had chatted and laughed, but now they were silent, almost self-conscious. Indeed, they looked even a little lost, as well they might, Mitchell decided: the neatness of these restored trenches, with their mathematically precise rows of concrete sandbags and clean-cut concrete duck-boards must be as far removed from the Vimy Ridge of far-off memory as the smooth grass, and dark ranks of fir trees which surrounded them. Nowhere, not even the most well-ploughed and cultivated farmlands of the Somme, was further from the reality than this restoration of what had never been.

He watched Colonel Butler work his way from the back towards him, very upright and soldierly in his uniform and a living commentary on his own definition of what made a soldier: he had never looked quite right in any of the civilian clothes he had worn, they had been as false on him as was the uniform on Mitchell. Now he looked himself at last.

'Over here, sir,' called Mitchell.

Butler looked around him unconcernedly, flicked a piece of orange peel out of his path with his stick, and made his way into the German trench.

'Where's Audley?' Butler's eyes clouded at Mitchell's salute. 'Belay that – no one can see us here. Where's Audley?'

'Up at the Canadian Memorial on the top of the ridge, sir,' said Mitchell carefully.

'With the woman?'

'Yes. We split up because – because that way she can't watch both of us.'

Butler's mouth tightened. 'And naturally she went with Audley – he intended that?'

'We reckoned she would – sir.'

'So you want to talk to me, then?' Butler cut straight to the point. 'Make it quick then.'

Mitchell swallowed. Compared with Audley's oblique approaches, Butler's directness was unnerving. 'We think we've got a lead. If you've got any Poachers in the coach I want to check it out with them as soon as possible.'

'What lead?'

'Some of the officers carried shotguns in the attack on Hameau Ridge. The French have got one of them, I think – one that was carried by a particular officer.'

'Which officer?'

'H. J. V. Bellamy – Second Lieutenant Harry Bellamy.'

'Bellamy?' Butler shook his head. 'I've got one 29th Battalion officer, but not – ' He stopped. 'But there was a Bellamy on the War Memorial at Elthingham – a second lieutenant.'

'That's the man. The squire's son. You've got a good memory –'

'Damn my memory. The man's been dead for half a century.'

'But he had a particularly beautiful gun, General Leigh-Woodhouse said so.' Mitchell refused to let himself be outstared. 'And if this is his gun it's been round here for half a century too.'

'So what? He was killed and anyone could have picked up his gun, particularly if it was a good one. What the devil can it tell you now?'

'I don't know. But Charles Emerson found something here, and if this gun was it then it told him something.'

'And if it is?'

'Bellamy was in "D" Company. That's the one which went in with the North Berkshires in the first assault – the one that disappeared over the ridge and never came back.'

Butler stared at him in stony silence for an elongated moment. 'Very well. I can give you two men who reached Hameau Ridge, Mitchell. Captain Faversham – he was a subaltern in "B" Company in '16. Wounded on the edge of the wood, but he'll have known Bellamy right enough . . . and Sergeant Hayhoe – he was sanitary corporal in "C" Company in the Somme attack.'

'*What* corporal?' Mitchell exclaimed incredulously.

'Sanitary corporal – in charge of the latrine men,' snapped Butler. 'But don't get the idea that's funny, because it isn't, not by a long chalk. Need a good man for that, a man who doesn't shirk. You can sum up a unit by its latrines just as much as by the shine on their boots. And the sanitary men backed up the stretcher bearers in action out here – Hayhoe won the Distinguished Conduct Medal at Ypres in '17 for pulling wounded men out of the mud under fire.'

'I wasn't laughing,' protested Mitchell defensively. 'But you've found nobody from "D" Company?'

He realised as he asked the question that it was a stupid one: by dawn on that autumn day on Hameau Ridge there was no 'D' Company. No officers, no sanitary corporals, no riflemen. And even of the rest of the battalion there were only a handful left on their feet, the bewildered conquerors of the Prussian Redoubt. After two more years of war and nearly sixty years of wear and tear they were lucky to have any Poachers to talk to at all.

But Butler was no longer listening to him anyway; he had climbed onto the firestep of the trench and was staring across the huge craters of the fifty-yard strip of no-man's-land which separated it from the British line.

'Now's your best chance to talk to Hayhoe on your own,' he growled. 'See the little one over there by the notice-board – the one all by himself? Always keeps to himself when we get to the battlefields and the cemeteries, Hayhoe does. Joins in the talk and the sing-songs in the coach and the hotel, but keeps to himself in the open. You go and talk to him now while I go and get Faversham.'

Mitchell studied the little man narrowly as he walked down the path towards him.

Sergeant Hayhoe, DCM, sometime sanitary corporal . . . that would be a problem, getting rid of the shit in the trenches when the fighting was static: weeks and months in the same place, going in and out of the line, you couldn't just chuck it anywhere – and couldn't do anything with it during daylight. So it would be another part of the busy night routine. It was odd that in all his researches he'd never thought of finding out about so basic and important a fact of life.

Little, but not frail: Hayhoe was wiry and compact, like a jockey, with a shock of badly-cut grey hair above a face weathered red and brown by wind and time, a Hobbit of a man who gave the impression that in his day he'd always been big enough at a pinch.

And a little old man now who took in Mitchell from head to toe carefully with a clear eye.

'Mr – Hayhoe?' Mitchell thrust out his hand. 'My name's Lefevre – Royal Tank Regiment.'

Cold, bony hand. But the grip was firm.

'Pleased to meet you.' Hayhoe nodded easily, the relationships and differences of age, rank, class and occasion all computed and balanced gracefully so that there was room neither for deference nor condescension in the greeting. 'Goin' to show us round tomorrow, the Colonel said – right?'

'I don't think I'd presume to do that, Mr Hayhoe. I think you know it all better than I do. I thought maybe you'd show me a thing or two, to be honest.'

Hayhoe examined him briefly for signs of insincerity, and then showed a couple of yellow teeth in a lopsided smile, shaking his head. 'Might have done once, one or two places, not now though. Don't recognise it now.' He shook his head again. 'First time I came out again – that was for the unveiling of the memorial at Thiepval, in the old King's time, King George V – didn't recognise it then. All gone, what I remember . . . an' good riddance, too.'

'You mean the trees and the grass had come back?'

'An' the smell had gone. Always had a good sense of smell I had – still have, too. Wished I hadn't *then*, worse than the mines, an' I never liked them either.'

'The mines?'

'Ah, I was in the pits when the war started, an' glad to be out of 'em at first, I was. But then it was out of the fryin' pan an' into the fire, an' no mistake.' He grinned ruefully at Mitchell. 'I'd of liked nothin' better than a good deep pit when Jerry was givin' us what for.'

'But you joined the 29th Rifles – the Poachers, I thought?'

'That I did – 'cause my elder brother did. A keeper on Lord Studley's estate he was – when he joined up a dozen of us lads from the pit went along with 'im an' two others from t'estate.'

'And they took you – obviously.'

'An' glad to. Wanted to make a good showing – an' the head keeper said he'd rather 'ave us shooting Germans than his lordship's pheasants, bein' as how he was going to be short-handed.'

A genuine poacher, he'd got, Mitchell realised. And of course that must have been how it had worked: if you were losing your young keepers for King and Country it was only common sense to take the young poachers out of circulation at the same time.

It was an added irony that the poachers had thereafter taken over the battalion in the popular estimation.

He grinned at Hayhoe. 'I've heard you got yourselves a reputation for a bit of poaching over here – until the Australians arrived.'

Hayhoe grinned back at him wickedly. 'Arr – the Aussies – Anzacs we called 'em then – they were the boys! Steal the shine off your buttons, they would. Good lads, though – Jerry was scared of them, I reckon. Don't blame him.'

'It was the Australians who relieved your battalion on Hameau Ridge, wasn't it?'

'That's right. Came through Bully Wood at the double when I was helping with the wounded – cor, and they were fightin' mad then! "No prisoners" they were shoutin' – "No prisoners". They'd had some trouble with prisoners, that's what one of 'em told me, though I reckon it was more likely snipers – the wood was still full of them, like. No one really knew what was happenin', not us and not Jerry neither, it had all happened so quick. An' I was in this shell-hole with Mr Leigh-Woodhouse, all covered with blood – '

'General Leigh-Woodhouse?'

'That's him. But he was just a boy then, of course, though he was a good officer, mind you – brave. Those officers then, it was all "Follow me", not like later on . . . you could get bad ones then an' it'ud be "After you, an' don't let me see one of you hold back" . . . but in the old Poachers they was all brave – too brave. They had different uniforms, see, an' carried revolvers, and Jerry picked 'em off like flies.'

'I've heard tell that some of them carried shotguns – is that true?'

'Shotguns?' For a moment Hayhoe seemed not to understand the question. 'Now you've mentioned it, some of 'em did – like young Mr Dyson in our company. An' he was lying dead in that same shell-hole, too, with Mr Leigh-Woodhouse. There was this

Jerry prisoner too, just a kid, and this Aussie comes up and says "Stand up", and Jerry stands up – and I *knew* what he was goin' to do an' I says "You can't do that" an' he says "You just watch me, mate" and he poops him.'

'Poops him?'

'Kills him – shoots him. "That's settled the bugger", he says, and off he goes cool as you like. I remember that just like it happened yesterday – "That's settled the bugger", he says. Cor!'

If Sanitary Corporal Hayhoe had felt any disapproval at Australian behaviour in 1916, the passage of time had erased it, reducing it to history. There was even a faint suggestion of admiration, a tacit acknowledgement that maybe the killer had been acting with instinctive logic better suited to conditions in Bully Wood at the time.

But that was a blind alley now.

'Do you remember the names of the other officers?'

'Of the old Poachers?' Hayhoe looked at him. 'Well, Lord St Blaizey commanded the battalion, of course – he was killed that morning, just outside the wood – him and the adjutant together. An' my company commander was Captain Ashley, that was Lord Riding's younger son – he was wounded. Lost an eye and a hand, he did, and he was back in France a year later – killed at Messines in '17, he was.'

It looked as though *Burke's Peerage* and *Debrett's* would have required substantial re-editing after Hameau Ridge.

Hayhoe closed his eyes. 'Then there were our other company officers: Mr Leigh-Woodhouse and Mr Dyson – an' Mr Ellison – he was killed by a shell, he was.'

'What about the other companies?'

'Arr, don't remember them so well ... "A" Company was commanded by let me think – that was Captain Pardoe, "B" Company was Captain Gordon. An' "D" Company was Captain Barbury – Viscount Barbury, of course. That was my brother's company, that was.'

'"D" Company?'

Hayhoe nodded. 'Most of my friends, them I'd joined up with was in "D" Company. Best company in the battalion to be in, too.'

'Why was that?'

'Why?' Hayhoe cocked his head. 'Well, we were always having to dig these trenches – they had to be seven foot deep, four foot wide at the bottom and seven foot wide at the top. An' when you'd done it – when you'd dug two yards of that – you were right for the day . . . Well, you see, there were a lot of miners in that company, my friends an' some lads from the Forest of Dean an' also from up Durham way, an' they was just the kids for digging. Ordinary chaps, they couldn't dig worth a damn, but us miners – we used to say "Come out of the bloody way, give us the spade", an' then we'd finish the job in half the time . . . I'd 'ave given anything to 'ave been in with them. But, of course, I wouldn't be here now speakin' to you if I had have been.'

'Why not?'

'Arr, because they was all killed, see.'

'All?'

'Every man jack of 'em. They went up ahead of us with the North Berks Fusiliers for some reason, I never knew what for, an' that's the last time we ever clapped eyes on 'em – never saw not one of 'em again, not one – Bill, my brother, an' my cousin Bertie, and little George Brett, an' Herbert Bidwell, an' Arthur Hough – ' Hayhoe's voice quavered suddenly ' – good lads, all good lads – all from our village. I was the only one left, an' when I went home for Christmas in '16 Herbie Bidwell's mother came up to me, an' she looked at me an' she said "Why you?" Just that – she just looked at me an' said "Why you?" and not another word.' He wiped his hand across his face. 'I never went home on leave again, not while the war was on, not until after the Armistice. Stayed at the YMCA in London instead.

'An' I never went back to the pits neither, though there were jobs waitin' in 'em in 1919. I went up to Lord Riding – not to his agent, mind you, to the old man himself – an' I said I'd served with his son, Captain Ashley that was, an' I wouldn't go down the pits, never again. I wanted a job in the open, by myself if possible.

'An' he said "Why, are you afraid of the dark?" An' I said "A miner's never afraid of the dark. It's because there aren't any of my mates left, that's why." An' he said "Weren't you a poacher before you were one of the Poachers?" An' I said "Yes", an' he said "Well, now you'll be a keeper" an' I was one of his keepers for fifty years, nearly, right down to two or three years ago.'

Mitchell remembered the tractor and trailer he had seen bumping across the fields sloping northwards from Bully Wood and Hameau village that very morning – fields where Bill Hayhoe and George Brett and Herbie Bidwell, and all the rest of "D" Company had vanished in the half-light.

And H. J. V. Bellamy.

'There was a Bellamy in "D" Company, I've been told – a second lieutenant, wasn't there?'

'Bellamy? Bellamy?' Hayhoe screwed up his face. 'Can't say as I remember him. I knew 'em all once, but it's a long time ago, y'know ... I do remember that in "D" Company they were all proper toffs – that's what we called them then – toffs, I do remember that. You ought to ask Mr Faversham, he'd remember him, sure to.' Hayhoe turned to survey the British trenches on his left. 'There he is now – with the Colonel. Mr Faversham, sir!' He swung back to Mitchell. 'We'd best go over to 'em. Mr Faversham's not so quick on his legs now,' he confided.

Mitchell followed him back down the path between the parapets of concrete sandbags to where Butler stood straight-backed beside a kindly-looking old gentleman supporting himself heavily on two sticks.

'Mr Faversham, sir, this is Captain – ' Hayhoe faltered, 'Captain – '

'Lefevre. Royal Tank Regiment.'

'I recognise the badge.' Faversham's eyes lit up with impish good humour. 'How do you do, Captain? I gather from Butler here that you are about to take up the responsibility of conducting us from here on – to be photographed in the interest of public relations and army recruiting . . . though how Hayhoe and I are likely to attract young men to the colours I must confess I fail to see.' He chuckled. 'Not with tales of our famous victories, I fear.'

'Sir . . .' Mitchell floundered for a reply. 'B-but they *were* famous victories.'

'They didn't feel like it at the time, though, dear boy – but then I was generally too frightened to notice, I suppose – and don't you snort like that, Hayhoe.'

'I was thinking you were a good play-actor, sir.'

'Ah, now *that* may be. But then most of us were play-acting – pretending to be soldiers. There wasn't really very much choice, you had to pretend to be brave. In fact the only time I told my company commander I was scared he thought I was pulling his leg. He thought it was a great joke – "That's the spirit", he said. I must say I didn't see the funny side of it at all. But I pretended I did.'

Mitchell summoned up his own courage. 'We were just talking about the battle of Hameau Ridge, Mr Hayhoe and I – about "D" Company. Did you know Harry Bellamy, by any chance?'

'Harry Bellamy?' Faversham looked at Mitchell curiously. 'Do you know the Bellamys, then?'

'I was down in Elthingham a few days ago – ' Mitchell was about to embark on an elaborate lie when he realised that he didn't even know whether the Bellamy family was still in possession of their ancestral domain ' – that's where the family lived in 1914, I believe.'

'That's right – good shooting country there. But the Bellamy fortune was founded on the coal mines up north – squires who became capitalists during the nineteenth century, they were. All nationalised in 1945, of course . . . Did I know Harry Bellamy? For a brief time – just under two years – very well. Being in the same battalion is like being in the same family, if it's a good battalion – and ours was, wasn't it?'

Hayhoe nodded vigorously. 'The best. I never served in a better one.'

'No, not the best,' Faversham shook his head slowly in disagreement. 'We were rank amateurs, beginners. If we'd been driving instead of fighting, we'd have had big "L" plates front and back at Hameau Ridge. I commanded a company in 1918 when we breached the Hindenburg Line on the St Quentin Canal – '

'Bellenglise?' The name came out involuntarily.

'That's right.' Faversham's eyes were bright. 'You've read about it?'

'My – I had a relative in the West Mercians.'

'Yes, they were in the division. That was the finest thing I ever took part in – a famous victory, if you like, dear boy. Except no one in England has ever heard of it, that is. But a famous victory all the same.'

'More famous than the capture of the Prussian Redoubt on Hameau Ridge?' said Butler.

'Accident, mere accident, Colonel. At Bellenglise we knew what we were doing. But Hameau Ridge was a triumph of incompetent gallantry.'

'Incompetent?' Butler frowned. 'That sounds a little harsh.'

'But true. The North Berkshires and the Poachers were supposed to cause a diversion – I rather think we were a sort of forlorn hope to annoy the Germans . . . But before we'd even got started they caught the North Berks in close order while it was still pitch black – shelled the stuffing out of them so that we had to reinforce them with "D" Company before they started.'

Faversham caught Mitchell's eye. 'That was Harry Bellamy's company, dear boy, and that was the last I saw of Harry.'

'What happened to them?'

Faversham spread his hands. 'Lord knows. They didn't get to the wood, that's certain. Their colonel was dead before they moved – direct hit on battalion HQ – and the tanks hadn't kept up with them. I'd guess they got on the wrong axis between the village and the wood and went on over the top, slap into the German reserves. In the dark no one knew what was happening – I never knew what was happening even in broad daylight in those days, most of the time. We did meet up with some Berkshires who'd got lost and they went into the wood with us. The rest of them probably ran into our own bombardment once they were over the crest.'

'But your battalion did a pretty competent job in the wood,' observed Butler gently.

'Well, I suppose you could say we were in our element there. Snap-shooting in the half-light, we were originally the Game-keepers' Rifles, you know. It was pretty much every man for himself. But I was hit quite early on – what would you say, Hayhoe?'

Hayhoe nodded. 'It was like you say, sir. The lads could shoot a treat, quick like. I mind what Tanner said afterwards – Rifleman Tanner. "There's a few brace of Jerries won't goose-step no more, corporal" he said to me.'

'Initiative, but no experience,' agreed Faversham, 'that's what we'd got. And more than our fair share of luck. That's what took Bully Wood and the Prussian Redoubt.'

Mitchell could contain the vital question no longer. 'Did you carry a shotgun, Mr Faversham?'

Faversham smiled, and then sighed. 'So you've heard of our affectation, have you? Yes, dear boy, I did. Half a dozen of us subalterns did – I rather think it was Harry's idea, too. I bitterly regretted it afterwards.'

'Why?'

'Because I didn't shoot any Germans – and I lost an exceedingly fine weapon even though I wasn't badly wounded.'

'You lost – ' Mitchell's voice cracked. 'You mean a special gun?'

'That's right. Lost it when I was knocked out by a lump of chalk – the adjutant warned me something like that would happen. He was all for stopping it, but the Colonel rather liked it. I think he thought it added a touch of distinction to a rather vulgar occasion. So I lost my Holland and Holland for nothing.'

Mitchell swallowed. 'Your Holland and Holland.'

'Lovely thing. Present from my father on my eighteenth birthday – that's what comes of giving boys presents too good for them ... But poor old Harry went out with an even better one – a Charles Lancaster.' He smiled sadly. 'Everything Harry Bellamy had was the best: Savile Row uniforms, Zeiss field-glasses, gold cigarette case and hip-flask, Charles Lancaster shotgun. He was worth a fortune on the hoof – we used to warn him that if the Huns ever heard about him they'd mount a special offensive. He said they'd only get it after he'd been killed, so it didn't worry him. Which they did, I suppose, poor fellow. But he didn't play-act at being brave. It was the real thing with him.'

'B-but you know he carried the Lancaster on the day he was killed?'

'Know?' Faversham seemed puzzled. 'How do you mean?'

'You moved out at night – and he was in a different company.'

Faversham nodded. 'Oh, I see what you mean ... Well, as it happens I packed up his kit afterwards – all our servants were killed or wounded. He'd had a pair of guns, of course, in a beautiful leather case with brass corners, I remember. One was still in it – Number 1. Number 2 was always his favourite. Made me sad to think some German had got it by then.'

7

The pale golden leaf took several minutes to drift past Mitchell. First it was caught in a sluggish back-current which took it in a slow circle; then it snagged on a waterlogged willow branch which in any ordinary October would have been well below the surface. But the little Ancre was low for the time of year, full of hazards for the falling debris of autumn; the little leaf would be trapped long before it was ready to sink. Nothing from these quiet headwaters would carry any message downstream to Albert, or beyond Albert to Corbie, where the Ancre joined the Somme and headed for the far-off sea.

That other October it had been very different . . .

Somewhere in his mind, he was sure of it, was that thing Charles Emerson had found. It was there, but he couldn't find it, no matter how he ransacked the facts.

. . . That other October the Ancre would have flowed high and fast, fed by drenching, torrential downpour . . . *would have* flowed high and fast if it had been able to flow at all – if its banks hadn't been shelled out of existence and its course hadn't been choked with the bodies of men and animals and the wreckage of their equipment, until the whole valley had become one vast swamp, an inland lake of mud and water . . .

The answer was there, but the only discovery he had made so far had been about himself, and it was hardly a palatable one.

It was Charles Emerson he was thinking about, and this was Emerson country, so it wasn't surprising that it was an Emerson theory he found uppermost in his mind. Indeed, this was the ideal moment to put it to the test – that there was always a spark of pure intuition which distinguished the true historian from the competent researcher. If they were right about what had happened a few days before then something had sparked Emerson: stumbling unexpectedly on a new piece of truth he had instantly recognised it for what it was. But if it were so then Paul Mitchell lacked the spark, seeing nothing except disjointed, inconclusive facts.

'Time's up,' said Audley from behind him.

So soon? thought Mitchell; his half-hour alone by the stream had passed like a dream, his thoughts drifting and circling as helplessly as the leaf in the cross-currents of the past forty-eight hours.

'Our time too, Paul – it is almost up,' said Nikki. She looked at her watch. 'This time tomorrow the meeting will have started.'

'Between whom?'

Audley shook his head. 'Don't ask – she doesn't know and nor do I, even if I could make a damn good guess. The rule with Neutral House meetings is that nobody talks outside and nobody asks questions. It isn't even Ted Ollivier's business, all he does is to make sure it stays private.'

'Then how do you know it's starting so soon?'

'Because French Security has already started the handover count-down. From now on the other two sides'll be moving men in, vetting the place, and Ollivier's men will gradually pull out. And as they pull out they clamp down on the outer ring, so they can jump on anything they don't like that moves in a twenty-five mile radius. It's a routine count-down procedure now.'

Mitchell shivered at the word. Count-downs launched rockets to the moon, but they also blew the horizon apart with their mushroom clouds: they were starter's orders for progress or armageddon. So they were the right words for a secret summit, which could lead to either of those things.

'And we are a long way from Bouillet Wood here, Paul,' said Nikki. 'What is so special about the Ancre that we should come here?'

The Ancre . . .

Nothing special about the Ancre. A sleepy little river bottom, with its lagoons and reeds and water-grass, and its villages nestling in the ridge-folds on either side: Hamel and St Pierre Divion, Beaucourt and Grandcourt and Miraumont. It looked for all the world as though nothing had ever happened, or could ever happen, along this quiet stream.

'This is where Emerson came last week.'

'Why here?'

'Because this is where we slogged it out with the Germans, October, November, January, February – '

The most terrible place on the whole Western Front, worse even than Passchendaele, where the mud had been like a beast which gulped living men in the darkness: how could he tell them that about this gentle place?

'This is where he thought we finally won the battle, when we made them pull back to the Hindenburg Line.'

She frowned at him. 'But the Poachers weren't here.'

So Audley had told her, as he'd said he would. 'No, they weren't.'

'And it is the Poachers who matter – the man with the gun, Sous-Lieutenant Bellamy, and the men with him who disappeared, they are the ones who matter most of all.'

' "D" Company,' said Audley.

' "D" Company, yes. Supposing they had taken the Prussian Redoubt – would that not interest Professor Emerson?'

'But they didn't take it. The other companies took it, we know that. And they came through Bouillet Wood to do it. As far as we know Bellamy's men never even entered the wood.'

'But could they not have come round the back of it – into the ravine? Then they could have attacked the redoubt from behind.'

Mitchell stared at her, unwilling to admit that he had already considered that very possibility – in the darkness and the confusion anything was remotely possible – and had discarded it.

Finally he shook his head. 'It's not on, Nikki.'

'Why not?'

'Too many Germans, too few Englishmen – too few to make an attack on the redoubt anyway. And there isn't a shred of evidence.'

'What about the gun – the sous-lieutenant's gun?'

'That's evidence of a sort all right, but that's not what I mean. Suppose Bellamy did all you say – suppose "D" Company did attack the redoubt from the rear. I don't believe for one moment that they did, but suppose they did – it still doesn't help us one bit.'

She looked at him uncertainly. 'But it would have interested Professor Emerson – and is that not what you have been looking for?' She turned towards Audley questioningly. 'That is what you said?'

Audley rubbed his chin. 'Yess ... but I can see what Paul's driving at: it would have grabbed Emerson – or any other military historian. But it wouldn't have mattered a damn to anyone else ... You mean maybe we've been barking up the wrong tree, Paul – the wrong tree all along?'

'I'm not sure – I don't know,' Mitchell shook his head. 'Somehow I don't think we're wrong.'

'Nor do I – and nor did they, by God,' said Audley grimly. 'Nobody kills the way they've been killing without a damn good reason. Whatever Emerson found out, it was dynamite.'

That was the point Mitchell had come back to himself: either there was something he had overlooked or there was something he didn't yet know. But there surely was *something*.

He gazed over Audley's head at the rising ground of the

Thiepval ridge, towards the ugly red-brick memorial which carried the names of all the men who might have supplied the answer to his questions, the lost men of 'D' Company: *Bill, my brother, an' cousin Bertie, and little Georgie Brett, an' Herbert Bidwell, an' Arthur Hough . . . all good lads.*

And H. J. V. Bellamy, the sous-lieutenant with the gun.

'But we're a long way from Bouillet Wood, you're right, Nikki,' he repeated to himself.

'So whatever Emerson found out must have come to him, he didn't find it down here,' prompted Audley.

The big man was looking at him intently, almost as though he was willing him to stretch his wits to their furthest extent. For an instant Mitchell was unbearably reminded of Emerson, whose encouragement had always stirred him to try to excel. Both men had in common that quality of leadership which had burned so brightly on this very ground: he remembered how one ancient survivor of the St Quentin canal crossing had summed up his company commander – *he made me act braver than I really was.*

The man Turco had had the map – Emerson's map – and the gun – Bellamy's gun . . .

'Someone could have offered him that Charles Lancaster – offered to sell it to him.'

'Did people offer him souvenirs?' asked Nikki.

'It wouldn't be the first time.'

'Did he buy them?' asked Audley.

'No. Not unless they went with information.'

'Like what, for example?'

Mitchell shrugged. 'There was one chap who offered him a piece of a tank's engine he claimed to have found in Triangle Wood. He didn't buy it, but he paid the man to show him where he'd found it – no one knew how far that tank went into the wood before it was knocked out, you see. That was the sort of thing which interested him.'

They both stared at him expectantly.

'Maybe Bellamy's gun was offered to him. That would get him back on Hameau Ridge sure enough.'

'To find out where it came from? Would he have known it was Bellamy's gun?'

'He'd have known about the Poacher junior officers carrying them, I'm certain of that.'

'Provenance!' exclaimed Audley triumphantly.

'Provenance?' Nikki looked at him. 'What is that?'

'It's the archaeologist's first question, mademoiselle. If you give him an old coin or a potsherd, like as not he'll be able to tell you what it is because that's his business. But what he'll want to know is where you got it from – that's its real value to him.' He nodded at Mitchell encouragingly. 'You're right, Paul – I'd never have guessed the same was true for a modern historian, but I can see how it could have been. The gun would make him ask the question.'

Nikki said quickly: 'But we don't know who answered it.'

Again they both stared at him.

Stretch –

'There is a reason why he could have visited Hameau Ridge, or pretty close to it,' said Mitchell suddenly.

Stretch –

'He had friends out here – ordinary people he'd got to know who were interested in the war. Not scholars, just local people – though some of them know a great deal, actually. There's one in Bapaume and another just outside Arras, and a couple in the town itself, and one at Albert – '

Just as it was possible to be made braver than you really were, so you could be made sharper.

' – but the one I'm thinking of lives in Vaux, just beyond the ridge on the Beaumetz road. It's the one place he's sure to have visited. I should have thought of it before, darn it.'

'Why is it the one place?' asked Nikki.

'Because he bought his petrol there – it's a garage run by two brothers named Jarras. They sell petrol and repair farm machinery, and that sort of thing.'

'But he'd be going out of his way to get petrol there.'

'That wouldn't make any difference, he always bought it from them.'

'Because they were interested in the war?' cut in Audley. 'Is that why?'

'One of them is, the elder one – Etienne. And he's not just interested, he's got an incredible collection of stuff from the battlefield. Guns and shells and all sorts of things. He does buy things, too.'

Nikki regarded him with a flicker of suspicion. 'You've researched Professor Emerson remarkably thoroughly, Captain.'

'Never mind – ' Audley waved his hand at her dismissively ' – the point is the man's a collector and every farmer on the ridge must know it. So if anything turned up it would come to him, eh?'

'More than that. He pays for it too – the other brother's married, but Etienne's a born bachelor. He spends half his – ' Mitchell broke off abruptly as he saw the expression on Audley's face change. 'What's the matter?'

For a moment Audley looked at him bleakly, then the cold logic transmitted itself.

Emerson. Emerson and Mitchell. Emerson and George Davis – *Emerson and Etienne Jarras.*

'We'd better go and see for ourselves,' said Audley.

8

'How did it happen?' said Audley.

Marcel Jarras finished pouring the wine before looking up, and then methodically pushed each of the glasses to its place across the oilcloth-covered table before speaking. 'Who can tell, m'sieur? The road is lonely there and it was very dark – and there were no witnesses. We shall never know.'

Mitchell watched the bubbles on the rim of his glass pop one by one. Etienne Jarras was dead and already buried, and there was nothing they could do about it. Murdered and buried, to put it more precisely, although this was one accident the bastards had got away with successfully – at least until now.

They were too late again, as they had expected to be; the only consolation was that once again there was nothing he could have done about it. He could kick himself for taking so long to point Audley in the right direction, but Etienne Jarras had been dead before Audley had even received his fragment of Somme map. Indeed, he had been the first unknowing victim of the whole business.

'But what sort of accident was it?' Audley's French accent was execrable but his grammar was impeccable.

'He had the break-down truck –' Marcel Jarras's shoulders lifted ' – as one leaves Tilloy Wood the road is steeply embanked to the right, with a drop of three metres or more. It was there he left the road. Perhaps he swerved to avoid something, that is what the police suggest – another vehicle, maybe. But they do not know because there is no sign to say what happened. And even if there was he would still be dead.'

Audley nodded sympathetically. 'That is true . . . And it was a break-down he was attending, then?'

Jarras nodded back at him. 'On the other side of Tilloy. Some imbecile from Paris had stalled his car and couldn't start it again. Me – I would have let him stew, but Etienne was good-hearted always. He was a Samaritan, a true Samaritan. He would go out no matter when or what.'

'I see. So when he didn't return you naturally became alarmed?'

'I was not here, monsieur. We were on holiday, my wife and I. We were – ' Jarras trailed off, frowning suddenly at Audley as he did so. 'You are a friend – you were a friend of Etienne's, you say? I don't remember you.' His gaze shifted from Audley to rest on Mitchell. 'Now *you*, monsieur – I do seem to remember that we have met . . .'

'No, Paul!' Audley cut off the half-truth Mitchell was about to offer, turning to Nikki. 'There's no more time for games. If you would care to introduce yourself, mademoiselle, I think we shall save time.'

'Certainly, Dr Audley.' Nikki reached inside her bag. 'Police, Monsieur Jarras – Bureau of Liaison with the SDECE. And these gentlemen are of the British Ministry of Defence.'

Jarras's jaw dropped open as if the muscles holding it had been severed. He stared first at Nikki, then at the card she held up to him, and then again at her. Remembering his own consternation of the night before at the photograph in *With the Tanks to Cambrai* Mitchell could well understand that look: in a male chauvinist pig's world secret policewomen were bad enough, but secret policewomen looking like Nikki MacMahon were downright unfair.

With difficulty Jarras wound up his jaw to its correct position, but the effort required to speak was still too much for him.

'You were on holiday?' said Audley.

The Frenchman looked at him, still speechless.

'You were on holiday?' repeated Nikki sharply.

Jarras gave a start. 'Yes. On holiday.'

Mitchell remembered the way she had simulated fear at the approach of the two motor-cycle police on Hameau Ridge. No need to ask where she'd learnt that role: she'd obviously been the cause of it often enough herself.

'Where?'

'At Lyons. My wife – that is to say, my wife's parents live there – '

'You were called back from holiday?'

'Yes, that's right,' Jarras nodded. 'It was on the Saturday – we were not due back until the next Wednesday.'

Nikki looked at Audley. 'You have further questions, Dr Audley?' She paused. 'Monsieur Jarras will answer them.'

Or Mademoiselle MacMahon will know the reason why. *And not so long ago I was planning a cosy evening with Mademoiselle MacMahon*, thought Mitchell. *Phew!*

Audley considered the Frenchman for a moment.

'What happened to the imbecile from Paris?' he said mildly.

'The imbecile – ?'

'The man whose car broke down.'

'Oh – him.' Jarras bobbed his head. 'He telephoned later to say he'd managed to start his car by himself.'

'Telephoned?'

'But yes, m'sieur. He telephoned both times. First to ask for help, and then – '

'Telephoned who?' Audley's voice was still mild. 'If your brother was already on the way, and you were on holiday – who answered the telephone?'

'Who answered?' Jarras looked at him questioningly. 'The boy answered, of course.'

'What boy?'

'The boy – Pierre. He helps with the odd jobs in the workshop and looks after the pumps when we are busy.'

'Is Pierre here now? Can we speak to him?'

'But yes – he is here.' Jarras glanced at his watch. 'He is on the pumps now, until nine o'clock.' He looked at Nikki uncertainly. 'Do you wish me to get him?'

Nikki caught Audley's nod. 'Yes, Monsieur Jarras.'

Mitchell watched the little man scuttle out, waiting until he had closed the door before speaking. 'You think the boy could know something?'

'He'll know nothing of value, that's for certain.'

'What makes you so sure of that?' asked Nikki.

'Because if he did he'd be dead, mademoiselle – like Etienne Jarras.'

Etienne Jarras among others. All of them innocent and unknowing, and all dead; it was as though Charles Emerson had carried the plague on his breath, infecting one person after another with the disease already in his own bloodstream.

All dead except *one*.

'But he may have seen something all the same, you never know,' continued Audley. 'They had to leave him alive to take that phone-call, so there wouldn't be any mystery why his boss was on the road. A calculated risk, you might say. But a very small one, I'd guess, because I have the distinct impression that somebody knows exactly what he's doing, which is more than we do. We're just picking up the pieces.' He frowned at Nikki. 'I think your boss is taking one hell of a risk not cancelling this meeting, you know.'

'And I think you under-estimate him, Dr Audley.'

'I don't under-estimate Ted Ollivier, young woman – I know

him better than you do, and I know when he's being pushed from behind against his better judgement.' Audley scowled at them both horribly. 'There's something that doesn't smell right about this thing – it smells of politics, not security. And if there's anything that knocks the hell out of good security it's political necessity . . . So what we want is something the politicians will understand, something that'll scare the daylights out of them.'

'Don't dead men do that?' said Mitchell.

'The only thing that'll do it is proof that their security has gone really sour. It's like Ted said, you expect the wasps to buzz round the jampot.' He jabbed a finger towards Mitchell. 'We've got to prove to them that the lid isn't sealed properly – because I'm damn sure it isn't.'

Nikki gestured towards the window, through which the red neon lights of the garage sign were now bright against the gathering darkness of the evening. 'You are running out of time for that – '

The outside door banged and there was a sound of hobnailed boots clumping down the passage to the office.

'Unless you think an apprentice mechanic can give it to you, that is.'

Audley shrugged. 'Apprentice lads have been known to have sharp eyes.'

The door banged open.

Mitchell's heart sank: *but not this apprentice*, he thought, taking in Pierre's vacant expression, which significantly remained unchanged as the lacklustre eyes shifted from Audley to Nikki. If the sight of her couldn't raise a spark in this shambling creature, then there was no spark there.

'Come in, Pierre,' said Audley.

'Uh?' Pierre advanced three steps, stooping a little as though the ceiling was close to his head.

'I want to ask you one or two questions . . . about Monsieur Etienne Jarras, Pierre,' Audley said slowly.

'Uh?' Pierre frowned.

'Monsieur Etienne Jarras – '

''E's dead.'

'We know that. You were working with him on the night he died.'

'What?' Pierre looked at Nikki. 'What's 'e say?'

Audley cast a hopeless look at her.

'You were working with Monsieur Etienne on the night he died,' said Nikki.

''E died . . .' The boy nodded.

'You were working with him that night.'

'On the tractor, we were – Monsieur Morel's tractor. Wanted it next day, 'e did . . . Didn't get it did 'e – wasn't ready, that's why.'

'Monsieur Etienne was called out on a breakdown – called on the telephone?'

'Yeah.' The small head nodded – big body, big feet, big hands, but small head: it looked as though in assembling Pierre, God had done his best with the left-over parts.

'Did you answer the telephone?'

Pierre looked at her pityingly. 'Me? What for?'

Nikki smiled at him dazzlingly. 'The second time, after Monsieur Etienne had gone, you answered the telephone very nicely, didn't you, Pierre?'

'Oh – that time. Yeah. 'E'd gone though. But 'e'd got the car goin', 'adn't 'e – '

'Who?'

'This other fella. Don't bother to come, that's what 'e says. 'E'd gone though.'

'You told him that?'

'Yeah told 'im that. 'E said not to mind "Tell 'im I called, Pierre," 'e says.'

'He – called – you – Pierre?' said Audley.

The boy looked at him pityingly. 'Yeah – well that's my name, ain't it.'

Back on the ridge the count-down to the summit was ticking away. Somewhere, in the West or the East or the Far East, the jet engines on military airfields were warming up and the top security men were checking their weapons and their watches. And here there wasn't one goddamn thing they could do to stop it: their fears and suspicions and fragile clues had led them finally to a moronic youth with an IQ of 70 minus.

'Ask him – ' there was a note of weariness in Audley's voice ' – ask him if there's been anyone like me here – a foreigner. If he works on the pumps he may have filled Emerson's tank.'

Pierre listened to the question from Nikki with an air of incomprehension. Finally he shook his head.

'A little man – with white hair – ' Mitchell pointed to his head.

'Uh?' Pierre ran his oily hand through his own hair vaguely.

' – In a grey Jaguar – '

'Aw – *him* – ' The nearest thing yet to intelligence showed in Pierre's face ' – Jaguar XJ6, that's a smashing car – I'd like one of them.'

'He was here?' said Nikki quickly.

'In a Jag – sure. A little old fella. 'E went round the back with the boss – and stayed there jawin' for hours – made me late for supper, they did.'

'Round the back?' echoed Audley.

Pierre jerked a blackened thumb. 'Round the back,' he repeated with a touch of exasperation, as one trying to explain the obvious to a simpleton. 'Made me late for my supper, didn't they.'

'A foreigner?' said Nikki.

'Yeah. English.'

'How do you know he was English?'

'Got "GB" on the back it had, didn't it, the Jag had – that's English. An' right hand drive – that's English too, isn't it.

Smashing car – had a good look at it while they was round the back. Do 200 on the straight easy.'

Mitchell caught Audley's eye. 'The museum's round the back – ' He remembered as he spoke that Captain Lefevre had never visited the Jarras garage, so that he was once more exhibiting suspiciously exact knowledge.

Audley nodded slowly. 'You go on back and have a look at it, Paul. We'll join you in a minute or two.'

Nikki frowned, clearly suspicious at Mitchell's sudden detachment. 'What are you going to look for, Captain?'

Audley answered before he could speak. 'We don't know. But Paul's an expert and if there is something, then maybe he'll see it when it won't mean anything to either of us. So I want him to have a clear run at it first, all by himself.'

Another long shot – and doubly so if those who had silenced Jarras had thought it necessary to check over his possessions. But long shots were all that was left to them.

Nikki was looking at him warily. She hadn't missed the museum slip and she must by now be well aware that Captain Lefevre knew more about Professor Emerson than any casually conscripted outsider ought to know. But before she could register her objection Audley had turned again to Pierre.

'Now, my lad – who else has been "round the back" with your boss in the last week or two, eh?'

Pierre wiped his nose nervously. 'Uh?' He looked bemusedly at Nikki. 'What's 'e on about now?'

Mitchell picked his way gingerly between the piles of rusty scrap metal towards the old Nissen hut behind the workshops.

Memory was a mysterious thing, and his own capacity for recall the most mysterious of all, automatically activated as it was by any chance sight or sound or smell. Here it was the smell, that peculiar mixture of oil and metal and damp earth, so that although it was twilight and he had been this way only once before he still knew exactly where to go. Two years before, almost to the day, he had followed Emerson and Jarras along this same path, between these same heaps. He had scratched his ankle on a projecting piece of metal and had been absurdly relieved that his anti-tetanus booster shot was only a few weeks old . . . for after all this was the home of gas gangrene, the killer which had horrified the medical corps in 1914.

Back then he had been struck by the irony in that: the researcher struck down by the old war he was studying. But now the irony had caught up with him just as surely, and he was the only survivor of the three men who had come down this path that October afternoon.

The door wasn't locked, as it had been that other time, but somehow he had expected that. What took him by surprise was the red-gold flash in the darkness ahead of him, the reflection of the neon sign at his back caught on polished brass.

Then, as his fingers found the light switch, the flash activated his memory again so that as the unshaded bulbs blazed he wasn't ambushed by the gleaming Maxim gun which stood trained on the doorway, the pride and *pièce de resistance* of the Jarras Museum.

Time telescoped and the same first thought he had once had on this spot was duplicated: there was enough here to equip a small private army.

Nothing had changed. To the left was the well-stocked rifle rack – Lee-Enfields, Lebels, Mausers, Mannlichers and even a stubby Moisin-Nagent cavalry carbine, strayed from some Russian battlefield; to the right, the light machine-guns, Hotchkiss, Lewis, a twisted Parabellum from a fallen Fokker, and the anachronistic Bren left by the retreating British in 1940.

There was the little old safe beside the desk, still stuffed no doubt with rusty handguns of a dozen different makes; there, above the rifles, the line of bayonets and swords; and there, above the machine-guns, the artistic display of Mills grenades and long-handled *Stielhandgranaten*.

Ammunition pouches and moth-eaten webbing; steel helmets of every shape and size and a lonely, faded glengarry; the crude devil's faces of primitive gas-masks, nightmarish with their blank, fogged eye-pieces; entrenching tools and heavy wire-cutters; and those strange echoes of medieval chivalry, the tank crewman's chainmail face protector and the iron visor and breastplate of the sniper . . .

At his feet was a heap of skeletal rifles, nearly unrecognisable with their wooden parts rotted away; when brother Marcel came to clear this place they would go straight onto the scrapheap outside the door, for Marcel shared nothing of his brother's magpie obsession. It was all junk to him.

He stared round the hut again, aware now of a second thought which had come to him two years ago and which now came to him again even more strongly. Only then it had been sad and now, wtth the darkness pressing in from outside, it was eerie.

Marcel was right: it was all junk, empty, rusted and useless. It had belonged to the men who were buried in a hundred cemeteries and it was fit only to equip a private army of ghosts.

He opened the drawers of the desk one by one, with a growing sense of the hopelessness of his task.

Boxes of buttons and badges, British, French and German.

A collection of battered tobacco and toffee tins, decorated with flags and cheery soldiers and dreadnoughts and kings and queens . . .

Nose cones from a variety of shells, some bright and clean, others corroded into unidentifiable lumps of rust . . .

A carved lump of chalk bearing the badge of the Sherwood Foresters and the date 10–9–16 . . .

A drawer full of maps, carefully labelled and filed. He rifled through them until he found one of Hameau Ridge and spread it out on the desk-top.

It was a British Army issue, corrected to the end of August, but Jarras had evidently worked hard on it, plotting the trench lines behind the German lines and meticulously marking in the movements of the units which had stormed the ridge. It was even possible to trace the crab-like progress of the tank 'Euclid' through the British trenches to the edge of the wood, where it ended with a red crayoned question mark. Poor Euclid had no doubt become an aiming mark for every German gun in the area once dawn had revealed her stalled on the crest.

But there was nothing here which was not already in the history books. The green line which marked the advance of the doomed North Berkshires and unlucky Company 'D' petered out in the dead ground beyond the crest with another question mark, while the blue arrows of the other Poacher companies curved leftwards through the wood, over the open ground and into the Prussian Redoubt. Following them, the fierce crimson arrows of the Australian battalions plunged into the two ravines . . .

Nothing there.

And nothing in the safe either. Even the door swung open at a touch, revealing the jumble of revolvers and automatic pistols in every stage of dissolution. Two years earlier Jarras had unlocked it with a flourish to produce the battered remains of an Austrian Steyr which he had bought from a quarryman that very morning. The Steyr was still there on the top of the pile.

All there and all junk . . .

He looked up as the doorknob rattled.

And junk to Nikki MacMahon – childish junk. He could see it in her expression as she took in the room – no woman could ever be expected to understand any man's innocent obsession with weaponry, ancient or modern.

'Good God Almighty!' exclaimed Audley, coming to a halt in front of the Maxim.

'And he was a bachelor – ' Nikki's lip curled ' – it is too Freudian for words, I think.'

'I don't know about Freudian, but it certainly wouldn't do back in England,' murmured Audley. 'They'd have this lot off him in no time, and he'd likely get six months for possession.' He bent to examine the gleaming machine-gun. 'What a beauty!'

Nikki looked down sidelong at him with a flash of amusement instantly extinguished as she realised she was being observed in her turn by Mitchell. As their eyes met he knew that in any other circumstances it might have been a moment of shared amusement – that there was a childish streak in Audley and that they had caught each other noticing it. But the taste of present failure was too sharp for them to share anything now.

Nikki tossed her head arrogantly. 'You've found – nothing?' She managed to make it sound like an accusation.

Audley looked up from the Maxim, first at Mitchell, then at Nikki. 'Of course he found nothing,' he said equably. 'The age of miracles is long past.'

'Miracles?'

Audley nodded. 'Luck, if you like. And we've had our share of that, m'dear. If there was anything here – maybe there was, maybe there wasn't – it's long gone. Right, Paul?'

They were the childish ones, thought Mitchell. It was the big man who knew his Kipling, and could treat those two imposters, Triumph and Disaster, just the same. That was another lesson to be learnt.

'The door was unlocked, the safe was unlocked – ' he shrugged, ' – and I don't even know what I'm looking for.'

Audley took in the whole hut with one swinging, 360-degree sweep. 'Well, they didn't come for the weapons, that's for sure.'

'None of them work, anyway. They're all rusted up.'

'Even the grenades?' Audley pointed to the wall.

'They're harmless.' Mitchell rose from the chair and went over to the grenade display. 'Tricky things to leave lying around, but Jarras wasn't a careless man – these haven't any explosive. And they haven't got igniters and detonators either.' He lifted one of the Mills bombs off its hook. 'Just good for a paperweight, that's all.'

'And what the deuce is that?' Audley pointed to a weapon displayed above the bombs.

'This?' Mitchell put the grenade back and reached above it. 'It's a sawn-off Lee-Enfield – someone's taken twelve inches of barrel and six-inches of butt. Used for trench raiding, probably.'

Audley took the wicked-looking thing from him and examined it critically. 'Well this is certainly in working order – ' He jerked the bolt up and back. 'Smooth as butter – as good as new.'

'Oh, sure,' agreed Mitchell. The trench rifle had been Jarras' newest toy two years before; he had just finished cleaning it and was looking for somewhere to display it to advantage. It had been Charles Emerson who had suggested the vacant space above the bombs. 'But he'd got that when I was here before. It came from – '

He stopped suddenly, staring at Audley.

'When you were here *before*?' Nikki jumped on the word.

Mitchell continued to stare at Audley. At him and through him and beyond him out of the window into the darkness which had fallen over Hameau Ridge. And also through the darkness of the years into which Second Lieutenant Harry Bellamy and his Poachers had passed so long ago.

'You were here before,' repeated Nikki accusingly. 'What – '

'Be quiet, woman!' ordered Audley. '*Yes, Paul – ?*

'The age of miracles . . .' Mitchell managed to focus on him again '. . . it isn't past after all.'

9

Audley sniffed the night air as though he disagreed with him. 'How much further?' he said irritably.

'Not far. Just a few yards,' said Nikki.

'Can't see why we can't drive up to the door like Christians,' grunted Audley. 'Nothing Ted can do about it now except make the best of a bad job.'

'My orders were precise,' said Nikki defensively. 'In the event – '

'Precise nonsense. In the event of our doing his job for him – did he reckon that was likely, eh?'

'He thought it was . . . possible,' she admitted. 'He said you were good at puzzles.'

'Not me, mademoiselle, not me.' Mitchell sensed that Audley was pointing at him now. 'Paul's the smart one, not me.'

Mitchell felt an odd feeling of anti-climax. 'I think I was a bit slow, actually. I should have got it this morning.'

'Just in time is quick enough, my lad. No one expects better than that in our business, we're mostly like that little wizard in the Thurber fairy-story, who never knew whether what he was saying was true or false.'

' "The Gollux",' Nikki laughed in the darkness. 'I've saved a score of princes in my time. I cannot save them all" – I'm surprised you know "The Thirteen Clocks", Dr Audley.'

'And I'm surprised you know it, mademoiselle. A very Anglo-Saxon tale, I've always thought.'

'Not at all. A French one – as a child I loved it.' She paused. 'I loved how the tears of sorrow turned to jewels which lasted, but the tears of laughter turned back to tears again very soon – it was so often true.'

'And still is, in my experience. But this time Paul has saved your princes, whoever they are – ' Audley stumbled in the dark, swearing under his breath. 'How many yards did you say?'

Instead of answering, Nikki fell back beside Mitchell. 'And am I still to believe that you are just a soldier, a simple soldier?'

'Plain cannon-fodder, ma'am.' It was equally curious how comforting a well-sustained lie could become: he had become quite fond of Captain Lefevre. 'I just happened to know Emerson and the battlefield, that's all. Sorry to disappoint you.'

'But you don't.' She reached for his arm. 'I told my boss that you were what you seemed to be – that you were a soldier. I thought you were perhaps a decoy. He said I was a fool to be taken in so easily. But I was not so wrong after all, I'm glad of that.'

But still not entirely right; and since her most recent coolness had apparently stemmed from a dislike of being conned by a mere male it was now far too late to come completely clean, reflected Mitchell sadly: she'd never forgive him twice . . . So this was one potentially beautiful friendship he was never going to develop as he would have liked. But then it never could have developed, because she was no more just a pretty French girl than he was any longer an ordinary unattached Englishman.

Strange thought, that: the worm was all bird now.

Bouilletcourt Farm loomed up ahead of them suddenly, a solid nucleus against the starry skyline of the ridge. Mitchell realised with a pang of recognition that they had been walking up that dreaded sunken road which had featured in the accounts of the assault on the strongpoint. At this point, possibly on this very spot, had been the German machine-gun which had scythed down three attacking waves, until a sharp-shooting corporal of the East Anglians had picked off the crew one by one.

'What's the matter, Paul?' said Audley.

There had been twelve dead Germans in the gun-pit at the end, and each of the last five had been shot through the head; they must have known what lay in store for them as each one in turn pulled his predecessor away from the gun and took his place. Yet they had gone on firing the gun until the last man all the same.

'What's the matter?' Audley spoke out of the darkness.

'Nothing,' said Mitchell. 'I'm coming.'

Nothing: that was true. To know what had happened was one thing, to feel it in the guts and understand it was another, and it still eluded him. It was his knowledge which had told him where they were, not his instinct.

Nikki led them along a high blank brick wall – this was the back of the enclave of buildings, of course – until they came to a small postern door which opened instantly to her knock. Yellow light flooded out over her, throwing her shadow onto the field behind.

'*Entrez, entrez – vite, vite.*'

Mitchell hurried after them, stopping to avoid the low lintel and blinking in the glare of the naked light on the wall just above him which illuminated an empty barn. No sooner was he through than the door was slammed shut behind him by a black-uniformed policeman helmeted and armed like those who had interrogated him the previous day.

'My David – Captain – ' Ted Ollivier acknowledged them brusquely ' – we have been waiting for you.'

'The hell you have!' Audley snapped back. 'And we've been tramping halfway across France in pitch darkness because of your crazy order.'

Ollivier brushed aside Audley's anger. 'Your message indicated an emergency. What is the emergency?'

'There's no emergency.'

'No – ?' Ollivier frowned at Nikki. 'What is this?'

'No emergency – ' Audley was his old cool self again ' – so long as you hold your summit somewhere else, that is.'

For a moment Ollivier's frown embraced them all, then his face became expressionless.

'We have a deal, David, you and I – and this is not the time for little jokes.' He paused. 'You have something?'

Audley nodded slowly. 'We surely have, Ted. It's to do with that jampot of yours, the one with the lid screwed down so tight.'

'Go on.'

'Screwing the lid down isn't much use when there's a hole in the pot – ' Audley held Ollivier's gaze for an instant before turning to Mitchell. 'I think it ought to come from you, Paul. You found the hole.'

The Frenchman's grey eyes switched to Mitchell with an intensity which took him aback: the reflection of the bulb at his back was caught in the centre of each pupil as a pinpoint of light which seemed to bore into him. For a second he was a rabbit transfixed by the murderous stare of a weasel, incapable of action.

'Put him out of his misery, man – tell him about the chalk and the cheese.' Audley's voice broke the spell.

'The chalk?' Ollivier's eyes clouded. 'The cheese?'

'This whole ridge is rotten with tunnels,' said Mitchell. 'Like a piece of cheese.'

'Tunnels?' Ollivier whispered the word. '*Tunnels?*

'It's a chalk ridge – all this land is chalk. It's perfect for tunnelling, dry and clean, very little timbering needed. Not like the clay at Ypres. When they were mining and counter-mining each other here they had trouble with noise – they could hear each other digging in chalk much easier – and they had to get rid of the spoil so it didn't give the game away . . . But when it came to straight tunnelling behind the lines, it was easy.'

Fought like lions and dug like moles: General Leigh-Wood-house's voice echoed in his memory. And his own words too: *But the Germans used to dig deep . . . They had two years to dig into the Somme . . .*

God! How could we have been so dim, so slow to see what the Audleys and the Olliviers could never see because there was nothing to see – what ought to have been all the more obvious to him because they couldn't be expected to see it: all the other deep and secret paths of the Somme.

Ollivier was looking at him, grey-faced.

'There are twenty miles of tunnels at Vimy – there's a whole ammunition train still down there in the chalk, no one dares touch it. They found dugouts full of Germans when they put the motorway through the Hindenburg Line just north of here – they were still down there in the chalk. It's *all* still down there – tunnels, men, supplies, equipment. The galleries in the chalk don't fall in, they'll still be there in a thousand years.'

For a moment nobody spoke, then Audley gave a low apologetic sound, half grunt, half sigh. 'Galleries under Hameau Ridge, Ted – if there are, then the seismic equipment you've had plugged into the ground won't have registered a whisper, because they were all there readymade.'

'If there are?' Ollivier grasped fiercely at the straw of uncertainty. 'You mean you don't know that there are these tunnels?'

'My God – Ted everybody who could have told us has conveniently had his mouth shut, don't you see?' rasped Audley.

'Then how do you know?' Ollivier persisted obstinately. 'You haven't a shred of proof, that is what I can see. You have a theory – not a suspicion, only a theory. So I must go to the Président and say "M'sieur le Président, there are twenty miles of tunnels in the chalk outside Arras, and Hameau Ridge is made of chalk too, so you must pick up the hot phone and say "I'm sorry, my friends, but tomorrow is not convenient" – is that what I must tell him?'

'You can tell him that, sure. And while you're about it you can tell him why Charles Emerson had to die – and George Davis and Etienne Jarras – and I'll give you odds on that peasant of yours in the ravine, too, the picker-up of unconsidered trifles who maybe picked up one thing too many.'

'All right.' Ollivier held up his hand. 'So why did they have to die?'

'Probably all for the same reason. But Emerson's the one who matters, because he – ' Audley stopped, turning again to Mitchell. 'I'm sorry, Paul, I keep on stealing your thunder. You tell him how the Poachers took the Prussian Redoubt.'

Mitchell drew a breath. It was decent of Audley to want him to have his moment. Except that it wasn't his moment, it was Emerson's . . . Except that it wasn't Emerson's moment either: it belonged to men who had been dead and lost for half a century under the edge.

'They got into the German tunnels – '

He no longer saw the Frenchman, another image in his brain was momentarily stronger than present reality, so strong that it dried up all other words and thoughts.

'They must have come round the north of the wood, where the ravine starts. In fact they must have run right into the British barrage as they came into the ravine – that's where the entrances to the German tunnels must have been. And there were quite a few miners in "D" Company – '

A miner's never afraid of the dark . . .

' – even only a handful of determined men in those tunnels could have caused chaos underground – '

And by God, they had been determined, those volunteers of the Somme, making up in sheer courage what they lacked in military skill – remember the Tyneside Irish who had broken through in Sausage Valley on the first day of the battle and had disappeared just like 'D' Company, fighting to the last far behind the German lines.

' – they would have been enough to block the tunnels, anyway. And that would have stopped the Germans getting their reserves up to the redoubt during the bombardment. Instead they probably had to start blowing up their own dugout entrances there. That's why their gunners started shelling their own people, maybe – they wouldn't have known what the hell was happening – '

The Germans had been brave, too. Their enemies in the rear and underneath them, shelled indiscriminately by both sides and then attacked by the Poachers from Bouillet Wood, they had fought it out to the last man.

And in dying had kept their secret for half a century.

'*Captain!*' Ollivier's voice cut through Mitchell's dream. 'How do you know this? How do you know it?'

Mitchell stared at him stupidly. How was it possible to know something with certainty yet without certain proof; it was dead against his whole training.

'Man – didn't you see the look on his face?' snapped Audley. 'Look at him now – that's the look I've been waiting for, and I'll bet that was the look on Emerson's face too.'

But it was the look on Ollivier's face – doubt and puzzlement struggling with acceptance – which roused Mitchell out of 1916. 'It was the shotgun.'

'The shotgun?' Ollivier frowned. 'What about the shotgun?'

'You said it was slightly damaged in the car explosion – you said the gunsmith almost wept because of it.'

'That's right.'

'So it was *undamaged* before the explosion – that's why Jarras didn't buy it when it was offered to him: he couldn't afford it.'

Ollivier looked at him intently. 'It wasn't damaged much, that's true . . .'

'The weapons they dig up out here are almost always rotted and rusted to hell, though.'

'So – ?'

'Almost always. But there is one way a weapon can survive and not rot: if it's in a deep dugout or a tunnel. We saw one less than an hour ago, a British trench rifle. Etienne Jarras bought it off the foreman of a motorway construction gang – and he'd found it in a German dugout they broke into on the Hindenburg Line, a deep one. The entrance must have been blown in when we broke through in 1918. There wasn't a mark on it, it was as good as new.'

As he stared into Ollivier's face he felt their roles had been reversed: the rabbit had become the weasel. 'Jarras asked the foreman if there was anything else down there. The man said "What do you want? We can let you have a complete German if you like, we found seventy of the poor sods intact". It was all there – weapons, equipment, men – everything.'

'And in our case one man in particular,' murmured Audley, 'Second Lieutenant Harry Bellamy of the Rifle Brigade – your 'H.J.V.B.' and our Harry –

> *I saw young Harry, with his beaver on,*
> *His cuisses on his thighs, bravely arm'd*

– and that's how someone found our Harry, armed with a Charles Lancaster shotgun.'

Ollivier shook his head in wonderment, looking from one to the other of them. 'And you've deduced this from a single weapon – a single weapon? It could have come from a hundred different places – from anywhere in France.'

'Oh no it couldn't, Ted old buddy,' Audley shook his head. 'That gun meant something to Emerson, and I wouldn't mind betting it wasn't the only thing he was shown – identity tags, personal belongings enough to tie the gun to the owner and tip him off where the owner might be. Enough to make him think of tunnels under Hameau Ridge, anyway. Tunnels someone else had found again. He didn't have time to check his theory out here, but he started checking it as soon as he got back to England . . . By which time the killers were already after him.'

'But still there is no proof – '

'Proof? Are you crazy?' Now Audley was puzzled. 'Man, I don't know what your special rules for neutral houses are, but I know damn well that one strong suspicion of insecurity is enough to put Bouillet Wood or anywhere else in quarantine – and you know it too. And if you won't act on it, then the only thing left for me is to put a call through to Gensoul in Paris and I'm going to tell him Bouillet Wood's at risk and Ted Ollivier has gone round the twist.' He shook his head sorrowfully. 'I haven't got any choice – and nor have you, old buddy. No choice at all.'

Ollivier looked at them, then half turned away, his shoulders drooping. 'No choice . . .' He echoed the two words softly. 'No choice at all . . . *Sorel!*'

There was a quick, dry rasp of leather against PVC, punctuated by a sharp click, and the policeman's machine-pistol was suddenly covering them all.

'Easy now,' said Ollivier, looking directly at Mitchell as though he was the unknown quantity among them. 'Just stand quite still, Captain.'

Mitchell glanced at Audley.

'I said "quite still", Captain. Just look at me, not at anyone else.' Ollivier began to circle to the left, the policeman moving with him.

'I never carry a gun, you know that,' said Audley in a flat voice. 'Neither does Lefevre.'

'I – know . . .' Ollivier patted Audley's coat gently. 'But – never . . . is a big word . . . Now you, Captain – fortunately – your uniform fits – very snugly . . . Good enough . . . Now, mademoiselle, your bag if you please – thank you . . . Just the one little pistol, I think – yes . . . So now you can all relax.'

He retraced his route, to stand beside the policeman. 'No choice. I'm glad you said that, my David, because I want you to believe me when I say that what I am doing fills me with sorrow. I want you to understand that although I have no choice I shall never cease to regret this necessity.'

'"Never" is a big word,' murmured Audley. 'But in this case I think you may be right.'

'You thought I was "round the twist"? My poor David – c'est une grande habileté que de savoir cacher son habileté – La Rochefoucauld should have warned you, eh?' Ollivier nodded. 'Let's say your mind was on other things, as I intended it should be. I didn't think it could be done, but I had to be sure.'

'And if it could be done I could do it?' Audley paused. 'No, that's not quite right, is it? If it could be done it had to be done through me because you could rely on me to bring the answer straight back to you.' The big man pivotted towards Mitchell, admonishing him with a finger. 'Now there's a lesson for you, Paul: in this business you must never let anything make you behave predictably, least of all friendship.'

'Friendship?' Ollivier's lips twisted in a half-smile. 'Say rather I knew you never could resist a problem, David. Particularly one that didn't concern you.'

'We all make mistakes. Even you.'

'*Vraiment.* I have made two serious ones.'

'You let Bellamy's shotgun slip through your hand – I take it that was the first one?'

'I employed *canaille* with itchy fingers, you might put it like that. It never occurred to me that Turco would explore the galleries and find something of value.'

'Turco?' Nikki spoke for the first time, so huskily that the name was hardly more than a whisper.

Ollivier nodded. 'Yes, mademoiselle. Turco was mine. And it was Turco who offered the gun to Jarras – the gun, a gold cigarette case and a gold hip flask, among other things.' He glanced at Audley. 'You were quite right. All conveniently inscribed with the same initials. There was even a letter in the cigarette case the young officer had written the day before he died. Chapter and verse, one might say. Unfortunately Turco did not understand what it all meant, only what it might be worth – and Jarras could not afford his price.'

'And so he offered it to Emerson?'

'Jarras knew Emerson was here. He thought at least he would find it interesting, so he led Turco to believe the rich Englishman might buy it.'

Audley nodded. 'But in fact he was only interested in where it came from, eh?'

Provenance.

Ollivier looked at him in silence for a moment. 'He offered one hundred francs for the letter – and a thousand francs for a mark on his map to show where it had been found. That was when Turco started to worry about what he had done. So he took the map – he had enough wit to say that he did not know exactly where it had come from, but he would try to find out.'

'But instead he tried to sell the gun somewhere else?'

'He was taking it to a dealer in Amiens when the Surveillance du Territoire spotted him. He lost the gun and the map – he was carrying the other objects in his pockets.'

Audley grunted. 'And then the cat was out of the bag, because they reported straight to Gensoul, I take it . . . And your second error?

Ollivier pointed at Mitchell. 'You found another military expert who knew Emerson well. Our information was that there was only one, the young man Mitchell.'

'Whom you had killed.'

'With regret. But in war there are always casualties, civilians as well as soldiers.'

'But whose war, Ted?' Audley's voice roughened. 'Whose war?'

Whose War? A sudden hideous understanding gripped Mitchell as he stared at them, from Audley to Ollivier to the policeman to Nikki. And to Nikki, her face as white as the chalk of the Somme, most of all – Nikki who was now disarmed and lined up with them, not with Ollivier and the man with the gun.

'France's, of course – '

'Liar!' Nikki's eyes blazed. 'Traitor!'

'You are a child – '

'But not a traitor. You – '

' – A child in a very old world. A very old, very wicked world.' Ollivier's voice deepened. 'You can be forgiven for not understanding it.'

'It is a neutral house. We have given our word – we have a solemn undertaking, I understand that.'

'Save your breath, mademoiselle,' said Audley. 'This has nothing to do with France and nothing to do with honour. France doesn't need to use characters like Turco – the late Turco, I presume, since he seems to have moved into the past tense. Another war casualty?' He considered Ollivier silently for a moment. 'In fact I'd guess Turco was that farm labourer of Paul's, the one who got himself blown up so conveniently in Rattlesnake Ravine yesterday. Two birds with one stone again.'

Nikki frowned at him. 'Two birds?'

'Yes ... Turco couldn't be trusted any more. But they couldn't just kill him and leave him lying around in case his body was identified, and if he was established as a farm worker he couldn't just disappear off the ridge without questions being asked. By blowing him up they solved both those problems – and they flushed us out into the open too, come to that. *Three* birds.' He nodded at Nikki. 'He always was a shrewd operator, your boss. Ex-boss.'

Ollivier gave Audley a cold little smile. 'And you were always a good guesser, my David.'

'One of the best, old buddy. Give me a start and I'll guess you right the way back to Moscow ... or Peking ... or one or two other less well-known places, depending on who's meeting at Bouillet Wood tomorrow afternoon. And depending on what you've set up for them.'

The bogus policeman stirred uneasily. '*Patron, il se fait tard* –'

Ollivier raised his hand. '*Oui* . . . And for you, my David, too late.'

Audley regarded him coolly. 'Getting rid of us is going to cramp your style, Ted.'

'You think so?'

'I surely do.' Audley shook his head slowly. 'If we're not out and about bright and early tomorrow morning there are sure to be questions asked, and you won't have the right answers. And if you've another tragic accident – another three tragic accidents – in mind, I don't honestly think anyone would swallow that, do you?'

Ollivier studied Audley intently. For one congealing instant of time they were like two men turned to stone by the same Gorgon image of failure. Then the big Englishman gestured so abruptly that the bogus policeman's machine-pistol jerked towards him by reflex action.

'Christ, Ted – it won't work any more, whatever you've cooked up, don't you see? There are too many things that can go wrong now.' Audley's thumb jabbed vaguely over his shoulder. 'Jack Butler's out there, so is Hugh Roskill – they're not fools – '

Oh God! thought Mitchell despairingly. Hugh Roskill was in Paris and Colonel Butler was on his way back to England. All this coolness, this confidence, was nothing but the purest bluff, the last bid for time in a game already lost.

'You say you're sorry, and I believe you, Ted,' Audley's voice changed gear to a matching regret. 'I can't think you ever wanted to do what you're doing – I think you've got a death-wish. That's why you called me in: not because you wanted to succeed, but because you wanted to fail. But it doesn't have to be fatal – for either of us. There's still time to get out.'

'Time?' Ollivier's face relaxed slowly. 'A good try – but you're wrong, David: I shall succeed. And with just a very little luck I shall survive too.'

'But what will you have achieved? A bit more chaos in the world – is that what you want?' The bitterness in Audley's words smelt of defeat. 'When we've both spent half our lives trying to prevent it?'

Ollivier's smile returned. 'That's exactly right: half our lives and a little more chaos. Only this time perhaps more than a little.'

'Why? For Christ's sake, why?'

The Frenchman shrugged. 'Because our way is wrong.'

'And their way is right?'

'Who is "they"?' Ollivier cocked his head on one side. 'When we were young there was "us" and "them" but now we are all the same – all "them" and all wrong ... When I realised that, I knew I had spent my life trying to repair something not worth repairing. So I have stopped being a repair man: now I am in the business of demolition. I am putting a match to the fire from which the phoenix may rise.'

Audley stared at Ollivier in blank disbelief. 'It looks more like a vulture from where I'm standing.'

Ollivier accepted the jibe tolerantly. 'It's all in the mind, my David – a little adjustment, no more. But unfortunately I don't have time to adjust you to reality.'

'Not in a million years, old buddy,' Audley's moment of bitterness had passed very quickly, to be replaced by what Mitchell guessed was a false unconcern. 'But in the meantime do we get to know how you plan to demolish a summit meeting? Or do we go straight on to the casualty list?'

'My dear David!' Ollivier raised his hands in a gesture of surprise. 'That I should be so so crude, so barbarous ... when it is quite unnecessary. It is enough that you are taken out of circulation for a few hours.'

'I'm most relieved to hear it.'

'And I am most disappointed that you should need to be reassured. If you – ' Ollivier glanced at Mitchell and Nikki in turn ' – if you are all sensible, you have nothing to fear. A little inconvenience for a little while, no more than that, I promise you.' He smiled at Mitchell. 'And you, Captain, will be more interested than inconvenienced.'

'I will be?' Mitchell attempted to sound as casual as Audley had done.

'Undoubtedly. You've been so very clever already, after all to deduce the existence of my tunnel from so little. Would it not interest you to learn that you are standing five metres from its entrance?'

10

Would it surprise you?

W Mitchell looked around the barn slowly.

It didn't surprise him, now he knew it, that there was a tunnel entrance somewhere in Bouilletcourt Farm; if there were tunnels running the length of the ridge, from Bouillet village to the wood, from the wood to the Prussian Redoubt, and from the redoubt back to the ravine, then there would certainly have been shafts down to them from the strongpoint in the farm.

That was not surprising, it was obvious; and equally it was obvious that any surviving entrance could not be in the open, where it would be too well-known if time and weather hadn't called it in. Only under cover could such an entrance survive and remain secret, and the farm buildings provided the only cover within a mile of the house in the wood.

But it was not obvious here in the barn, because the barn was completely empty; around him were four blank walls, windowless and broken only by the postern at his back and a pair of heavy double-doors at the opposite end. Thick ropes of ancient cobwebs sagged across the rough brickwork and the plank floor beneath him was scuffed and scarred with years of hard usage. Cobwebs and dirt were the barn's only visible contents.

'In the corner, Captain.' Ollivier pointed past Mitchell's right shoulder. 'On the floor in the corner you will find a trapdoor – go and see for yourself.'

From where he had been standing the furthest corner had been in shadow, seeming no different from the rest of the barn except for a rusty iron hook hanging from a staple in the wall at waist-height. But as he moved towards it he could make out the outline of a large trapdoor; it was flush with the floor, but the gap around it was a fraction wider than the gaps between the floorboards. The accumulation of dirt on it was no less than elsewhere, helping to mask it and suggesting that it had not been opened for weeks, but the spread of such camouflage could be achieved in seconds with a few sweeps of a broom.

'It looks promising, does it not?' Ollivier prompted him. 'Then open it.'

Mitchell hesitated. There was a recessed grip at one end, like the hand-hold in a manhole cover, but the size of the thing and its position close to the angle of the corner meant that it would have to be lifted not from the back, but from the side or the front.

'Go on, Captain. It isn't too heavy, and there is a hook on the wall to hold it.'

Mitchell had just come to the same conclusion about the hook. He braced his legs and thrust his fingers into the handhold.

In fact the door was by no means light: it was made of the same inch-thick planking as the floor. But it came up all the same, revealing the first treads of a substantial stairway, broad and wide, which fell away into the darkness. The sharp smell of artificial fertiliser rose out of the hole.

'A cellar,' said Ollivier. 'A large cellar, too, with almost the floor area of this barn. You could hide a lot in such a cellar – the Gestapo were pleased when they found that trapdoor back in '43. They knew there was a Resistance Group operating in this area and they even suspected its headquarters might be on Hameau Ridge. They had great hopes of finding something down there. They knew they were – how do you say – "hot"?

'But they didn't find anything – not a smell, not a trace,

although they were very good at finding things . . . And do you know why they didn't find anything, Captain?'

Mitchell looked up at him.

'Because there was nothing to find.' Ollivier's smile broadened. 'When they found that trapdoor they were so hot – they were so close – we were in the palm of their hand, six of us. And yet they could not find us because – because they did exactly what you have done, Captain: *they opened the trapdoor. And when they did that they covered up the entrance to our hiding place.*'

Mitchell stared at the heavy door which he had hooked on to the wall a minute or two before.

'They were always so ill-mannered, the Gestapo – close the trapdoor, if you please, Captain – they never thought to close the doors they opened . . . Good! Now you will see what they obscured in their eagerness to examine the cellar.'

Between the strip of wood on to which the trapdoor's hinges were screwed and the wall lay a narrow continuation of the wooden floor, four boards wide.

'It looks as if it's nailed down, but it isn't really. Count off the nails from the left,' Ollivier ordered. 'The fifth one – when old Jacques Billot came back to his farm in October 1918 there wasn't one brick standing on another – that's the one. Pull it up, it's not firm – '

With his finger nail Mitchell scraped the dirt from around the head of the nail, gingerly at first and then, as he felt it move, with a growing sense of excitement.

'Billot and his son rebuilt their farm all by themselves, you see – that is, his surviving son; the other two had been killed at Verdun. He got round to this barn in 1924 – go on, pull it, Captain – and he came on this shaft when he was digging the foundations for the outer wall – '

It was a large nail with a wide flattened head, the sort of thing the local blacksmith might have made. The first inch or so of it came out easily, but then it stopped and as it did so the whole section of floor between the trap and the wall shivered.

'He was a prudent man, old Billot, his son Pierre was fond of recalling. He remembered the past and he didn't trust the future – "*Les Sales Boches* were here in '70 and again in '14. They'll be back a third time, you'll see." So he decided to make a place for his money and his valuables and his family, a place no one else would know about – *lift*, Captain. It won't bite you.'

Mitchell took hold of the protruding nail firmly between his thumb and forefinger. The four short lengths of floorboard came up together to reveal a cavity, a black hole just big enough for a man to squeeze through. At first sight it seemed quite shallow; then, as he levered the boards to one side he saw that a deep shaft slanted away under the wall of the barn, which was supported below ground level on a length of steel girder.

'Et voila! Old Billot's handiwork. It beat the Gestapo in '43 and it beat our experts in '69 just as easily when they checked out this place – I watched them do it. Just like the Germans, they couldn't resist the celler . . . Nothing like a peasant to out-think the clever ones, eh? Not even the farmer who lives here now knows about it, and he's been in this barn a thousand times.'

'The farmer who lives here now?' Audley repeated slowly. 'So what happened to the Billots?'

'The old man died in his feather bed in '35, and the son – '

'Don't tell me,' cut in Audley. 'Let me guess again . . . Before a Gestapo firing squad?'

Ollivier smiled. 'Very good. He was the leader of our Resistance Group, Billot *fils* – we kept our arms and equipment down there in his father's strongroom. And ourselves too on occasion . . . in fact I was down there alone the last time, when the Germans raided the farm. For three days I was there, waiting for them to go away, with just a torch and a packet of candles . . . And that was when I found out where the tunnel went, my David – I was looking for a way out, but I didn't find one. It was not . . . very pleasant.'

'But better than being above ground,' said Audley drily.

The only survivor of his group . . . And here also was the answer to the question they had brushed aside as being irrelevant back at the Jarras museum: of all the empty houses in France which filled the requirements of a neutral house, security had chosen one with a fatal defect. They had dismissed it as the purest bad luck, but luck hadn't come into it. It had been Ollivier.

'And where is the present owner now?' Audley looked around him. 'Is he conveniently deaf as well as blind?'

The bogus policeman stirred. '*Patron –* ' the anger was plain now ' *– il gagne du temps seulement.*'

'Of course,' Ollivier nodded. 'Sorel thinks you are playing for time.'

'He underrates my insatiable curiosity.'

'But naturally . . . The farmer is visiting a young woman in Arras. A most attractive young woman who has taken a surprising liking to him – for the time being.'

'A fortunate coincidence. You seem to have thought of almost everything, Ted. I give you that.'

'Not "almost", my David. Everything.' Ollivier was unsmiling. 'You were the only risk, but a calculated one.'

'You'll never know how lucky you've been, as a matter of fact. But being in charge of an operation's security does give you an unfair opportunity to lay on its insecurity.' Audley gave a small yawn. 'So let's get on with the calculated risk, eh?'

'I was almost about to suggest as much. As I said, I was looking for another way out in '43. But I didn't find one – I found something very different.'

Audley waited very politely for a moment. 'Am I expected to ask what it was?'

'On the contrary. I propose to show it to you, my David.'

*

Mitchell watched Ollivier squeeze himself into the hole. It was a fairly tight fit, but unfortunately not too tight, and when he had almost disappeared the Frenchman twisted round to look back up at them, his face at floor level.

'There now! You see that you will not find it too difficult, just a little dusty. I will prepare the way for you.' Ollivier's eyes met Mitchell's steadily. 'And don't get any ideas about jumping Sorel, Captain. Don't even talk to him, he won't understand you and it will make him nervous. Then he might shoot you, and that would be a great pity, eh?'

As Mitchell watched the Frenchman disappear he sensed within himself a curious feeling of unreality. His eyes had been watching, his ears had been hearing; their information was still being relayed to his brain to be analysed. But somehow he couldn't believe that he was really part of what was happening. It was the man Lefevre who was here, not the man Mitchell; what would happen, would happen to Lefevre, not Mitchell – Mitchell would get up tomorrow morning and pick up the threads of his life, regardless of what happened to Lefevre.

Because Lefevre would be dead, he was very sure – because that promise of safety and survival was a lie and an afterthought betrayed by the whole line of Ollivier's earlier questions. They had been directed towards one answer and one answer only: the nature of the clue which had led to the knowledge of the tunnel.

But of course there was no clue. Or, at least, Harry Bellamy's beautiful shotgun was by itself an insufficient clue until added to his own special knowledge of the war and Charles Emerson – and the odds against anyone else being able to duplicate that were infinite. Indeed, that had been the Frenchman's twin objective in involving Audley: to find out if such a clue existed and then to destroy it.

Mitchell shivered involuntarily as he realised he was staring into the black hole of the shaft. His death was down there. He had spoken his own sentence and authorised his own execution. He was the clue which had to be destroyed.

His death and Audley's and Nikki's: that had been the mad glitter in Ollivier's eye, not the reflection of the naked bulb: they would all be casualties in Ollivier's war, their innocence or guilt irrelevant because they were the necessary price of secrecy and survival.

No one had seen them come; by morning the pink car would be far away. Once they were underground –

'I owe you an apology, Paul,' said Audley conversationally.

'*Ferme ta gueule*,' snapped Sorel.

'Screw you, friend.' Audley inclined his head towards Nikki, ignoring the man. 'And I must apologise to you also, mademoiselle. I have been unpardonably stupid.'

Mitchell saw that the expression on the big man's face belied the gentleness of his voice.

'Nevertheless . . . while there is life . . .' Audley turned slowly towards Sorel as though calculating exactly how many words would be too many, '. . . there is hope.'

The muzzle of the machine-pistol was now pointing at Audley's chest. For an instant Mitchell waited for the man to fire, then the muzzle swung slowly back to cover them all again.

He breathed out gratefully. Audley had gone to the limit, to the very last syllable, to risk passing on his message that their lives depended on their taking the first chance that presented itself. But now there could be no more words.

'Sorel – *je suis prêt*.' The voice from the shaft took him by surprise as he was measuring the impossible distance between himself and Sorel. 'You first, Captain Lefevre.'

If there had ever been a chance above ground, there was none now.

The shaft was wider than it had seemed from above. Twisting as he remembered Ollivier had done, Mitchell found regular ledges for his toes – a miniature stairway in brick – which prevented him from sliding. At first he could sense rather than see the roof close to his head, but when he looked upwards after having descended ten or twelve feet he could see that it had been arched for greater strength in the same brickwork that was beneath his fingers and toes.

This wasn't German work. But of course this upper part of the entrance had certainly been blown up by the British assault troops in 1916, like every other bolt-hole along the ridge – except presumably the dugout and tunnel entrances in the Prussian Redoubt and Rattlesnake Ravine which the Germans themselves had probably blown in to isolate the Poachers underground.

So this must be about where the old farmer had rediscovered the shaft while digging out the foundations for his wall or his cellar . . .

Suddenly his foot hit an obstruction which quivered at the blow. There was a dim light coming from below and in it he could just make out the topmost rung of a ladder lashed to the twisted metal rods protruding from a shattered section of reinforced concrete. The shaft beneath was steeper and timbered; it was nothing like any photograph he had ever seen of German underground work, but then he knew he had never particularly remarked such pictures anyway. Down the timbers to his right ran a collection of wires, two thick old electric cables and a number of what must be telephone wires.

'Come on, Captain. No time to admire the scenery.'

The voice came from nowhere – from somewhere still some distance below him. He clambered off the brickwork on to the ladder, dislodging a few small pieces of debris which pattered on to the rungs below. His hands were covered in dust and cob-webs which he could feel rather than see: everything was bone dry down here, even the air had a dry, chalky smell about it where he would have expected mustiness. It was like a tomb which had long passed through the stages of rottenness and decay to reach an equilibrium in which all other smells had been neutralised.

He stepped off the ladder on to the firmness of the tunnel's floor.

'Call Mademoiselle MacMahon, Captain.'

Mitchell stared upwards. He seemed to have descended an immeasurable distance, so that the real world was even further away than the distant suggestion of light far above him.

'Very good. Now I want you to stand to the left of the ladder. I have a Sten gun – a gift from Britain thirty years ago, but none the worse for its age, I do assure you. We have any number of them down here, still as good as the day they were made. Turn and face the wall, if you please – that's right.'

Mitchell fought the lethargy of the prisoner whose position was only hopeless because he had given up hope. In the brief moment in which he had been able to look around him he had been aware of a chamber perhaps ten feet square with two exits. A beam of light, head high, had stabbed at him out of one of the entrances.

Miner's helmet.

That was better. He was thinking again.

Ollivier was wearing a miner's helmet and he was standing in one of the exits.

The other exit had been piled with boxes . . . *We hid our arms and equipment down there . . . I have a Sten gun – a gift from Britain thirty years ago.*

Would a Sten fire after thirty years? Packed away in the dry down here, there was no reason why it shouldn't work after a hundred years, damn it. And no reason why Ollivier should need to bluff him, either.

He reached out to touch the plank wall in front of him.

'Don't move, Captain – please.'

It had a strange springy feel, the wood, like sorbo-rubber. Probably unseasoned green timber when the Germans had brought it to the front, but a thousand times better than anything the British bothered to use. Panelled rooms and elecricity and telephones: all the comforts of home the Germans had built for –

Mustn't think of things like that. Must *think* . . .

A fragment of something from above struck him lightly on the cheek. Nikki was coming down the ladder. He watched her legs out of the corner of his eye: lovely legs and a breath of that same perfume he had first smelt in the car yesterday – was it only yesterday?

Nothing like those legs and that perfume – nothing like Nikki MacMahon – had ever been in this hole before. But that was another thought as useless as it was incongruous. The trouble was that his brain had already computed the chance of getting to where Ollivier stood in the tunnel and had rejected it as impossible.

The Frenchman repeated his instructions to her, and his warning.

'Call David now, Captain.'

Their time and their chances were draining away. A sickening suspicion was growing inside Mitchell that there were not going to be any chances, that there never had been any, that Ollivier was too professional not to have calculated the thing exactly. Perhaps there was even a vestige remaining of the old friend who had shared a staircase at Cambridge with Audley and who didn't relish cutting them down in cold blood: perhaps he was hoping that Audley would take his chance against Sorel and that Mitchell would risk his against the reliability of that thirty-year-old Sten – perhaps that was why he'd gone out of his way to challenge him with the weapon's antiquity.

But now even those non-chances had passed: he could hear Audley's shoes scrape on the rungs of the ladder just above.

The big man came down slowly, peering around the chamber and then catching his head with a dull thump on one of the supporting beams.

'Easy, David,' came the voice from behind the beam of light.

'Easy? For God's sake, I can't even stand up straight!' Audley brushed the cobwebs from his hair. 'I can see why the Germans gave up wearing those spiked helmets.'

His voice was only mildly angry, almost bantering.

'Against the wall beside Mademoiselle MacMahon, if you please.'

As Audley turned towards the wall Mitchell caught a glimpse of his face before it was lost in shadow. It was very different from his voice; it was stamped with an expression of ferocious danger quite unlike anything he had ever seen on it before. If Audley was frightened, as he ought to be, he gave no sign of it; what he was showing was the look that went with his words at the top of the shaft – *I've been unpardonably stupid* – the look of an arrogantly clever man who had allowed himself to be out-smarted and was almost incandescent with rage at the discovery.

'That's very good – you are all being sensible,' Ollivier murmured encouragingly. 'So now we will go for a little walk – just a few steps to start with, so that Sorel may join us without . . . without tempting you not to be sensible, shall we say? You first, Captain. Then Mademoiselle, and then you, my David, last but not least . . . Just remember to move slowly, Captain – remember that however fast you can move it cannot be fast enough.'

Suddenly Mitchell was very frightened indeed, but more that Audley would explode and get them all shot there and then than that Ollivier would squeeze the trigger.

'Come on, Captain. We can't wait – ' Ollivier bit off the end of the sentence. 'Steady, my David – don't try it.'

It was as though he had picked up the vibration of Mitchell's fear and Audley's anger. But as he sensed the big man relax beside him Mitchell decided that some tell-tale movement must have betrayed the intention prematurely.

'That's just right . . .' The voice drew them one by one into the tunnel. The beam of light was blinding, but it was obvious that Ollivier was moving sideways, his back to the tunnel wall.

'Now we've come far enough. Just sit down where you are and we will wait for Sorel in comfort.'

The floor was uneven but not rough – smoothed by the passage of innumerable jackboots. Once they had left the chamber at the bottom of the entrance shaft they were surrounded by naked chalk, he had seen that much as he lowered himself out of the direct beam. It was over a yard wide and nearer six feet than five in height – more like the dimensions of the galleries the New Zealand tunnelling companies had cut, rather than those typical of the British and the German. And like those New Zealand tunnels it wasn't shored-up either . . . But then it was for communication, not mining or counter-mining; there would have to be room for fully-equipped troops to pass each other in it.

Ridiculous. Mitchell rubbed his eyes and blinked. He still couldn't comprehend the reality of it. Everything that had happened to him in the last couple of days was a dream full of strange sharp images. Butler's polished shoes catching the light in the Institute: *It is Mr Mitchell, isn't it?* and then the dark cold water rushing up, engulfing him; his mother's eyes wide with shock; his reflection – Captain Lefevre's reflection for the first time – in the hotel mirror; the line of council houses at Elthingham and General Leigh-Woodhouse's old manor rising out of the grass; Nikki's red-gold hair and the swell of her breasts which neither Mitchell nor Lefevre would ever touch.

The trench rifle. He had seen it two years before, fresh from the grave, and had never thought to see it again . . . never thought that it would be the death of him.

Him. Not Lefevre. Lefevre was a joke, Colonel Butler had been right there.

Mitchell.

'Get up.'

There was another light now, coming from behind. For an instant it threw the uneven walls of the tunnel into a jagged relief of white chalk and black shadow, framing the dark figure of Ollivier like a cyclops with a single glaring eye. Then the eye fixed its gaze on Mitchell and he was blind again.

'Get up.' The politeness was gone from Ollivier's voice now; with Sorel at their backs he had no further need for false courtesy.

'Now we will continue our little walk. I will set the pace and when I say "stop" you will stop immediately, Captain. One step too far and I will fire, make no mistake about that. Do you understand?'

The little walk was a nightmare.

Nor was it a little walk. On the open ground above, the farm couldn't be much more than a quarter of a mile from the edge of the wood. But underground, shuffling and stumbling at a snail's pace and hypnotised by the light which never left his face, Mitchell lost all sense of distance. He knew only that he was being drawn on and on irresistibly, able to think of nothing coherently but the need to steady himself first on one wall, then the other.

Sometimes his feet encountered unidentifiable objects which crunched as he trod on them or rattled as he kicked them out of his way. Once he nearly tripped on what he was sure was a steel helmet, a mishap which roused in him the sudden hope that Ollivier might trip also. But although he was virtually backing down the tunnel, the Frenchman was either exceptionally sure-footed or already knew the extent of the hazards.

Mitchell wiped his face again with his free hand and was surprised to find it covered with sweat, yet clammy to the touch.

He was still wasting his precious time on foolish thoughts: of course Ollivier knew the tunnel's hazards. He had explored it for three days years ago, long before he had discovered a new use for it.

But what use?

That was irrelevant too. All that mattered now was that Ollivier knew what he was doing, where he was going, and they didn't. All along he had planned what he was going to do if they had come up with the fatal answer. Now he was simply putting his plan into operation.

They were as good as dead.

'Stop.'

Mitchell stopped so abruptly that Nikki stumbled into him, almost throwing him off his balance.

'We take a little rest here,' said Ollivier. 'Just ahead on your left there is an opening, Captain – you will lead the way into it. It is only a short passage, seven or eight metres, no more. Then a dead end.'

Dead end . . .

'There is a place to sit. You will sit there. In a little while we will go on. Now – move.'

Mitchell blinked into the light. 'I can't see a thing, you're blinding me.'

'Feel your way along the wall.'

Mitchell turned half left and began to feel his way along the wall of the tunnel. Before his eyes had become accustomed to being out of the direct beam his right hand fell away into the emptiness of an opening in the wall. It was narrower and lower than the main passage, so that he was forced to stoop as he entered it. As he did so he felt a sudden contraction of fear in his chest: it was like entering total darkness and for all he knew there might be a bottomless shaft at his feet.

'I can't see anything,' he protested abjectly. For a moment he lost the left-hand wall, and then his hand touched something quite unlike the hardness of the naked chalk – it yielded to his fingers with a dry rustle. He recoiled in horror towards the opposite wall, striking his head on the low roof as he did so and crying out.

'What is it?' Nikki's voice was shrill with fear also.

'I don't know – '

'There are only a few old coats hanging on the wall, Captain.' Ollivier's tone was scornful. 'Nothing to be afraid of.'

Old coats? Mitchell swallowed the lump in his throat. That yielding something had been tattered cloth and canvas: he had known that in the back of his mind instantly. What he had been appalled by was the thought of what might be inside it.

'That's far enough.'

A measure of light illuminated the narrow passage. It came from behind and was largely blocked by their own shadows, but he could see that Ollivier had risked nothing by directing them into the opening: it petered out just ahead of him.

'Sit down.'

Mitchell peered about him. On his left a low bench-like ledge had been scooped out of the chalk; above it, on a line of spikes driven into the chalk, hung a line of coats faded and thick with the dust of ages, waiting for owners who had themselves been dust for two generations. He sat down carefully on the very edge of the ledge, unwilling to set his back against the rags.

There was a low murmur from the opening to the main tunnel: Ollivier and Sorel were co-ordinating the last phase of their operation. Operation Dead End . . .

'Paul . . .'

Audley had no inhibitions against pressing himself back against the coats. As he whispered Mitchell's name a small cascade of dust and tiny pieces of chalk rained down on him.

'We've got to jump them,' Audley hissed. 'There's no alternative. Listen – '

But Mitchell was no longer listening. Every sound, every sight, had been blotted out by the hardness of the thing which had pressed into his spine as he leant back to catch Audley's words.

Very slowly he twisted his left arm behind his back to explore the object.

Folds of material ... buttons ... the harsher, stiffer feel of canvas ... He fumbled along the outlines of the object, his fingers searching –

Jesus Christ!

Mitchell's hand froze, one finger trapped in a ring of metal. He felt his chest expand into another wider band of metal which held him in a straitjacket of panic. His death was not only out there in the tunnel, it was here under his hand an inch from his spine. His finger was hooked through it: absolute, shattering, irrevocable death.

His whole body was bathed in sweat. He could feel it standing out on his face and dripping from his armpit down the side of his body like blood from a wound.

He mouthed the one word, very softly, staring past Audley at the single light shining down the passage towards them.

'Cover me,' he whispered. 'Take his attention.'

Audley's face was in deep shadow and there was no sign for a moment that he had understood. But then he turned away, looking straight ahead, and leant forward to block out the light.

Slowly Mitchell withdrew his finger from the metal ring. He concentrated his thought fiercely: if it had been sensitive to a touch, then it would have already happened. But if it hadn't happened it might never happen ... Mustn't think of that ... must pray that someone long ago had done his job properly, knowing that other men's lives depended on his care.

And must remember that it was dry down here – dry, dry, dry.

Besides, there was nothing left now to lose. That was the lonely advantage they had over Ollivier: they had nothing to lose which wasn't already forfeited.

Audley cleared his throat. '*M'sieur!*' he addressed the light at the end of the passage. '*M'sieur, excusez-moi . . . mais . . . j'ai envie de pisser.*'

Without waiting for an answer he rose from the ledge, facing the light and blocking it entirely from Mitchell's sight.

'*J'ai envie de pisser, mais pas en face de mademoiselle,*' Audley hissed in an embarrassed tone, taking a step towards the light.

Mitchell pushed aside the stiff folds of the ancient German greatcoat to get at the thing behind it, forcing his fingers to move slowly. Even if Sorel found Audley's delicacy surprising he could hardly expect his prisoner to pee sitting-down, for God's sake.

It was a carrying waistcoat, as he thought it would be; a carrying waistcoat of the sort British raiding parties and assault troops used, with ten pockets. Nine were empty – but the canvas webbing was stiff with age and his fingers were clumsy. He could feel the drops of sweat racing down his face like insects running for safety.

It wouldn't move, it wouldn't move!

'*Asseyez-vous!*' snarled Sorel.

No more time for delicacy. Push with the left hand – pull with the right.

Suddenly it was heavy in his hand. He straightened, hugging it under his left armpit, his eyes tightly closed.

Five seconds.

He counted them with heartbeats.

'Sit down, David,' he croaked. 'You'll get us all shot.'

Audley subsided back on to the ledge, grumbling under his breath. 'Give it to me,' he mumbled out of the side of his mouth, making it sound like a final complaint at not being allowed to finish what he had started in decent comfort.

Mitchell opened his eyes. He could hear Nikki breathing faster next to him. She must have heard what he had said, but either she was a young woman of iron nerve or she didn't fully understand the extent of the risk. For her peace of mind he hoped it was the latter.

He shook his head slowly from side to side without turning towards Audley. For better or worse the thing was his. He'd found it – and they'd want him out of the passage first. It was a simple matter of common sense.

He stared at the chalk wall in front of him. The last man to sit on this ledge had been a German soldier, maybe one of the ill-fated 450th Reserve Regiment who had defended the wood with such courage. He would have sat here and wondered if this was the day when his bullet was being loaded, or his shell was being carried from its dump.

'Captain Lefevre.' Ollivier's voice sounded far away. 'We go on now.'

As Mitchell stood up, crouching under the low roof of the passage, the direct beam of Sorel's light vanished, leaving him in almost total darkness again. Only the main tunnel was illuminated now: obviously Ollivier and Sorel had drawn back from the passage entrance, one on each side, waiting to take up their positions again at the front and rear of their prisoners.

The bastards weren't taking any chances. But then they'd never taken any chances, not with Charles Emerson, not with Paul Mitchell walking home from work, and not with poor old George Davis walking home from his evening pint at the pub.

'Paul!' said Audley urgently.

Etienne Jarras, too – the Samaritan who'd never leave a stranded motorist. He would have been easy too.

Pin out.

'Come on, Captain.'

'Get down on the floor, Nikki,' said Mitchell. 'We're coming.'

He stepped carefully towards the opening. Two sorts of dangers there were: the sort you couldn't do anything about made you frightened, but this was another sort –

He poked his head out of the passage, looking left towards Ollivier then right towards Sorel. The twin beams blinded him, but not before he could see that they were quite close.

Sorel was closer, he decided in the last split-second as he released the striker arm behind his back.

Five seconds –

Four

He tossed the grenade at Ollivier's feet and threw himself backwards down the passage, scrabbling with fingers and toes for extra inches of safety. His head struck a hard ridge of chalk with an explosion of pain which was lost in a tremendous eardrum-shattering concussion of sound inside his head.

Grandfather –

Part three
Operation Mitchell

Why, there's Colonel Butler!' Corporal Hayhoe pointed a gnarled finger over the cemetery wall. 'I thought you said he was going back home today, sir.'

There was nothing gnarled about Hayhoe's eyesight: it was Butler striding across the field towards them.

'Maybe he's fixed for us to see the wood after all,' said Hayhoe hopefully.

Mitchell watched a French army lorry skirt the edge of the wire on its way to the entrance of the wood. It was the third he'd seen since he'd led the party slowly up the hill, and there were both soldiers and uniformed police patrolling the perimeter fence ostentatiously.

'I wouldn't bet on it,' he replied carefully. 'But you wait here, Mr Hayhoe, and I'll go and find out.'

For the life of him he couldn't bring himself to salute Butler this time, not if there were a thousand Frenchmen watching. But mercifully Butler took no exception to the omission: he stopped five yards short of Mitchell, hands on his hips, and shook his head in wonderment.

'Couldn't keep away then?' Butler's lip twisted in what might just be a smile. 'You're a glutton for punishment, Mitchell, I'll say that for you.'

'What do you mean?'

Butler gestured towards the scene behind him. 'Your handiwork, man, your handiwork – Audley told me. But don't worry – it's all sorted out at this end. There wasn't any need for you to come back.'

'I haven't come back.'

Butler's eyebrows lifted. 'No?'

'I'm showing the Poachers the Prussian Redoubt.' Mitchell ignored the look of disbelief. It clearly hadn't occurred to Butler – or presumably Audley either – that life beyond Hameau Ridge had gone on as usual; that the unspeakable Whitton should rouse him at dawn with a wink and a nudge, less than two hours after he had collapsed into bed –

'Eh, you look proper knackered, lad – looks as though she gave you a right going-over, an' no mistake.'

– and drag him off to carry out his official duties.

'Indeed?' Butler gave the cemetery a quick glance. 'Well that does at least account for why Audley couldn't get through to you this morning. We wondered where you'd got to.'

'Let's 'ave you, then. Got a lot of walking today, lad.'

'Where's Audley?'

'In Paris by now, with the woman of theirs. I said we've got things sorted out here, but there's the devil to pay there, I can tell you.' Butler paused. 'But I've got a message for you from him.'

'A message?' Mitchell tried, but failed, to keep the eagerness out of his voice.

Butler looked at him curiously. His heavy features and fierce colouring seemed to Mitchell ill-designed for conveying nuances of expression, but the eyes betrayed a suggestion of sympathy.

'A message?' Sympathy he could do without. 'Go on.'

The eyes went opaque. 'You killed two men last night.'

Mitchell was taken totally aback. For a moment he could think of nothing to say.

'How certain were you that the grenade would go off?'

Mitchell stared at him, still nonplussed. 'I didn't know. It all depended how careful the battalion bombing officer had been – back in 1916.'

'The battalion bombing officer?'

Mitchell nodded slowly. 'It was in a British waistcoat carrier – the Germans must have captured it – killed the chap who was wearing it, when we raided their trenches most likely. And if it was from a raid then it was a good bet our chaps would have checked their grenades carefully first. They wouldn't have used any with the wax seal round the top of the striker broken, for instance, because then the damp might have got in and the charge would've deteriorated. But if it was on the top line in 1916 – if the base plug had been treated with vaseline, and so on – it was absolutely dry in the tunnel, you see . . .'

'You thought it would still work.'

'There was a fair chance, yes.'

Butler nodded. 'How do you feel about it – now?'

Mitchell felt a touch of irritation, but he could hardly admit that. 'I don't know what you mean – how do I feel? There wasn't any choice.'

'There's always a choice,' Butler shook his head. 'Maybe not at the time, but afterwards sometimes you wonder.'

'There wouldn't have been any afterwards for us, for God's sake,' Mitchell could hear the anger in his own voice: Butler was the last person from whom he expected such idiotic questions. 'If you mean do I regret it – '

Butler pounced. 'Do you?'

'Why the hell should I?' This time he had the anger controlled.

'No reason at all.' Butler relaxed. 'You did what came naturally to you . . . so I'll tell you a little story which may amuse you.'

'You said you had a message.'

'Oh. I have –' the lip twisted again in a Butlerian smile-substitute ' – but that comes at the end. First comes an apology, though.'

Mitchell frowned. 'An apology?'

'From Audley. He nearly got you killed because he made a mistake about Ollivier. He doesn't usually make that sort of error, I can tell you. Ollivier wasn't so clever, he was just lucky.'

'Lucky?' Mitchell searched Butler's face for evidence that he was being mocked in some obscure and macabre way. It seemed to him that Ollivier's only luck had been to catch the full blast of the grenade. Sorel hadn't been so fortunate.

For an instant he was back in the tunnel, with the man's gurgling cries of agony rising out of the echoes of the thunder-clap. They had not continued very long, and his own senses had been reeling, but they were not something he wanted to remember.

'Lucky?' He repeated the word to drive out the memory. 'I thought we were the lucky ones.'

'Aye, at the end you were. But if Audley's job had been to help the French you wouldn't have been there at all.'

'Audley's – job? What do you mean?'

'We've enough problems of our own without sticking our noses in theirs.'

'I don't follow you. We were helping them – you were helping them when you first brought that map to me.'

'A little thing like that we'd do for anyone, even the Russians. If it has nothing to do with our security it has nothing to do with us, Mitchell.'

'But what about Charles Emerson – and George Davis? That had nothing to do with you either, are you saying?'

'Not with us. With the police perhaps, but not with us.'

Mitchell stared at him. Not the French and not Emerson. But that left nothing at all.

Except the one question. 'So what was Audley's job, Colonel?'

'You were.'

You were.

Not the French. Not Emerson. But Mitchell.

He'd take it slowly. 'What sort of job was I?'

Butler drew a deep breath. 'Ollivier sent us a piece of map and Emerson's name, but we couldn't get through to Emerson. Then we were told a young man named Mitchell would probably know where Emerson was, and even if he couldn't he'd at least identify the map for us.

'So we did a little routine checking on the young man. And then a little more. And then quite a lot.'

'From my old tutor, you mean – Forbes?'

'Among others. He gave us a pretty fair specification – it interested us quite a lot.'

'It interests me too. But I wouldn't have said Archie Forbes was one of my admirers exactly.'

'He isn't. But he said you had a superb memory, for one thing.'

'That was big of him. And what else?'

'Remarkable application to detail and objectivity in assessing it.'

'He makes me sound like a computer.'

'Only a computer lacks intuition, and you don't.' Butler's eyes narrowed. 'And a wide streak of bloody-minded ruthlessness, you don't lack that either. He said you were potentially a very dangerous young man, in fact.'

'Forbes told you that? I wouldn't have thought it was apparent in my essays on the Cromwellian settlement.'

'He said that given the right circumstances you'd show it.' Butler paused. 'So we thought we'd have a look at you. And after we'd seen you – and after Emerson had been killed – we thought you were worth a try-out.'

'A try-out?'

Butler nodded. 'Yes. You've got to face it, Mitchell: you may be a scholar, but you're also a born intelligence officer. You'd be wasted on anything else.'

'You must be bloody short of manpower,' Mitchell sneered.

'We are – of your sort.'

'My sort?'

'Aye. In wartime it's easy. We can pick and choose who we want from the professions. But in peacetime ... You know, Mitchell, of the ten truly outstanding intelligence officers of the last war, nine were civilians – they were civilians in 1939 and they were civilians again by 1946. Your tutor Forbes was one of them, as it happens. We wanted him to stay on, but he wouldn't.'

'Isn't the pay any good?'

Butler ignored the jibe. 'We catch them too old and we can't hold them – they've already got careers. So usually we have to make do with second best.'

'Like colonels?'

'Captains and majors usually,' said Butler coolly.

'And is Audley second best?'

'Audley's a rarity – like you. He enjoys it.' Butler sniffed. 'Like you.'

Touché! Mitchell remembered Audley's warning about Butler belatedly; the mighty memory had let him down for once.

'You're very sure of me, aren't you.'

'I'm sure you're right for the job, with a little more discipline and a little less arrogance yes,' said Butler.

As a result of the try-out, of course, thought Mitchell dispassionately. That had been Audley's job, quite simply: to try him out in the field, the best test of all. And the fact that he was being tried out on someone else's problem was the bloody masterstroke, because if he made a hash of it the British had nothing to lose. In just the same way the Germans had tested their Stukas in Spain and the Russians their Sam missiles in the Egyptian desert, Paul Mitchell had been tested on the unfortunate French.

'Whether you want it is another matter, naturally,' continued Butler. 'Which brings me to the message ... I gather Audley's already made you an offer. He says you accepted, but after last night you may feel differently. So as of now you have three days in which to make up your mind. Then Audley will be getting in touch with you – that's the message: three days.'

The sound of another lorry revving up on the edge of the wood broke the silence on the ridge. Butler turned towards it momentarily, then swung back towards Mitchell.

He stabbed a finger towards the Prussian Redoubt abruptly. 'In the meantime, get those old men off this hill and right away from here – double quick.'

Mitchell frowned. 'What do you mean?'

'What I say. They shouldn't be here.'

'Why the hell not? They've more right to be here than anyone alive.'

'Then if they want to stay that way, get them out of here. There's enough explosive under this ground to blow us all halfway back to Enghand.'

'Explosive?'

'Aye.' Butler regarded him. 'You didn't get round to discovering what Ollivier had in store for this afternoon's meeting, did you? A hundred tons of ammonal – or whatever the Germans used back in 1916. All packed in airtight tins and sandbagged in ready to blow. And the French reckon it would have blown, too, though I'm no expert.'

Ready to blow?

Mitchell stared at the wood, hypnotised by the thought of two hundred thousand pounds of ammonal. A third of that had opened a hole one hundred and fifty yards wide at La Boiselle ...

'Ollivier thought so too, anyway,' went on Butler. 'His detonator was set for 6 p.m.'

Bouillet Wood would have disappeared off the map.

And the summit conference.

And Paul Mitchell.

Ready to blow since 1916: So that was why the Germans had held Bully Wood so lightly – and why no counter-attack had been mounted until too late. They'd planned to draw the attack into the wood and then blow it to kingdom come from the safety of some deep dugout in the Prussian Redoubt.

Only Harry Bellamy and his Poachers had spoilt the plan.

'It would have gone up right enough,' he said.

'Indeed? Because your Mills grenade went up?'

'Not just the grenade, no.' Mitchell watched the lorry on its way thoughtfully. 'There were two big mines at Messines in '17 which were never exploded, and afterwards they more or less lost track of them – somewhere near Ploegsteert Wood they were.'

'You mean they're still down there?'

'One is. The other blew up of its own accord during an electrical storm ... in 1955. Fortunately it was still in open country.'

Come to that he had a little mine of his own now, large enough to make a respectable bang in academic circles: the truth about the battle of Hameau Ridge, no less.

And in popular circles too, suitably edited – just right for the front page of the *Sunday Times Weekly Review*, say.

The Heroes of Hameau.

In its way that would be a memorial to Harry Bellamy and his Poachers; and it would certainly establish the future author of *The Breaking of the Hindenburg Line* most satisfactorily in the public eye: Paul Mitchell, the rising young military historian.

And after that there would be Charles Emerson's unpublished masterpiece. For if the manuscript had gone up in flames the ideas were still intact, safely locked up in the rising young historian's memory.

That future was his for the taking, the survivor's inheritance.

*

Except that he had no more use for it than they had for a memorial. Or if they had they could afford to wait for a better man (or at least a worthier scholar) to build it for them. It was all the same to them – last year, next year, sometime, never.

Whereas Paul Mitchell had suddenly acquired a taste for the unconquered present.

He grinned at Butler. If he asked whose summit they'd saved he'd be told that it wasn't any of his business. Which it wasn't – so he wouldn't ask.

Not for the next three days, anyway.